HEALTHY WEALTHY
& DEAD

HEALTHY WEALTHY
& DEAD

by Suzanne North

NeWest

Canadian Cataloguing in Publication Data

North, Suzanne, 1945-

Healthy, wealthy & dead

"A Phoebe Fairfax mystery"
ISBN 0-920897-55-X

I. Title.
PS8577.O77H4 1994   C813'.54   C94-910054-4
PR9199.3.N67H4 1994

Credits
Cover & Interior design: Brian Huffman
Editorial Assistant: Kathleen McLean
Editor for the Press: Doug Barbour
Financial Assistance: NeWest Press gratefully acknowledges the financial assistance of The Canada Council; The Alberta Foundation for the Arts, a beneficiary of the Lottery Fund of the Government of Alberta; and The NeWest Institute for Western Canadian Studies.

Printed and Bound in Canada by Best Gagné Book Manufacturers

NeWest Publishers Limited
#310, 10359-82 Avenue
Edmonton, Alberta
T6E 1Z9

For Don

Thanks to the Saskatchewan Western Development Museum, custodians of the only steam calliope still whistling in western Canada, and to Debbie Massett and Dave Kinzel who introduced me to its workings.

CHAPTER 1

"The Ranch. Monday morning. Ten sharp." Ella's was the last message on my answering machine. I could hear the click of her computer's keys in the background as she summoned our shooting schedule from its memory. "You should have time to finish the exteriors before you have to meet Candi and me at the swimming pool at four." Click, click, click. "We'll tape the Morrison interview by the pool. It won't bother you to go back to the pool again, will it, Phoebe? It's been almost six months. You should be over it by now." That computer is like an extension of Ella. "I really don't know why the whole thing upset you so much in the first place. After all, the woman was already dead when you found her. It wasn't as if you could have done anything." Except the computer has a slightly warmer personality. As usual, her message ended without a goodbye.

I'm a television photographer. Ella's my boss. I work two days a week for a Calgary station, mostly for a program that Ella produces called "A Day in the Lifestyle." As its unfortunate title suggests, "Lifestyle" provides its surprisingly numerous viewers with a weekly glimpse into the lives and haunts of local trend-setters. Generally, the camera work is pretty routine stuff but "Lifestyle" pays some of my bills and leaves me with a good chunk of the week free for my own projects so I have no complaints. Even working with Ella doesn't bother me any more.

I arrived at The Ranch's wrought iron gates at three minutes to ten on Monday morning. By three minutes after I'd started work. The Ranch is a small, exclusive, and very expensive health resort located in the Rocky Mountain foothills an hour's drive southwest of Calgary. It occupies what was once a private estate built in the twenties by one of Alberta's millionaire cattle barons as a wedding present for his daughter. As the years passed and the dollars dwindled, both the daughter and her estate declined into shabby gentility until The Ranch's parent company, one of those American conglomerates that seem to own at least one of everything, bought the old lady out and she happily removed herself to a California condo.

The estate originally consisted of a handsomely proportioned sandstone and timber house, a spacious stable of the same material, and a swimming pool, one of those tiled and sculpted masterpieces built in an era when pools were works of art and not just plastic-lined holes in the ground. At the time of the sale its cracked tank hadn't held water for years. The rest of the estate was similarly dilapidated. Immediately, The Ranch began a series of renovations that banished the antiquated wiring, the crumbling plumbing, and all the other chronic miseries of structural neglect from the old place and restored it to a warm, comfortable version of its original twenties elegance.

I set the camera on its tripod and began to work my way down Ella's list. After two years on "A Day in the Lifestyle" we've evolved a perfect way of working together by staying apart. At the start of every job, Ella scouts our locations and prepares a detailed list of the shots she wants. Then she sends me out with the list and a camera. Alone. Her list for the job at The Ranch was very long but, given good light and a little good luck, I could work my way through it in a day and a half. As it turned out, that Monday I got both.

It was a perfect autumn day in the foothills. A rime of frost had covered the ground overnight but, by the time I began shooting, the sun had melted its lens-flaring sparkles and underfoot was wet with dew. A slight breeze stirred the poplar trees. The scattering of gold leaves left on their branches fluttered with a rush of tiny clicking sounds. The earthy smell of fallen leaves mingled with the aromatic scents of spruce and pine. The poplars grew sparse and the spruce more dense as the hills climbed toward the Rocky Mountains. Tricks of air and altitude made the mountain peaks seem deceptively close. They shone blue and white in the west, drawing my lens like a magnet. I found myself framing my shots to include as much of them as possible.

I started with a wide shot of the house. In spite of Ella's forebodings, I was enjoying the opportunity to have a good look around The Ranch. As a child, I'd known both the estate and its old owner very well. Until I started high school, I had spent most of my summer holidays in the district and had passed many happy afternoons prowling round Mrs. Malifant's place while the grown-ups talked and drank tea. Mrs. Malifant is nearly ninety now but she still keeps in touch. I can always count on an envelope with her firm, blocky handwriting and a San Diego postmark to appear in my mailbox every Christmas and birthday. I'd have to write and let her know what The Ranch had done to her old home. I thought she'd be pleased. I certainly was. Mrs. Malifant's estate had begun its decline long before I was born so I'd never seen it looking as prosperous and solid as it did that Monday.

By mid-afternoon I had completed most of the exterior shots on Ella's list and worked my way around to the stable. There I began with a shot of the corral where a dozen guests had assembled for The Ranch's regular afternoon trail ride. I moved closer as eleven of them, all looking trim and athletic in The Ranch's form fitting kelly green sweat suits, swung lithe legs over the backs of their trail ponies. They sat relaxed and at home in their saddles while they watched the twelfth rider, a man a little shorter and a lot plumper than they, gallantly make his third unsuccessful attempt to scramble aboard a pony. His fourth try said he wasn't a quitter. The fifth proved he wasn't too proud to accept help. Propelled by a boost from The Ranch's head cowboy, he at last made it into the saddle. Backwards. There he sat, bemused and bewildered, gazing over the pony's tail. The whole sequence was pure Laurel and Hardy. I couldn't resist moving in for a close-up even though I knew that Ella would never use the shot. She suspects that anything funny is probably not in good taste and on "A Day in the Lifestyle" good taste counts.

"Don't worry, Reg," the cowboy called encouragingly. "The first time is always the toughest. By the end of the week you'll be leaping into that saddle quicker than a flea can hop on a coyote. Jump off and try that manœuver again."

But Reg could not dismount. He was shaking with laughter. His flushed round face and the placid pony's hind end filled my viewfinder. All in all, Reg didn't seem to be taking the business of self-improvement very seriously. This was not typical. The Ranch takes itself and the services it sells very seriously indeed. So do its customers. The Ranch had found a perfect market in the wealthy middle-aged, that group poised on the brink of realizing their own mortality but possessed of enough cash to enable them to teeter a little longer on the youthful side of the abyss.

None of the guests I had seen so far on my rounds with the camera seemed in need of a session at a health spa.

They all looked perfectly healthy. Even Reg, his twenty extra pounds aside, was pretty much in the pink. However, those twenty pounds did put him in a class of his own because it was the only surplus podge on view at The Ranch. All the other guests were incredibly svelte. In spite of this, almost all of them wanted to shed a few pounds. To this end they willingly submitted themselves to The Ranch's nutritionally balanced, beautifully presented, and portionally minute meals. I had eaten today's lunch myself, a tiny helping of imagination on a bed of raw spinach. By mid-afternoon it wasn't even a memory.

His laughter finally under control, Reg attempted to turn right way round in his saddle without resorting to the desperate measure of dismounting. The pony snaked its head around to check his progress. Ponies at The Ranch are so well trained and so well behaved that this one's upper lip only curled slightly in the merest suggestion of a horse laugh. Everyone who worked for The Ranch, man, woman, or beast, possessed a similar impeccable professionalism. With more laughter and a final boost from the cowboy, Reg at last sat right way round in his saddle, facing earward in triumph. Then the ponies set off in single file for their afternoon amble along the dappled foothills trails.

The cowboy led the procession. His name was Byron and he was The Ranch's version of a Greek statue in a Stetson. Byron of the broad shoulders, the slim hips, and the slow seductive smile, was the embodiment of masculine beauty in its youthful prime, a shining example in chaps. But gorgeous as he was, the cowboy was simply one of a crowd of impossibly good looking young men who worked for The Ranch. I had already photographed half a dozen similar Apollos busy supervising the activities that centred around the gym and tennis courts. Byron supervised the guests' equestrian endeavors. He rode at the head of the daily morning and afternoon rides, guiding his charges along the maze of trails through the hills near The Ranch. He also managed the stable and, with the help of a couple of wranglers, saw to the welfare of The Ranch's string of ponies.

As that afternoon's group filed out of the corral, I focused on Byron's prancing Appaloosa mare. The placid trail ponies followed in her stylish wake. I waited until the last one had trotted into the trees and out of sight before I turned off the camera. I could still hear the jingle of bridles and the soft thud of unshod hoofs. On still autumn days, sound seems to carry forever on the foothills air. I straightened my back and stretched. The sun shone warm on my shoulders and the pleasant smell of horse and saddle-soaped leather lingered in my nostrils.

"Hello, Miss Fairfax. It's good to see you again." Mr. Reilly, The Ranch's business manager, startled me into action. "Do you have time for a cup of coffee?"

"I'm supposed to be lugging this stuff over to the swimming pool to shoot an interview with Dr. Morrison. I should have been there ten minutes ago so I guess I'd better pass on the coffee. Thanks anyway." I took the camera off the tripod. "Besides, isn't caffeine frowned on at The Ranch? Kind of like booze at a Baptist hall. That's the impression I got at lunch."

"Ate with the guests, did you?" Mr. Reilly laughed. "I assure you, the staff dining-room is quite a different place. We can't ask people to put in a hard day's work on what we feed the paying customers. Here, let me carry some of that equipment for you. I'm going in your direction." He took the tripod and slung it over his shoulder. We started up the path to the pool.

Mr. Reilly and I had met once before, on the morning that I found the body in The Ranch's pool. He was in his sixties, tall, straight, and very distinguished with his shock of white hair and neatly trimmed moustache. He looked like Hollywood's idea of a British officer and a gentleman, and I knew from personal experience that the gentleman part was true. That morning last April, after the police arrived, he'd found me a blanket and a hot drink and sat with me in front of the fire until I stopped shaking.

"You've got a beautiful day for your work," he said. "But then I'm prejudiced. I think every day in these hills is beautiful. I wish I'd moved here years ago."

"Where do you come from?" He had an intriguingly indeterminate American accent.

"Here and there, I guess. I've worked for the company that owns The Ranch for nearly forty years and I went wherever they sent me. They sent me a lot of places but this is the best." He took a deep breath. "Can you beat that air?" I had to hurry to keep up with his long strides. "I understand we're working together tomorrow."

"I'm shooting interiors at the main house and in one of the guest cabins tomorrow morning." No one actually lived in the old mansion any more. It now housed the dining- and social-rooms plus The Ranch's business offices. The guests stayed in small, luxuriously appointed log cabins. The Ranch had built a series of these, each tucked away in its own private clearing in the woods. "You're my guide. I hope I'm not imposing on you. I'm sure it won't take too much of your time."

"You won't be imposing at all, Phoebe. I have plenty of time. Take as much of it as you want. I'll enjoy it." He wasn't just being polite.

"I thought running a place like this would keep you pretty busy."

"The Ranch?" He seemed amused. "I'm used to running the kind of hotel where you could put The Ranch in one corner of the fourth floor and never notice it was there. Then I was busy. For me this place is like retiring to the country."

We arrived at the swimming pool. "Thanks very much." I reclaimed the tripod. "Will I see you at dinner?"

"Not me, I'm afraid." Mr. Reilly grinned enigmatically as he held the pool door open for me. "I'm far too old to dine with The Ranch's guests. It's one of the few benefits of growing old that have come my way and I treasure it."

I hauled the gear the length of the pool to where Ella and Candi sat in two patio chairs near the water. Candi Sinclair is "A Day in the Lifestyle's" on-camera host and interviewer. The two of them were having their ritual pre-interview chat in which Ella issues stern instructions about sticking to the script and Candi smiles agreeably. Before each interview, Ella prepares a carefully ordered, meticulously worded set of questions for Candi. During the interviews, Candi manages to make a shambles of Ella's list and usually rounds out the destruction by flinging a few extemporaneous inquiries of her own into the rubble. To her credit, Ella rarely utters a word once the camera is rolling. Instead, I have become familiar with the feel of her silent screams as she stands behind me and the camera, grinding her teeth and clutching a stop-watch in her white-knuckled hand. Right now, her hands and jaw were as relaxed as any bits of Ella ever get, and the stop-watch hung around her neck on its leather lanyard. She wore one of her working habits, an impeccably cut navy business suit and a cream silk blouse. Ella's attractive enough in her starched and tailored way, but somehow she manages to make herself look older than her thirty two years.

Candi is just the opposite. She's twenty-five but she always seems younger. Maybe it's her eyes. They look out from under her masses of ash-blond hair, so blue and honest and innocent they might belong to a child. According to Ella, Candi's eyes aren't innocent, they're simply vacant. Ella claims that Candi combines the beauty of a Botticelli Venus with the intellect of a Dürer rabbit. I don't agree. Candi isn't stupid. She just doesn't think the same way Ella does. Actually, I've never met anyone who thinks quite like Candi. She's got a one of a kind mind that's capable of such dizzying leaps of logic that it's really not safe to try following. I'm out of danger anchored behind the camera, but I've watched many a "Lifestyle" guest miss Candi's verbal flying trapeze and fall to gibbering incoherence. As Candi herself once remarked in a monument to understatement, "I guess I'm just not your linear type of thinker." She was dressed for the poolside interview in a bikini and one of The Ranch's green sweat tops.

"Well, hi there, Phoebe." Candi turned her smile on me, all five hundred watts of it. She is a virtuoso smiler. Ella says this is a result of having participated in too many beauty contests. She thinks that Candi's interviewing style may trace its origins to the public speaking sections of those same contests.

"Phoebe, you're late." Ella, on the other hand, is not much of a smiler. "Set the camera up there." She looked up from her clipboard and pointed to a spot beside the closest of the two stone dolphins that spouted water into either end of the pool's mosaic-tiled tank. "I want as much of the rocky part in the background as possible. This place is too beautiful to waste."

Ella was right. The Ranch's pool was a glass-domed marvel. Its designer had made such ingenious use of the surrounding landscape that even in winter when the dome's huge doors were closed against the cold, it still looked like an outdoor pond. Part of a hillside had been blasted out to accommodate the deep end and the resulting exposed rock provided walls on two sides. In one corner the rock sloped gently to the water's edge. Here the builder had added soil and planted the same kinds of shrubs as those that grew wild on the hill outside. The vegetation's uninterrupted sweep up the slope made the glass line separating inside from outside seem to disappear. In her preparations for the coming interview, Ella had positioned the patio chairs so that we would need a minimum of artificial light. Instead, we could use the afternoon sunshine that poured through the dome.

"We'll need some reaction shots after Candi wraps up the interview and after that you can move back for a medium shot because she and Dr. Morrison are going to end the interview by diving into the pool." Ella continued rattling off instructions. "Make sure you get that dive on the first take Phoebe because we don't have time to go through make-up and hair again. And be careful you don't fall in yourself." It's moments like these that remind me why Ella and I work best apart. "And Candi, whatever you do, don't mention that woman who drowned in here last spring. Phoebe is probably having a hard enough time as it is without you bringing the whole thing up again and I know Dr. Morrison doesn't want to hear any more about it either."

I had forgotten to think about the woman in the pool but, thanks to Ella, I could see her once again floating face-up a few inches below the surface of the water. It was as if the six months since I found her had never passed.

"That was an awful thing, wasn't it?" Candi said. "I don't know how you managed to handle it so well, Phoebe. Getting her out of the water, trying to revive her. . . . I couldn't have done what you did. Did anyone ever find out what really happened to her?"

"Don't be so morbid, Candi," Ella said. "The poor woman drank too much and drowned. That's all there is to it. She wasn't even a guest at The Ranch." In its barest outline what Ella said was true. The woman was not a guest at The Ranch, at least not at the time of her death. However, she had spent a couple of weeks there about six months before she died. The Ranch had done its best to hush this up. Health resorts frown on death. The realization that there is no cure for mortality is bad for business. The customers find it disheartening.

"What about it, Phoebe?" Candi asked. "Is that really all there was to it?"

"I honestly don't know," I said. "All I did was find her." I'd come to the pool just before dawn to get some shots of the sun on the dome at first light. I saw her drifting near one of the stone dolphins. The gently spouting water billowed her hair. Its long brown strands rippled out from her head like tendrils from a sea creature.

"Too bad you were the one that got stuck with shooting that stuff," Candi said. "I know it wouldn't have changed what happened to that woman but at least you wouldn't have had to be the one who found her."

I had drawn the assignment of shooting some footage for one of The Ranch's promotional videos. The New York firm which produced all The Ranch's advertising did not consider our station's photography department grand enough to handle a whole production. However, they occasionally condescended to sub-contract us for a little of the catch-up stuff.

"Somebody had to find her," I said. I had jumped into the water and dragged her out. I did my best to breathe life back into lungs I knew were already dead. "At least Dr. Morrison was around to help." The doctor had examined the body and then we called the police.

"Did they ever find out why she picked this pool to kill herself in?" Candi asked.

"She was a guest at The Ranch sometime last year," I

replied, "But they never found out what she was doing back here when she died."

"The woman had a history of depression. The official verdict was suicide. She was very drunk when she drowned." Ella seemed to think that settled the matter.

"What a terrible way to die even if you were drunk out of your mind." Candi shook her head in pity. "Why didn't she just stay home in bed and take too many sleeping pills or something? That poor, poor lady. I wonder why she did it?"

"Candi, 'Lifestyle's' viewers are not interested in dead bodies." Ella's voice began to rise in pitch. "And Dr. Morrison has especially asked us not to mention the one Phoebe found." Volume climbed after pitch. "So I swear that if you so much as whisper anything about suicide when that camera is rolling, the next body they find floating in here will be . . ."

"She didn't even leave a note, did she?" Candi asked, oblivious to Ella's tirade. "Imagine, going to the trouble of coming all the way out here to kill yourself and then not even leaving a note to say why. I think that's really weird." The same point had troubled me. It was as if the drowned woman held her life in such small esteem that she regarded her own death as something of no significance. It had not been worth explanations or goodbyes. "Besides, if she didn't leave a note, then how do they really know she killed herself?" Candi continued. "Maybe it was an accident."

"It wasn't an accident," I said. "There was a half-drunk bottle of rye and an empty bottle of pills by the side of the pool. They both had her fingerprints on them. The police think that she must have taken the pills with the whisky and then just floated around in the pool until she lost consciousness and drowned."

"I guess she couldn't have done that by accident,"

Candi conceded. "But that still doesn't make it suicide. Maybe somebody pushed her. They could have forced her to drink the whisky and take the pills and then waited until she was unconscious and . . ."

Ella rolled her eyes in her most withering oh-God-why-me look. "Will the pair of you please get on with the job. In case you'd forgotten we have an interview to do." We were spared her further wrath by the appearance of Dr. Heather Morrison, The Ranch's managing director and our interviewee. She had arrived at the pool's entrance just in time to catch Candi's closing remarks.

"So sorry to be late." According to my watch Dr. Morrison was right on time. "I hope I haven't thrown your schedule into complete chaos, Miss Baxter. I've been caught up in conference calls all afternoon. I'm afraid that's the story of my life these days." She smiled ruefully, the falsely self-deprecating smile of one whose executive days are so much longer and more important than the ordinary twenty-four hour variety the rest of us live.

I hadn't seen Dr. Morrison since the morning of our sojourn over the dead body. Although I live on an acreage a couple of miles north of The Ranch which, I suppose, makes us neighbours, that was the only time we'd met.

"Miss Fairfax." The doctor offered me a hand. "How very pleasant to see you again." As we shook hands, she stared intently at a point about six inches from the tip of my nose. I found this oddly disconcerting until I suddenly realized that Dr. Morrison was not simply nearsighted but so acutely myopic that she couldn't have recognized her own face in a make-up mirror without corrective lenses. She'd obviously come prepared for the planned post-interview dive and swim with her bikini on and her contacts out. In the meantime, she was either too vain or too insecure to wear a pair of glasses. I couldn't believe it was insecurity. Our previous meeting had convinced me that nothing could faze Dr. Morrison. It had to be vanity.

To give the doctor her due, her looks could back up a good measure of vanity. She was a small, neatly made brunette and although she had a good ten years on Candi, she did her bikini equal justice. The two of them doffed their Ranch sweatshirts and settled their nearly nude bodies into the patio chairs. I put my eye to the viewfinder and started the tape rolling. Dr. Morrison fixed her foggy gaze somewhere in the limbo between her nose and the camera. Candi cranked up her smile a notch or two. Ella pushed the button on her stop-watch. Another "A Day in the Lifestyle" interview began.

CHAPTER 2

"Dr. Morrison, what exactly is The Ranch all about? I mean what is it that you do here . . ." Candi paused, "Exactly?" Candi is not what you'd call a barracuda-style interviewer.

"Well Candi, we call The Ranch a Lifestyles For Wellness Centre and I think that pretty well sums up our whole philosophy. We give each guest who stays here the time and space to examine his or her individual lifestyle. Hopefully, we can motivate every one of them to make a personal commitment not just to developing better physical health but to evolving a whole new way of wellness." Dr. Morrison was off and running. I could see she had already dismissed Candi as a dumb blonde. Many of Candi's interviewees did this. Most of them regretted it.

"What's the difference between health and wellness?" Candi saved Dr. Morrison the bother of a rhetorical question.

"I feel the term health is very limiting, Candi. It implies only the physical, when really there's so much more to our total well being. There's our mental health and our occupational health and even the health of our other-directed relationships. The word wellness encompasses all these aspects of health and this is very important when you consider that what we strive for at The Ranch is an holistic approach." Dr. Morrison stopped and waited for one of Ella's scripted questions.

"You mean The Ranch really isn't just a fat farm?"

Candi slipped in one of her surprises.

"A fat farm?" The doctor feigned innocence with a puzzled smile. I could feel Ella screaming behind me.

"You know, a fat farm. A place where people come to lose weight," Candi explained patiently, not in the least disconcerted.

"Here at The Ranch we *never* emphasize the negative," Dr. Morrison said, stressing the "never." "And, to my way of thinking, Candi, reducing diets most certainly are negative. So the answer to your question is no. The Ranch is not a place for the treatment of the pathologically obese." She made it sound like the criminally insane. "What we do emphasize is the positive value of good nutrition and the part it plays in a whole lifestyle. We all know just how easy it is to let ten or fifteen extra pounds creep on around our middles," Dr. Morrison patted her firm, flat stomach. "But a reducing diet really isn't the answer. Instead, here at The Ranch we help our guests to discover and maintain their ideal body shape." Dr. Morrison paused for breath.

"That's kind of like what they say at my aerobics class, 'If you want to keep your shape good, you've got to keep in good shape.'" Candi shot her comment into the pause. Ella did a little more silent shrieking. Dr. Morrison looked puzzled.

"That really is a fun way of putting it Candi, but I think there's a little more to the concept of body shape than that. At The Ranch, we view weight loss not as an end in itself but simply as a natural result of wellness."

I wondered how much of this stuff Dr. Morrison actually believed. For the next five minutes, Candi stuck pretty closely to Ella's script. It gave the doctor a chance to promote the benefits to be derived from a week at The Ranch with a vigour that stopped just short of the promise of eternal life.

"In conclusion I guess I can best sum up by saying that what we really try to encourage at The Ranch is nothing more than simple living. Simplicity," Dr. Morrison smiled ruefully. "Everybody knows what the word means but I'm afraid that not very many of us in our stress-filled modern lives actually know what simplicity really feels like." She aimed her unfocused gaze in Candi's general direction.

"I know what you mean Dr. Morrison," Candi stared back earnestly. "Lots of us know how to be simple in our heads but do we really know how to be simple in our hearts?"

Once again Dr. Morrison seemed a little perplexed, almost as if she had begun to suspect Candi of harbouring a secret shred of intelligence behind her guileless blue eyes. She shrugged off the suspicion and continued. "Here at The Ranch we help our guests to strip away the complications and stresses of modern life and come face to face with their simplest feelings and needs."

"Well, you sure do have a beautiful place to strip down to simple things in." Candi gestured grandly around the dome.

"Thank you, Candi. I appreciate your positive comments." Again the puzzled look flickered briefly. "We are very proud to offer our guests world-class facilities here at The Ranch's foothills estate. This estate has a lot of history too. Did you know that the Prince of Wales once went swimming in this pool? He stayed here on one of his trips to Canada.

"Prince Charles actually went swimming in this pool?" Candi gazed at the water with reverence.

"No, no Candi, not the present Prince of Wales. I was referring to Edward VIII, The Prince of Wales who gave up his throne for the woman he loved. He stayed here back in the twenties." Even Dr. Morrison had some regard for truth in advertising.

"Well, it's really not hard to imagine a prince swimming in this pool is it? I've never been in a swimming pool that was even close to being this . . ." Candi searched for an adequate word, ". . . this princely." She looked up at the dome. "What is hard for me to imagine is getting in touch with all that simplicity you talked about earlier. I mean, how can you manage to get in touch with simplicity in a pool that makes you feel like a princess?"

"I really don't think that pleasant surroundings preclude simplicity, do you Candi?" Dr. Morrison continued smoothly. "If anything, this kind of beauty is simplicity itself. Beauty relaxes us and promotes a reflective kind of tranquility if we are only receptive enough to appreciate it."

"I think I see what you mean," Candi agreed, all ingenuous enthusiasm. "What you're saying is that beautiful and simple are sometimes the same." By now it was obvious that Dr. Morrison considered her interviewer the living proof of that equation. "But really," Candi said, her enthusiasm giving way to earnest puzzlement, "It's not just simple simple here, is it? It's world class simple."

"Really Candi, I don't think you understand." Either by deliberate aim or a lucky shot, even I wasn't quite sure which, Candi had succeeded in provoking Dr. Morrison. "Simplicity is a very complicated thing," she continued, considerably irritated. "Maybe the easiest way to explain it to you, is by saying that I regard The Ranch as a working example of Mies van der Rohe's famous dictum, 'Less is More.'"

"Well, that's certainly true," Candi nodded in vigourous agreement. "It costs an absolute fortune to stay here, doesn't it?" I know Ella's wrong. There really is a brain hidden under that froth of spun gold hair.

"Miss Baxter, I thought we agreed we wouldn't talk

money." This time Dr. Morrison ignored both Candi and the camera and spoke straight to Ella. "I think you'll agree our guests have been more than co-operative—they've signed waivers, they've agreed to be photographed and interviewed—so I don't think it would be in the best of taste for us to repay their co-operation by quite literally broadcasting their financial arrangements."

Dr. Morrison was wrong. There was nothing most of The Ranch's guests would have liked better than to have the world know just how much they were able to shell out for their adventure in wellness. The outrageous prices it charged had actually helped The Ranch to establish the considerable social chic it presently enjoyed among the determinedly upwardly mobile.

"Golly, I'm so sorry Dr. Morrison. I guess I must have misunderstood that quotation of yours. Don't worry. Ella will edit that part out, won't you Ella? Sorry." Candi gave us her best silly-me shrug and a twenty-one tooth smile. "And I promise, I really will be careful not to mention that lady who got herself drowned in here. Trust me."

By the time Ella placated Dr. Morrison and put a firm lid on Candi there was nothing much left of the interview. Ella glanced at the rock wall where the late afternoon sun had begun to cast long shadows. "I think we'd better get on to the swim or we're going to have to set up more lights. And Dr. Morrison, if you still want to mention dressing for dinner perhaps you should do it now, before we move the camera." Candi opened her mouth to speak but Ella was quicker. "That's all right, Candi. You don't have to bother with a question. We'll put one in later if it's necessary." Ella was not about to let Candi drop another of her interrogative bombshells. "Tape still running, Phoebe?" I nodded. "Okay, Dr. Morrison, tell us about tonight's dinner at The Ranch. Now." Ella pointed to the doctor who hit her cue like a pro.

"Before we go for our swim, Candi, I should remind you that tonight is a special evening in our dining-room. You've probably noticed that dress is usually very casual at The Ranch but, one night every week, we dress formally for dinner. We thought your viewers might like to see one of those evenings because they are so much a part of our holistic approach to diet and health. You see, Candi, we feel that the pleasures of elegant dress, of a beautifully set table, and of good conversation are all equally important elements of enjoyable dining. As a matter-of-fact, at The Ranch we regard food as the least important part of a meal."

I moved the camera, got the shot of the pair of them diving into the pool and then continued with a few more shots of them swimming. I noticed, with some surprise, that a decidedly masculine third person had materialized in the viewfinder. An aquatic edition of cowboy Byron, this one in a bathing suit and a baseball cap, sat in the comfortable niche of rock that served as the lifeguard's chair. He must have made his silent appearance while I was shooting the dive. No doubt Dr. Morrison had given him careful instructions on when to make his perfectly-timed, unobtrusive entrance. While she might not be willing to talk publicly about last spring's drowning, it was obvious she wanted "A Day in the Lifestyle" to show that The Ranch was appropriately concerned with the safety of its guests.

I finished with a close-up I knew Ella would find particularly tasteless, a view of Dr. Morrison's briefly bikinied bottom as she wriggled it out of the water and plopped it on the edge of the pool. Candi climbed out and stood beside her, an addled Aphrodite in a hot-pink bikini. Her hand rested on one of the stone dolphins. Water glistened on her skin and ran down the strands of shining hair that clung to her shoulders and breasts. Candi is so beautiful that there's no point in even being envious of her. It would be like being jealous of a painting.

"Venus of the Foothills." A quiet voice with a soft Scots burr spoke from behind me. I turned from the tripod where I was busy dismounting the camera. A middle-aged man with grey flecked sandy hair and a stomach that was just deciding to become a paunch stood staring at Candi in open admiration. He wore a pair of baggy beige swimming trunks. "All finished being interviewed Heather?" he called to Dr. Morrison.

"Felix, you're here." It was a statement, not an exclamation. Dr. Morrison pulled on her sweatshirt and dutifully, if unenthusiastically, introduced us to Dr. Felix Sanders, The Ranch's visiting consultant psychiatrist who spent two afternoons a week tending to the guests' mental wellness. We all shook hands with Felix. He didn't bother to hide his disappointment when Candi's charms disappeared into her sweat suit before she offered him her hand.

"I wouldn't think there were many people at The Ranch who needed a psychiatrist." Candi smiled and allowed her hand to linger a little in his by way of consolation for the spoiled view.

"Indeed, Candi, there are not. That's why I can find the time to come bathing with beautiful women." He replied with the elephantine gallantry that often grips even normally sensible men when they first meet Candi.

"I'm afraid we've finished our swim, Felix," Dr. Morrison said briskly. "And we're going to be doing some more shooting for this television program at dinner so you'll have to excuse us while we get ready." It was a dismissal.

"Ah, Heather you fret too much. There's plenty of time before dinner." Felix could not be disposed of so easily. "Phoebe hasn't even finished packing up her camera equipment in here and you can't do anything without her." He turned to me. "That's a video camera not a film camera, isn't it?" I nodded an affirmative. Frankly, I was surprised he knew the difference between the two and I told him so.

"I'm by way of being an amateur film maker myself," he confided in his rolling Scottish r's. "I have some video equipment of my own—just stuff for the home market I'm afraid, nothing professional—but by God would I love to have a set-up like this. Could I have a look at it sometime?"

"Why not come a half hour early for dinner tonight?" I suggested. "I'll be setting up the equipment in the dining-room and you can have a good look at it then. Help me set up if you like."

"Felix doesn't usually stay for dinner," Dr. Morrison said quickly.

"But tonight I would be delighted to accept your gracious invitation, Heather." He was unfazed. "You can expect your new camera assistant at seven."

"It's a formal evening, you'll need a dinner jacket," Dr. Morrison warned.

"Thanks for reminding me," he replied.

"It's a sashimi night, Felix," Dr. Morrison played the last card in her bid to put him off.

"Raw fish. What a treat, Heather. I can't remember when I last tucked into a nice bit of cold cod. Just tell the cook to toss another flipper on the platter and I'll be there. See you all at dinner." He climbed into the pool and struck out for the deep end in an untidy crawl.

Dr. Morrison knew when she was beaten. She and Candi left the pool to change out of their wet bathing suits. Ella stayed behind to help me pack up the gear. The hunk in the baseball cap climbed down from the lifeguard's niche and walked toward us. He was almost as good looking as Byron although maybe the bathing suit gave him an unfair edge.

"Hi, I'm Marty Bradshaw. I'm the lifeguard here," he added unnecessarily. He smiled at Ella. "If you'd like to go for a swim we keep suits in every size especially for visitors. You too." He nodded politely at me but I was obviously an afterthought.

"That's very generous of you, Mr. Bradshaw," Ella shook his proffered hand, "I really think that . . ."

"Please," he interrupted, "Not Mr. Bradshaw, just Marty." He pointed to Felix now thrashing his way towards us. "I have to stay here to watch him, and lots of the guests will be coming for their pre-dinner swim soon so it won't be any trouble at all for me to watch you too."

"Thanks for the offer, Marty." I slid the tripod's legs up and strapped them together. "But I want to get this gear squared away and go home for an hour before I have to change and be back here for dinner." I don't think he even heard me. He was still smiling at Ella, inexplicably smitten by her tailored charms.

"It's really a wonderful pool if you like to swim," he added by way of persuasion.

Poor Marty was wasting his time. Ella never mixed business with pleasure and, if she ever did, it certainly wouldn't be with a nearly nude jock ten years her junior. She goes for the intellectual type. She's definitely a brains-before-brawn kind of woman.

"Thanks Marty, I'd love to go swimming," Ella said. "I'm a size eight."

I packed up the tripod and went home.

CHAPTER 3

A spectacular autumn sunset lit the three mile drive from The Ranch to my place. I drove the station's van through my gates just as the sun slipped behind the mountains. Its last rays backlit the peaks, outlining them for an instant in a filigree of gold against the indigo evening sky. Like The Ranch's land, my much more modest tract backs on to the government forest reserve, so the wilderness of the Rocky Mountain foothills is, quite literally, just out our back doors. However, because both front doors are within easy commuting distance of Calgary our stretch of foothills is prime gentleman ranchers' country and even small parcels of land are pricey. I can afford to live on my forty acres only because I inherited them from my Uncle Andrew.

The dog trotted sedately from his sleeping spot by the house to welcome me home. The dog is part of the unfinished business of my marriage. My ex-husband bought him shortly after we moved from Calgary and came to live here on my newly inherited property. I hadn't wanted a dog. My work demands a great deal of time and takes me away from home frequently so it has made me reluctant to encumber myself with domestic responsibilities. According to Gavin that is why our marriage failed. Who knows, maybe he's right. Gavin now lives in a no-pets apartment in Calgary.

The dog was to be a working animal not a pet, or so Gavin said. According to the man who sold him to us, our puppy came from a long line of wonderful watch-dogs. When Gavin brought him home he was a ten week bundle of tan fur and floppy ears. In less than a year he grew to be the most enormous German Shepherd I have ever seen, complete with paws that would do credit to a Siberian tiger and a set of teeth to match. But he's no watch-dog. Instead, he's the kind of animal usually advertised as "great with kids." He seldom growls or barks and he approaches the world with a bashful curiosity more appropriate to a fawn than a watch-dog. It was typical of my ex-husband to have picked the only poet from a litter of soldiers.

The dog sniffed my shoes. He ambled along behind me while I put the camera in the house and followed me to the corral where I stabled and fed Elvira and Pete. Like the dog, Elvira and Pete are unplanned encumbrances. They actually belong to my friend Cyril Vaughn. Cyrrie calls them my paying guests. Elvira is a retired race horse who deigns to grace my pasture with her elegant presence during the day and graciously occupies a box stall in my small barn at night. Pete, the pinto pony, is her humble companion. Elvira is a terrible snob. Even so, she sometimes condescends to touch noses with the dog or to give me a couple of patronising nudges as I put my hand through her halter to lead her to the barn. Pete loves everyone, especially Elvira.

Usually, my neighbour's teenage son looks after feeding and stabling them but on those occasions when he can't oblige he lets me know by leaving punctuation-free messages in my mailbox. This morning's note read, "You feed pm football Tom." I interpreted this to mean that he intended to stay late in Calgary, where he commutes to school every day, in order to attend a football game. Therefore, I should feed the horses this evening. A confirming phone call from his mother usually supplements Tom's cryptic communications. I hung the horses' full water buckets from the hooks in their stalls, closed the half doors and watched them munch their hay for a minute or two. It was very quiet in the barn except for the rhythmic sound of their contented chewing. There is something snug and comforting about watching the horses eat. I left before Elvira could remind me that she had earned more in one season at the track than I had in my eight years behind a camera.

It was pitch dark when I closed the barn door. Familiarity, not sight, guided my steps as I walked along the moonless black path through the trees to my small bungalow. I stopped in a clearing to look at the stars. Although the lights of Calgary now produce a diffuse red glow on the northeast horizon, a glow that grows in intensity every year as the city grows and spreads, the foothills sky is still awash with stars.

My stargazing was interrupted by the raucous shriek of a steam whistle. Its harsh sound ripped through the quiet evening. The dog began to tremble and I braced myself for the inevitable second blast. It came, followed rapidly by a third and then a fourth, each piercing screech pitched a grating fraction of a tone under the octave of the one before. The steam calliope needed tuning again. The steam calliope always needs tuning. I doubt there is an instrument that sounds worse than an out of tune calliope. I know there are none louder.

The calliope lives next door. It is the prized possession of Tom's father, a fanatic steam engine hobbyist. By day Jack is a high-powered lawyer with a Calgary oil company but, in the evenings and on weekends, his heart is in steam. He's always on the lookout for prizes to add to his collection of antique engines. Because much of the agricultural machinery used in the early part of this century was steam driven, rural Alberta is a good hunting ground. Even so, compared to the very practical tractors and threshing machines that make up the bulk of Jack's collection, the frivolous old instrument was an unlikely find.

Jack hit the collector's jackpot when he discovered the calliope's hundred-year-old remains oxidizing their way to oblivion in a barn near Cluny. How the old circus instrument came to be there remains a mystery. He hauled his find back to his workshop and spent the next year restoring the pile of tarnished brass and broken keys back into a working music machine. The calliope is now the jewel of his collection and the love of his life. Unfortunately, neither his family nor the neighbourhood dogs share Jack's passion.

A calliope's whistle is one of the happiest noises in the world but it is also one of the loudest. It can be heard for a distance of ten miles. Within five miles it sets off the dogs. Under a mile it curdles milk—in the cow. At point blank range it can shake the fillings out of your teeth. Therefore, according to an agreement he has with his wife, Jack is only supposed to play the calliope on Saturday mornings when she can arrange to be well away from their house and out of its direct line of fire. Actually, the whole neighbourhood was grateful to Barbara for negotiating this concession as we'd all been startled so many times by the haphazard shrieks that we were beginning to feel pretty unnerved. However, despite his best intentions to abide by the agreement, sometimes, usually when Barbara is out, Jack simply can't resist sneaking in a little mid-week tuning session in the evening after work.

One more banshee note shrilled its way across the pasture and then silence. It took a moment or two for the dog to collect his wits. He usually spends calliope concerts in the house hiding under my desk but the evening tuning session had caught him off guard. Finally, he stopped quivering and wagged his tail a couple of times. His cold wet nose touched my hand, a polite reminder that there was another animal dinner to prepare before I showered, dressed, and went back to photograph dishes of fishes at The Ranch. I took the hint.

Back at the house I gave the dog his food which he ate with his customary cat-like fastidiousness. The prospect of working for a whole evening on another of The Ranch's meagre meals drove me to making a life-sustaining peanut butter sandwich for myself. I ate it standing in front of my closet as I searched for something to wear that was elegant enough to pass muster at The Ranch's evening fashion parade yet practical enough to allow me to heft around the video equipment. It was a discouraging search.

I'm fond of clothes but, in my job, dressing for success means wearing things that allow me the complete freedom of movement I need to operate a camera. Constantly wearing slacks may be practical but it's also pretty boring. The best compromise between practicality and fashion that I've come up with to date is tailored culottes worn with roomy, raglan sleeved blouses and sensible shoes. My culottes outfits are hardly the height of chic but they have earned me a reputation among my fellow television photographers as a pretty snappy dresser. Since all of them are male and take a perverse pride in looking like mobile laundry bags, this is rather like being hailed as a musical genius by people who can't hum "Three Blind Mice."

I looked longingly at the dress Cyrrie had bought for me last spring on his annual trip to London. It's an original Molyneux that he found in an antique clothing store. Although it is over fifty years old, that dress is by far the most elegant piece of clothing I've ever owned. It is made of black silk, very clingy and très décolleté. The narrow straps and the ingenious way the material is cut and draped are sexy as hell. Sometimes I think it's too much dress for a mere mortal like me. Clothes should not have lived longer and more interesting lives than their occupants and the Molyneux has me beat on both counts. Cyrrie swears that shortly before the war he saw Gertrude Lawrence in a gown just like it having dinner at the Ritz with Noel Coward. He thinks that mine might even be that very same one. Cyrrie tells delightful stories.

The Molyneux intimidates me a little but nevertheless I'd been longing for a chance to wear it. Evenings calling for formal dress are not exactly crowding each other off my social calendar and The Ranch's dinner seemed to be as suitable an occasion as I was likely to encounter for some time. Even so, I nearly rejected it in favour of something more practical. Bare shoulders are no place to rest thirty pounds of camera.

Out of respect for the Molyneux, I took a little longer than usual getting ready. I showered, put on my make-up, beat my hair into submission, dressed, and left the house in just under fifteen minutes. The night was chilly. The Molyneux was probably accustomed to being swathed in furs on frosty evenings but there's a limit to the kind of second-hand clothing I'm willing to wear. If the original owner had to die to donate then count me out. The black silk did look a little silly peeking out from under the sausagey bulk of my down-filled coat but at least I was warm on my drive back to The Ranch. Except for my feet. They felt like blocks of ice in my flimsy shoes.

It was after seven when I arrived at The Ranch's floodlit gates. I peered into the lens of a closed circuit television camera mounted just above an intercom, pushed the buzzer, and identified myself to the disembodied voice that answered. I heard a click and the gates swung open in front of me. Big old pine trees lined the driveway and after a few lovely lungfuls of their scent I pulled up at the main house beside a small sign that discreetly requested me not to park in front of the door. It often feels like the greater part of a television photographer's life consists of hauling camera equipment from place to place so we soon learn to ignore signs, find the shortest distance between hauls, and send the parking tickets to the station.

I collected the tripod and a light case from the back of the van and climbed the broad stone stairs that led to the house's imposing pair of oak doors. In our district, Mrs. Malifant's old mansion is a three-storey sandstone and timber legend. Alberta's early cattle barons were never famous for their modest tastes and, even by their standards, the house had been considered madly extravagant for its time. Just hauling dressed stone from the quarry near Okotoks out here to the hills was a mammoth undertaking in 1923, especially as then the last ten miles were nothing but a dirt track.

The first two storeys were brightly lit, both inside and out. Floodlights shone up from the autumn-empty flower beds that flanked the stairs, illuminating the warm buff of the sandstone blocks. Light glowed from inside the tall, mullioned windows. The floodlights shone less brightly on the timbered third storey, whose gabled windows and sloping roof proclaimed it the former servants' quarters. With one exception, the windows of the offices it presently housed were dark too. The door in front of me sported a brass bull's head with a ring through its nose for a knocker. It fell on the oak with a satisfying thud and summoned Mr. Reilly.

"Good evening, Miss Fairfax. Here, let me help you with that." He reached for the light case. "Do you have much other equipment to bring in?" I had. "I expect you're dropping off your equipment on your way to the visitor's parking lot." I wasn't. "Do let me help you with the rest of your gear before you move your van."

Unpacked, legally parked, and with my coat stashed in a large closet off the main hall, I followed Mr. Reilly to the wood panelled dining-room where I began to set up the lights and camera. He left me in the company of two white-jacketed waiters who were busily putting the finishing touches to the place settings on the half dozen large oval dining tables. Because this was a sashimi night the place settings were Japanese style, complete with lacquered chopsticks and delicate porcelain tea cups. The waiters finished folding the last of the napkins and then left me alone to run the light cord under the edge of a pale rose Aubusson over to the nearest electrical outlet.

"Hello, Phoebe. Sorry to be late. It really doesn't make a very good first impression on the job, does it?" Felix bounded into the room. His ruddy cheeks were freshly shaved and he smelled pleasantly of soap. He wore a glittery blue dinner jacket that was too big in the shoulders and too small round the middle. Electric blue metallic threads woven into the cloth shimmered like the iridescent scales on a tropical fish.

"Ready for the sashimi? God-awful stuff to eat but very photogenic." He looked around him at the beautifully set tables. "I see we have a full house tonight."

"That's unusual?"

"It is on sashimi nights. Many of the guests just have a tray sent to their cabins but tonight is different. Must be the magic of television. I knew that you and your camera would inspire them to come and be seen even if it meant they had to eat raw fish."

"If the guests don't like it then why does The Ranch bother to serve sashimi?"

"Phoebe, Phoebe." He shook his head in mock amazement. "You are a naive one. The Ranch doesn't serve food because it's enjoyable, The Ranch serves food because it's good for you. Whether you like it or not is irrelevant. The fact that sushi and sashimi are very fashionable foods these days might just have a little something to do with it too."

"Is it still fashionable? I thought sushi was out." I make no claim to any sort of expertise in food fashions but Cyrrie says that raw fish is definitely yesterday's news.

"You may be right," Felix agreed. "If so everyone at The Ranch will be vastly relieved, including me. In my books, sashimi is strictly for seals."

"And you were willing to eat seal food just to get a chance to look at this stuff?" I pointed at the camera.

"Not just to look at the equipment. I'm taking a photography class at the community college and I wanted a chance to see how a real pro does it. You're famous, you know. I've heard a lot about you. I've even seen some of your films."

"Then you must be in Jerry O'Neil's class," I said. "Jerry's class is the one place I'm even remotely famous and that's only because I let him use my films for show and tell." Jerry is one of the best news photographers in the business but after fifteen years of filming every war in the world he decided a little peace might not be a bad idea so he took a job with one of the local stations. He also teaches an evening course in motion picture and video photography geared to amateurs and their equipment. His class was the only place I could think of where Felix might have seen my films. "Why didn't you tell me you were one of Jerry's students?"

"Why didn't you tell me that you're the Phoebe Fairfax who makes those amazing nature films?"

"Gosh. I should have mentioned it. Just think, you might have mistaken me for some other Phoebe Fairfax."

"I must admit, your name does tend to linger in the mind."

"You mean it sounds like something out of Gilbert and

Sullivan."

"Really, Phoebe, I'm not joking. Your work is good," he said. "It's better than good, it's wonderful. In the true sense of the word. It's full of wonder."

I mumbled my thanks. I am not used to basking in praise for my natural history work. Most of my films are about the more unglamourous, uncute and uncuddly bits of nature. They are not exactly hot sellers. Right now I'm working on one about a beaver pond. I'm hoping it might have a little more crowd appeal than my last effort on wolf spiders did.

"You look uncomfortable," Felix continued. "Aren't you pleased when someone appreciates your work?"

"Very pleased," I said. "And also surprised that you've seen any of it." Actually I wasn't surprised that he knew my work. I was astounded.

"Well, you shouldn't be surprised. Jerry's shown our class four of your films. I think the one about meadow voles was the best. Even better than the one that won the Canadian Nature Whatsit prize."

"The Canadian Conservation Gold Medal." I supplied the title of the very modest award I had recently received.

"That's the one. It must really be fun to do work like that. I still don't know how you managed to get some of those shots."

"It's mostly luck and patience. And time. Lots and lots of time." I looked at my watch. "Which is something we don't have right now. We'd better get this stuff set up." The equipment lay scattered around the dining-room floor.

"What's simple enough for me to do?" Felix asked. I put him to work setting up the tripod while I carried on with the lights. He looked up from unbuckling the straps and caught me eyeing his ill-fitting jacket. "It belongs to Byron," he explained. "It's his second best dinner jacket. He loaned it to me for the evening."

"I'm trying to imagine what the first best must be like."

"I'm crushed. You're not impressed," he laughed. "But really, there's nothing wrong with this jacket that my shedding ten pounds and twenty years wouldn't fix. Honestly, it looks terrific on Byron."

I had my doubts. Even the beautiful Byron couldn't redeem those brocaded satin lapels. "It's hard to imagine Byron in a dinner jacket."

"All the men who work for The Ranch have to own a dinner jacket," Felix said. "Generally there's a shortage of men among the guests so the staff is called on to help make up the difference at Heather's formal dinners. You'll see some of them tonight."

Most health resorts that feature weight reduction in their regimens, which is simply another way of saying most health resorts, attract greater numbers of women than men. The Ranch was no exception. There were always a few too many women and, without the resident Apollos to beef up the gentlemen's ranks, some nights the dining-room looked like a sorority reunion. Apparently, none of The Ranch's male employees objected to this duty and neither, it seemed, did the women whose tables they balanced so beautifully. I wondered if the stalwart studs filled any other gaps in the solitary ladies' lives but I couldn't think of a tactful way to put the question. "Do all The Ranch's employees live out here?" I asked instead.

"Most of them do, at least during their working week. Some of them have homes and families in Calgary where they go on their days off but most of the single ones live out here all the time."

"Dedicated?"

"Well paid," Felix stated bluntly. "Exceedingly well paid."

The ratio of staff to guests at The Ranch favoured the

staff, and every employee, from the medical people to the manicurist, was the best that money could buy. The Ranch demanded a high level of performance from its workers but, as Felix said, it paid them well. Besides a basic wage a good twenty-five percent higher than most of them could earn elsewhere, The Ranch provided comfortable accommodation, excellent meals, and a generous employee benefit package. One of the most popular parts of that package was a long annual holiday and cut-rate prices at any of the luxury hotels that The Ranch's parent company owned all over the world. In return, The Ranch got the dedicated service of a hard-working, well-qualified and relatively stable staff. Most of them had been with The Ranch since it opened and few employees resigned. Dental plans are all very well, but there's nothing like the promise of a cheap winter holiday at a luxury hotel in the tropics to buy a Canadian's loyalty forever.

Most of the full time employees were young and male. Besides the guests, the only people at The Ranch over forty were Mr. Reilly, the secretary he shared with Dr. Morrison, and the head chef. Women employees—the chambermaids, the nutritionist, the secretary, and one lone young woman who conducted aerobics classes—were definitely a minority group. The employees who dealt directly with the guests, mainly the exercise experts and the physiotherapy staff, were almost exclusively male and under thirty. It was this group that provided the manly touch at dinner.

"They eat with the guests every night?" I remembered my meagre lunch. "Why haven't they starved to death?"

"Not every night. Not even The Ranch could buy that kind of loyalty," Felix said. "They're only required to appear at Heather's weekly dress-up dinners. She's very picky about this formal dining business. I think she hopes the guests will concentrate so hard on dressing for dinner that they'll forget there's nothing to eat. And maybe she's right. Wait until you see some of the outfits that appear tonight."

"Will Byron be wearing his first best dinner jacket?"

"I assure you, it makes this one look conservative," Felix said. "Now what else can I do?"

Whether he meant about the jacket or the camera gear I couldn't tell but I found myself enjoying Felix's company. He was an immediately appealing man in a rumpled and funny and comfortable sort of way. He was also a very enthusiastic photographer and he quizzed me knowledgeably about the gear as we finished setting up. He actually listened to my lecture on increasing depth of field in slow motion close-ups. That takes dedication. It even bores me. He waited until I had droned to a finish before he spoke.

"I really should apologize to you, Phoebe," he said. I'm here partly under false pretenses. I didn't come just for the photography lesson. You see, I know you were the one who discovered the body in the pool last spring and I'd like to ask you about it, if you don't mind."

My heart sunk. "I'm sorry Felix, but right now I do mind. I have an evening's work in front of me and there really isn't time to talk about something that I'd sooner forget."

"It's important," he said. "Perhaps we could meet later."

"I can't tell you anything that isn't in the police report. They must have questioned me five separate times. Absolutely everything I saw and did is in that report. I just want to forget about it."

"The incident still bothers you, does it?" It was more a statement than a question.

"I guess it does," I admitted. As a television photographer, I'm no stranger to violent death. I've shot my share of accident victims on their way to the morgue via the six o'clock news. It's all in a day's work and, in the viewfinder of my camera, everything is small and far away. Through a lens, even death is distant and diminished. But finding this woman had been different.

"Can you think of any reason why it should still be so disturbing to you?" he asked.

"Maybe being back at The Ranch has something to do with it," I said. That morning, in the soft grey light of the spring dawn, there was no camera to hide behind. For me the woman I found would never be just another anonymous mound on a stretcher. She was a person. She had a face. She'd had a life. She had those awful staring eyes.

"Do you think that's the only reason?" Felix persisted.

"No, I don't," I snapped. "But unless you're prepared to conjure up a couch and bill me for your time I think I should get back to work." The anger in my voice startled me. It obviously surprised Felix too. He quickly apologized.

"I'm sorry, Phoebe. I'm being very rude. I shouldn't have brought the subject up. I apologize if I've upset you."

"And I apologize too. I shouldn't have overreacted like that." We stood looking at each other. There was an awkward pause.

"Apologies accepted all round?" He broke the silence.

"Absolutely," I replied.

"Good. Because, Phoebe, I truly didn't mean to . . ." The dinner gong interrupted him.

"Saved by the bell," I said. "Grab that light will you, and we'll get some shots of the guests having their drinks."

Felix picked up the portable flood. "I'll bring it along but I think you'll find it's superfluous. The Ranch's guests are all so dazzling you won't need any extra light."

CHAPTER 4

A small forest burned brightly in the huge brown-tiled fireplace. Its heat radiated far into the understated art deco living-room where the guests had assembled for drinks. Here, too, The Ranch's renovators had preserved the best of the original twenties' features, including a magnificent Lalique chandelier and the angular marquetry of the polished hardwood floor. A similar geometrical motif ran through the beige on beige drapes that covered the entire west wall and closed off a bank of floor to ceiling windows. The other walls were covered in a subdued, sandy coloured silk. Four large bowls of cut flowers, each one on a small, high table in its own corner of the room, provided the only real colour amid the meticulous monochromes. Unless, of course, you counted The Ranch's guests. As Felix predicted, they dazzled.

They wandered in all expensively and, for the most part, beautifully dressed. While the waiters served them their non-alcoholic cocktails, I hoisted the camera on to my shoulder and Felix and I started round the room. It was like photographing my way through a list of contemporary couturiers. Even some of the men had abandoned their traditionally conservative evening colours. A few had gone so far as to wear cummerbunds that matched their ladies' gowns. It marked them as a pair, like mated birds with matching plumage. Strictly speaking, I suppose this sartorial colour coding was in questionable taste, but I liked it. It was the one ingenuous touch in a room full of relentless sophistication. Not that the opinions of a woman wearing a dress so old it had been bombed in the blitz would count for much in this crowd.

Reg came in looking scrubbed and pink in his dinner jacket, his paunch held neatly in place by a conservative black cummerbund. A woman I presumed to be his wife accompanied him. She was a couple of inches taller than Reg and fashionably thin. Besides an expression of permanent irritability, she wore a shimmery black dress and a matching cape lined with red silk. Presumably the cape was her concession to a short walk in the chill night air. She looked like Dracula in drag.

Marty and Ella came in together, Ella in the evening equivalent of her business suit and Marty looking almost as gorgeous in clothes as he did in his bathing trunks. Byron's first best dinner jacket was everything Felix had promised and more. It was wine-red, high buttoned with western style arrow-cut pockets, a nipped-in waist, and gold lariats embroidered on the lapels. Beside it, his electric-blue second-best seemed like the quintessence of understated elegance. A pink ruffled shirt, a string tie, flared trousers and cowboy boots completed the costume.

Felix and I finished our lap with the camera, collected our drinks, and took ourselves and the camera equipment off to stand in a corner near a flower vase. I noticed that Felix had refused one of the cocktails and stuck to mineral water. I tasted my carrot juice concoction and wished I had followed his example. I hoped it wouldn't wilt the flowers.

As soon as all the guests were well launched into the drinks, Dr. Morrison and Candi made their entrance. Contacts in and clothes on, Dr. Morrison was a pretty spectacular sight but she was no match for "A Day in the Lifestyle's" intrepid interviewer. Candi drifted into the room in a cloud of sea green silk. I heard the collective intake of breath from all the men present. You could practically smell their testosterone levels rising. They seemed to have stopped breathing.

"Hi, Phoebe." Candi smiled and waved to me across the room. Every male eye followed her as she walked over and stood beside me. I could have been stark naked and painted blue and none of them would have noticed. Candi Sinclair, the Zuleika Dobson of the Canadian West, struck again.

"If I could have your attention please." Dr. Morrison broke Candi's spell and the collectively held male breath exhaled itself in a gusty communal sigh. "We have some guests at dinner this evening." Beginning with Ella, she proceeded to introduce the "Lifestyle" crew. A series of strangled little masculine murmurs followed Candi's turn. Undaunted, Dr. Morrison continued. "And now Miss Baxter would like to say a few words to you."

Ella stepped forward. "Thank you, Heather." I was startled. Ella rarely called the program's guests by their first names and Dr. Morrison seemed an unlikely candidate for such familiarity. "On behalf of all of us who work on 'A Day in the Lifestyle' I would like to thank all of you for your co-operation on this project." Since the total extent of the guests' co-operation had been to permit me to photograph them from becoming angles as they went about their normal round of activities, their stint before the camera had hardly been what you'd call a strain. However, I suppose it never hurts to flatter the foreground action a little. "It has been very gracious of you to allow us to interrupt your stay at The Ranch." Ella was pushing the flattery a little, I thought. "And by way of thanks, 'A Day in the Lifestyle' would like all of you to have a copy of the program that we are taping today. After this edition of 'Lifestyle' has aired we will be sending each one of you a video cassette."

I nearly dropped the camera. Someone must have put something in Ella's carrot juice. "A Day in the Lifestyle" never gave anything away to anybody. "A Day in the Lifestyle" regarded paying my salary as an act of flagrant profligacy. But, Ella wasn't finished. "And, of course, there will be a copy for each member of The Ranch's staff as well. You've all been just so wonderful to us."

Truly, Ella had taken leave of her senses. She smiled at the guests' polite applause that greeted her remarks. She beamed at Marty's enthusiastic clapping. "Thank you. My thanks to all of you." She spread her arms to embrace the room in a generous, spontaneous, and totally inappropriate gesture. By now, I was really worried about her.

"Phoebe, guess what? Ella's in love!" Candi whispered conspiratorially, her imagination in high gear again.

"Sounds to me like she's been drinking," I whispered back.

"She's in love," Candi insisted.

"Maybe she fell and hit her head on the edge of the pool."

"She's in love."

"She's deranged."

"Phoebe, Ella is in love with the lifeguard," Candi explained patiently. "Even you should be able to see that."

I don't quite know what Candi meant by *even* me, but experience has taught me never to ask what Candi means by anything she says. Her interviewees soon learn the same lesson. Dr. Morrison took the floor once again.

"Thank you very much, Miss Baxter. That's very generous of you . . . ," she hesitated, "Ella." She looked uncertainly at Ella who smiled back with an effervescence worthy of Candi. "I know we'll all look forward to receiving our videotapes." Even Dr. Morrison had noticed that Ella was not quite herself. "And now I'm sure that Chef Sugamoto wants us in the dining-room to start sampling some of his beautiful sashimi. I guess I should use the Japanese term and call him Itamae Sugamoto, shouldn't I?"

The doctor's rhetorical question fell on ears deafened by hunger. She hadn't finished speaking before The Ranch guests plunked down their cocktail glasses and marched smartly into the dining-room. The rest of us followed at a slightly less famished pace.

Candi and Ella and I completely disrupted Dr. Morrison's carefully calculated balance of the sexes. Obviously the doctor thought she could minimize this social calamity by concentrating us in one area so she sat all three of us at her own table. I also think she wanted to keep potential annoyance away from the paying customers and that afternoon's interview had branded Candi as a prime source of conversational grief. My constant coming and going with the camera marked me, too, as a definite dinner disrupter. Before Ella's crazed speech, Dr. Morrison had probably regarded our starchy producer as first-class formal dining material but now even Ella was tucked safely between the doctor herself and Felix. What Reg and Mrs. Reg, whose name was Deanne, had done to deserve exile with us I didn't know but they, and the beautiful Byron, completed our table of eight.

I noticed the other Apollos, including Marty, scattered around the room to decorative advantage. Their good looks glowed with the rude health of youth that no amount of money and perseverance could ever restore to their middle-aged dinner companions.

The waiters served soup in small blue and white bowls. Thin slices of carrot and green onion floated in a savory fish broth. Most of the guests guzzled their bowls down before any of us outsiders had taken more than a couple of tentative sips. Unfortunately, most of my soup grew cold while I got ready to photograph the ceremonial entrance of the sashimi carts.

All it lacked was a drum roll. As soon as the soup dishes were cleared away, the double doors to the kitchen opened and the Japanese chef and his assistants, immaculate in their starched whites, wheeled two large food trolleys into the dining-room. I got a good shot of one of the mobile work stations as it rolled past and an even better one of Itamae Sugamoto winking at me as he passed in front of the camera. "Hey, Phoeb," he murmured, his eyes fixed on the spot where I stopped and the Molyneux began. "You got the best looking dress in the room."

Itamae Sugamoto and I have been friends since high school. In those earlier and easier days he had been plain Ben Sugamoto, third-generation Canadian and star of the school musicals. He'd made a fine Modern Major General and an even better Music Man. Now he was a chef, a respected restaurateur and family man. Nevertheless, there was more than a touch of the old dramatic Ben in this well-timed entrance of Itamae Sugamoto, flamboyant sashimi artiste. It was a role he was well qualified to play since he had actually studied the art of sushi and sashimi preparation in Japan. Every Monday night Ben and his team packed their special knives and dishes and an assortment of fresh fish into a van and drove from Calgary to cater The Ranch's sashimi meal. Their appearance here coincided with the weekly closing day of Sugamoto's Japanese Restaurant, the family business Ben ran in partnership with his wife. Sashimi night also gave The Ranch's regular cooks a night off. I don't think Ben ever took a night off.

He and his two assistants worked with amazing speed assembling the highly intricate morsels of food and arranging them artfully on white platters that the waiters delivered to the guests along with minute individual bowls of brown rice, Japanese style salad, and large pots of tea. Sashimi is as much a form of visual art as it is food and the whole meal was wonderful to photograph. I simply let the tape roll as I wandered from table to table. I finished the sequence with a shot of Ben. Tonight, he seemed more conjuror than cook. His knife made a lightening pass over a small trout, instantly reducing its flesh to paper thin slices. I half expected him to pass his hand over the pieces and see the trout magically reform and swim away though the air.

"Ben, you should have been a magician. Thanks." I turned off the camera and prepared to return to my table.

"It's okay, Phoeb. For you, anytime." Ben didn't look up from the salmon rosettes. He always used the old high school diminutive of my name, Phoeb pronounced Feeb.

"Can't I be Phoebe in public Ben? Just once?"

"Can't run away from your past, Phoeb." He winked again and flourished a piece of tuna. "Talk to you later, eh? Come back to the kitchen after dinner." He sliced the tuna in a perfect domino pattern. "And Phoeb, make sure you try the blowfish. As us chefs say, it's the *dernier cri.*"

I returned to my table and helped myself to one of Ben's creations. The sliver of squid lay cold on my plate. Still, it was a good deal livelier than the dinner conversation at Dr. Morrison's table. Reg sat on my right. He hardly spoke. He hardly ate. Candi had him mesmerized. He simply sat and stared across the table at her. Ella, too, seemed to occupy a different dimension. From time to time, both of them beamed beatific but absent-minded smiles at their fellow diners, none of whom noticed.

Byron applied all his concentration to shovelling sashimi and rice into his mouth. He used his chopsticks like a culinary back hoe.

Dr. Morrison knew all the correct Japanese names for each kind of sashimi plus their English translations. The rest of us might get by with, "pass me one of those pink thingies with the green goo on it," but not the doctor. She could recite whole platters of the stuff and, what's worse, she did. Whenever there was a lull in the conversation— and at our table lulls outnumbered chat by an impressive margin—Dr. Morrison filled the gap by reading the fishy roll-call.

Deanne and Candi and Felix made attempts at something not even Candi at her most optimistic would have called conversation, but at least they tried. By the time I returned, they had reached a first name basis and the early stages of what seemed to be a discussion of socialized medicine. I believe it had begun with Felix's remark that sashimi, while it looked lovely, tended to make his after-dinner cigar taste funny. I sat down just as Deanne launched into a lecture on the evils of smoking.

"I wouldn't object so much to people smoking if they didn't do it around me and if I didn't have to pay for it." She stabbed the air with a scarlet fingernail by way of emphasis. Her bony, blue-veined hand seemed much older than her face, which had obviously achieved its present elevation with surgical assistance. "Those of us who are not tobacco addicts should not be forced to bear the medical expenses of people who smoke," Deanne's lecture continued. "Smokers shouldn't get one red cent's worth of medical assistance even from private health insurance schemes. They should have to pay the cost of their self-induced illnesses themselves. Why should I subsidize anyone's voluntary diseases?" She pinched a chunk of tuna in her chopsticks.

"You mean you'd do away with public VD clinics?" Candi asked in her best ingenuous voice.

"VD clinics? What on earth do VD clinics have to do with smoking? I don't think I understand what you mean." Deanne treated us to a patronizing smile meant to imply that Candi obviously had not quite got the point. Unlike Dr. Morrison, Deanne was not aware of the conversational pitfalls awaiting those who used this tactic on Candi.

"Oh, Deanne, you must know what VD is," Candi replied. "There's syphilis and gonorrhea and herpes and . . ."

"Of course I know what venereal diseases are," Deanne interrupted Candi's lugubrious litany. "I simply fail to see what they have to do with the topic we are discussing."

"Well," Candi paused for a thoughtful moment, squid-loaded chopsticks half-way to her mouth. "You see," she reasoned, "the way you get VD is just as voluntary as the way you get diseases from smoking. I mean, you're right, Deanne, no one makes you smoke," she conceded. "But then, no one exactly makes you go out and screw around either, do they?" She popped the rubbery morsel into her mouth and chewed cheerfully.

Any reply Deanne may have considered was drowned by Felix's laughter. He threw back his head and roared. Even Reg managed a smile with both eyes focussed. Felix finally regained enough composure to speak. "Candi, you are a marvelous woman and I salute your considerable powers of logic." He reached for his tiny cup and slopped a little tea over the tablecloth as he drank a toast.

"A woman is only a woman, but a good cigar is a smoke." Byron made his first conversational contribution to the meal. It stunned the table into silence. "I didn't make that up myself," he smiled modestly. "I heard it on TV and it just sort of stuck in my head."

"That's Kipling, isn't it?" Dr. Morrison asked. Byron stared at her with eyes as blank as those of the rainbow trout that gazed up from the platter in front of him. Nevertheless, the doctor grasped this slender conversational thread and attempted to weave it into a new beginning. "Do you like poetry, Deanne?"

"No."

"I do," Candi chimed in, but Dr. Morrison ignored her. "My favourite poet is Shelley."

"Hail to thee blithe spirit," Felix began.

"Bird thou never wert," Candi finished.

I'm hallucinating, I thought. Maybe Ben hadn't been joking about the blowfish and this was the beginning of the end.

"*Blithe Spirit*. That's a Noel Coward play. I saw it in London." Ella briefly rejoined the world.

"The blithe spirit in Coward's play is called Elvira," I heard my own voice say. "And I have a retired race horse who's named after her. At least, she lives with me, she doesn't really belong to me. Elvira really belonged to my uncle and his friend. They called themselves the Blithe Spirits Stable and Elvira . . ." I prayed that someone would interrupt my babbling. Deanne obliged.

"If we could get back to the point we were discussing." I was amazed that she could remember what it was. "I would just like to say that I still think people should pay the shot for all the health problems they bring on themselves through their own unhealthy habits."

"Would you be willing to pay your own medical costs if eating tonight's dinner made you ill?" Felix asked. "I'm sure you're aware that sashimi is a very high risk food."

"Felix, that's nonsense and you know it," Dr. Morrison said sharply. "Raw fish is an almost perfect form of protein. Add some complex carbohydrate like this brown rice and it makes a wonderfully healthy meal. What food could be less of a risk?"

"Something that wasn't quite so riddled with worms,"

Felix replied. Everyone but Byron stopped eating and stared at him. "Parasites are part of a wild animal's life and the fish we're eating tonight are wild animals. Normally the heat of cooking destroys all the parasites and their eggs but this flesh is raw. Whatever lived in these fish has now taken up residence in us." Felix definitely had our attention. We sat like rabbits mesmerized by a snake. "As a matter-of-fact, I was talking to a parasitologist at the hospital just last week," he continued. "He told me that life in Calgary was dead boring for him until the sushi fad hit town. Now he says he sees more worms in a week than he used to in a year. Claims raw salmon is sending two of his children through university."

"I've eaten sashimi dozens of times," Dr. Morrison countered staunchly, "And I've never contracted parasites."

"Not yet, you haven't," Felix said, managing to imply that Dr. Morrison was playing a reckless game of piscine Russian roulette. "But if you keep eating this stuff, it's only a matter of time. Come on Heather, you're a doctor. You know that all it takes is one infected piece and you've got a gut full of worms."

"And you know that The Ranch's fish is perfectly fresh and scrupulously clean. We also have one of the best sushi chefs in Canada to prepare it for us." Dr. Morrison would not give in but Felix had made his point. Small wonder he wasn't on her list of favourite dinner guests.

Despite the fact that I had only managed to swallow a nibble of squid tentacle, I wondered how many of the beasts that called the squid home were now setting up housekeeping in my intestinal tract. Deanne placed the salmon she held in her chopsticks back on her plate and peered at it suspiciously, searching for signs of alien life. At our table, dinner was at an end. Except for Byron, that is, who continued to consume the sashimi at a steady rate. People who dress like Byron can't afford to be squeamish.

CHAPTER 5

Dinner officially ended with applause for the chef and his assistants. I decided to let the dining-room empty of people before I packed up the camera gear. I followed Ben into the kitchen where he stood at a sink cleaning his sashimi knife. Ben never lets anyone else handle his cooking knives. They are handmade in Japan and very costly. I said hello to Marge and Carter, his two assistants who were already busy cleaning the food trolleys. I knew them from my visits to Ben's restaurant.

"You're a hypocrite, Phoeb." Ben washed the long steel blade with a soft cloth, carefully avoiding the razor sharp cutting edge. "What were you doing applauding? I know you hate sashimi."

"I wasn't being hypocritical. Just because I don't like it doesn't mean sashimi isn't very pretty to look at. I was applauding your visual artistry. The food was terrible. How are Marianne and the kids?"

"They're fine. I told Marianne you were going to be here tonight and she sends you her love. We haven't seen you for ages, Phoeb. Where've you been?"

"Working, Ben. Same place you've been."

"Ain't that the truth." He dried the knife and placed it on the counter next to its special carrying case. "Want to go for a walk? I'm dying for a cigarette and they don't let you smoke around here. Makes me feel about ten years old but I sneak off to a spot down by the stables. Coming?" He took off his chef's hat and apron, folded them neatly, and put them beside the sashimi knife.

"No thanks. I'm supposed to meet Mr. Reilly in the dining-room in a couple of minutes to set up tomorrow's taping. I'm doing some interior shots and he's going to show me around. I think he's really supposed to watch that I don't pinch the silver."

"Watch that Reilly doesn't pinch you, Phoeb. He's The Ranch's very own dirty old man."

"Mr. Reilly? Come off it, Ben. You've been into the cooking sake again."

"No, really, I'm not kidding you," he protested. "I had to go see him before dinner. He has an office upstairs and he was in there watching a porn movie on his VCR. I know he thought his door was locked but, when I knocked, it just sort of fell open and I got a pretty good look at his TV set. He sure turned it off in a helluva hurry when he saw me. Reilly and porn flicks. I nearly cracked up. We both pretended I hadn't seen anything but I don't know how I managed to keep a straight face."

"Mr. Reilly watches dirty movies? That's incredible. I like Mr. Reilly. I thought he was a nice man." I was sorry Ben had told me. I knew that I would not feel quite the same about Mr. Reilly next time we met.

"You're the one that's incredible, Phoeb. Just because he watches porn movies doesn't mean Reilly can't be a nice guy. All it means is that he watches porn movies. Haven't you ever watched a dirty movie?"

I shook my head.

"Well maybe you should. Round out your photographic education if you didn't die of boredom first. The one that Reilly was watching really stunk. The photography was awful and the woman in it was old enough to be somebody's grandma. Had a pretty good bod though."

"The world's oldest act starring the world's oldest

actress."

"You said it. But, you know what amazes me? No matter how tacky that stuff is, it always sells."

"I don't think the buyers are looking for artistic merit and trenchant social comment."

"Hey Phoeb, ever think of going into the business? With you as the photographer and Candi as the leading lady, you gals could make a fortune. I'll be your business manager. What do you say?"

"I hope they make you manager of a McDonald's some day, Ben."

"How much longer will it take you to finish here?" Ben asked Carter.

"Fifteen minutes, twenty tops. You got time for a smoke."

"See you at the van in twenty then," Ben said.

"Why would anyone go out into all that beautiful clean air just to fill their lungs full of crap?" Marge had recently quit smoking. She chomped down on her nicotine-laced chewing gum and glared at him.

"So they don't have to watch you chew gum, Marge. Better take it easy with that stuff or you'll pull out your fillings." Ben grinned at her. She threw a plastic bag full of fish scraps at his head. He ducked and caught the bag deftly in his left hand. "For Byron?" he asked. Marge nodded an affirmative and went back to scrubbing the food trolley.

"Byron eats fish scraps?"

"Come on, Phoeb," Ben laughed. "Even Byron couldn't eat this stuff." He held up the scraps. They had settled into an amorphous mass of grey sludge at the bottom of the bag. "Byron feeds it to the stable cats. Sashimi night, the barn cats' delight. They're probably lined up licking their whiskers right now." He put on his jacket and fished his cigarettes out of the pocket. "Come

to the restaurant and see us soon, Phoeb. And bring
Cyrrie. I'll cook you something special."

"And the operative word there is cook, isn't it, Ben?"

"Round-eyed barbarian."

"See you later in the week for sure," I promised. "Say
hello to Marianne for me." He waved and closed the
kitchen door behind him.

I returned to the dining-room and started to pack up
the gear. My faithless assistant Felix was nowhere to be
seen. Actually, everyone except a waiter clearing tables
had disappeared. Byron had left right after dinner to check
on the horses. Ella and Candi were off collecting their
things and changing clothes for the drive back to Calgary.
Dr. Morrison had retreated to her office, probably to get in
a hundred more important phone calls before bedtime.
Reg and Deanne were partners in a bridge game in
progress in the living-room.

At The Ranch, evenings were short and mornings
came early. Except for Sunday afternoons, the space
between their evening meal and bed was the guests' only
block of free time. Most of them returned to their own
quarters immediately after dinner. A few of the dedicated
went for a walk, although after sunset the paths around the
place were so dark that walking was pretty well limited to
a stroll up the paved driveway to the gates and back. The
rest spent the time before their bedtime hot drink playing
bridge or backgammon or just chatting in front of the fire.

The waiter tossed the last of the white linen table
cloths into a laundry cart and trundled it out to the kitchen.
I was packing the lights into their cases when Mr. Reilly
came into the dining-room. Byron's shimmery blue dinner
jacket hung from his arm like an empty reptile skin.

"That jacket really gets around."

"Dr. Sanders asked me to return it to Byron for him,"
Mr. Reilly handled the jacket as if he wished he'd worn

rubber gloves. "Would you like to go over the list of things you want to photograph tomorrow?" He looked very tired and very old. Perhaps watching dirty movies is wearing for the senior set.

"I think we could wait until the morning," I said. "I don't know about you, but I've put in a long day and I'd like to go home and get some sleep." It would have been cruel to keep him up. His face was grey with weariness.

"You are a very tactful young woman, Phoebe. And a very observant one," he added. "I think tomorrow would be an excellent time to start. Why don't you come and have breakfast with us?" I must have looked doubtful. "I promise you'll be well fed. Remember, the staff dining-room is very different from this one. We won't send you to work on an empty stomach."

We agreed to meet the next morning at 8:15 in the staff dining-room. Despite my protests and weary as he was, Mr. Reilly helped me carry the camera equipment to the front door. I flatly refused his offer to help me out to the van with it.

"I'll just bring the van around to the front door and load it here. No problem."

"If you won't let me carry anything then you must at least let me walk to your van with you. I'm off to the stables to talk to Byron and the parking lot's right on the way."

The night was cold after the warmth of the house and I was glad of my coat. I think the chilly air must really have bothered Mr. Reilly because he actually deigned to throw Byron's jacket around his shoulders. The moonless sky was bright with stars but they shed no light on the blackness of the driveway. It was so dark that I literally could not see to put one foot in front of the other. We aimed our footsteps at the light from a flood-lamp mounted high on a tree above the parking lot. I unlocked the van door and Mr. Reilly held it open while I climbed in.

"I'm looking forward to tomorrow, Phoebe. It should be an interesting morning for me."

"It's very dark out tonight," I said. "If you're walking down to the stables maybe I could lend you a flashlight. There's always one in the glove compartment of the station's vans."

"I've been at The Ranch for so long I could walk these paths blindfolded. But thank you for the offer. See you in the morning." He closed the van door.

As I drove to the house, I glanced in the rear view mirror and saw him standing in the circle of the floodlight's beam. His immaculately groomed white hair contrasted oddly with the lurid glimmer of Byron's jacket.

I parked the van in front of the *No Parking* sign and climbed the front steps. I found Reg standing in the entrance hall in the midst of my equipment cases. Candi's powers weave their spell in direct proportion to her proximity. Distance seemed to have restored his wits.

"Just thought I'd keep an eye on this stuff for you while you were out." The Ranch was not exactly a seething bed of thieves and vandals. It was obvious that he had been waiting for me to return.

"Thanks, Reg. That's very good of you." I wondered what he wanted.

"I'm dummy this hand," he said, explaining why he was at liberty from the bridge game. There was an awkward pause. "Did you have a good day, Phoebe? Get lots of good pictures?"

"Some not bad stuff, I hope. How was the trail ride?"

"Two hours long." He patted himself gingerly on the rump. "I saw you out there filming it all. I must have looked pretty ridiculous getting on that horse."

"I'd say you looked gallantly determined."

"And I'd say I looked like an idiot." He laughed his good-natured laugh. "Do you think that you're really going to use those pictures of me in your program?"

"It isn't my program, Reg. I just take the pictures. Ella decides which of them she wants to use and, honestly, I don't think you and your horse will make it in. You were too funny." I thought he would be relieved but he looked genuinely disappointed. "What I could do is try to get that bit of tape dubbed on to the end of your copy of the 'A Day in the Lifestyle' video Ella says the program is sending to everyone. Then you'd at least get to see it. I can't promise for sure, but I'll see what I can do."

"That would be great," Reg enthused. "I'd really appreciate it."

There was another awkward silence. He looked like he wanted to say something else and couldn't think how to begin. Finally, he spoke. "Do you think it would be possible for you and me to get together sometime soon? Please don't misunderstand me, I'm not coming on to you or anything like that. Not that you're not a very attractive woman, Phoebe, but . . ."

"What can I do for you, Reg?" I put the poor fellow out of his misery.

"I'd just like to talk to you about something. It's important."

"May I ask what it is?" Since we had only met today I couldn't think what Reg and I had to talk about.

"I'd sooner not say right now. I don't want to talk about it at The Ranch. I know this must sound a little nuts but please believe me, it is important. Is there somewhere we could meet? It won't take long."

"I'm free on Thursday afternoon." Now I was curious. "There's a tea house not far from The Ranch. Why don't we go there?"

"A tea house?" Reg's face lit up.

"Fifteen minutes drive south. Homemade scones and strawberry jam. I'll pick you up here about four."

"No, not here. I'll meet you out on the road. At four o'clock I'll start walking south until you pick me up."

Deanne came into the hall. She held the door to the living-room open behind her. "Reggie, darling, it's your deal and the table is waiting. I'm sure Miss Fairfax wouldn't want you to miss this hand, would you, Miss Fairfax?" She smiled but her scarlet nails drummed impatiently on the door. No wonder Reg wanted to keep our meeting a secret. He said good night as Deanne whisked him back to the living-room and his place at the bridge table.

I had just finished loading the equipment in the van and locking the back doors when Sugamoto's Japanese Catering van pulled up beside me. Marge rolled down the window and stuck out her head. "Hey Phoebe, have you seen Ben?" she asked irritably. "He said he'd meet us at the van. Carter and I've been sitting in here nearly fifteen minutes and he still hasn't come." She punctuated her sentences with vigourous snaps of her chewing gum.

"Sorry, I haven't seen him since he left the kitchen. Maybe he smoked an extra cigarette."

"Guess we'd better go back and wait. If you see him tell him to move it, will you?" Marge closed her window and the van headed back behind the house.

I walked around to the driver's door of my van, glad to be on my way at last, when Byron called to me from the top of the steps. At this rate I would never get home.

"Evening, Miss Phoebe. You off home now?"

Miss Phoebe? Maybe he had watched too many episodes of "Dallas" as a child. "I'm on my way now." I opened the van door.

"Wait up a minute, will you please, Ma'am?" He came quickly down the stairs and stood in front of me, just a little too close. His hand rested on the open door. His eyes were very blue and looked directly into mine. He smiled and the lines around them crinkled a little. It's called turning on the charm and, for Byron, it worked. Byron's charm definitely turned me on. I could feel my body responding to him as strongly as if he had actually touched me.

"Have you seen Phil Reilly? He said he'd come see me at the stable right after supper, as soon as he'd finished talking to you, but he never showed."

"I left him in the visitor's parking lot about twenty minutes ago. He had your blue jacket and he said he was on his way to see you." I took a step back and stumbled slightly. Byron's hand shot out to steady me. He grasped my arm and, corny as it sounds, at that moment I felt a surge of pure, powerful, totally surprising, and overwhelmingly genuine lust. I swear my knees buckled. No wonder Byron had achieved such popularity among the female guests. He might dress like a bad dream and not be much of a dinner conversationalist but Byron obviously needed neither clothes nor words to communicate his most important message. He was a male version of Candi.

"The last I seen him was before supper," Byron said. He kept his hand on my arm.

"Sorry, I can't help you." It came out a little breathless. I could feel the pressure of his fingers through the sleeve of my coat as he helped me up into the driver's seat. I probably had the same fatuous expression on my face that Reg had worn all through dinner. "I don't know where he is."

"That's okay, Miss Phoebe." He closed the van door. "See you tomorrow. Drive careful, eh." He waved as I pulled away from the curb.

I took a deep breath, leaned back in the seat and felt the tension start to leave my body. Near the end of the driveway, the van interrupted an invisible beam and the wrought iron gates opened automatically. The gates marked the end of The Ranch's private pavement. I turned north on to the public gravel.

I rolled down the window and the night scents blew in on the cold breeze. I heard the coyotes howling. Their eerie chorus made the back of my neck tingle and I felt the skin down my spine tighten. Humans still have hackles. The veneer of urbane elegance that The Ranch attempted to impose on its surroundings ended at the gates along with the paved drive. The van's headlights shone into the twin reflectors of a fox's eyes and I slowed down to let their owner scramble to safety. Once, in the late spring, I had seen a grizzly bear near this road. We might be just an hour's drive from Calgary but this was still the edge of the mountain wilderness.

My evening at The Ranch had given me a touch of the same feeling of unreality as flying the polar route to Europe always does. A few hours out of Calgary, when you're well over the arctic tundra, they serve a meal. And there you sit, sipping French wine and toying with your Air Canada dinner, in a fragile metal cocoon suspended five miles above one of the bleakest, most inhospitable regions on earth. It never fails to make me feel unreal.

The headlights picked out a car pulled over to the side of the road. A man in an overcoat and tweed hat stood by the back wheel on the passenger side and waved. It was Felix. I pulled in behind his car and got out.

"A flat tire I'm afraid." He walked toward me. "Can I catch a lift to town with you?"

"No spare?"

"That is the spare."

I laughed.

"I meant to have the other one fixed," he added a little sheepishly.

"Sorry, but I'm not going to Calgary. I only live a couple of miles from here but you're welcome to come home with me and use my phone."

He accepted the offer. "I saw you out by your van talking to Byron as I was leaving The Ranch. I thought you might be coming this way before long. Good thing for me that you did." We climbed into the van. "Is this what they call a mobile unit?" he asked.

"Nothing so grand I'm afraid. Mobile units are equipped to broadcast live from location and they cost a fortune. This is just a van full of camera equipment." We started down the road.

"How much would a professional camera like yours cost?" I had the feeling his question was not wholly academic.

"I think this one cost about forty thousand, but it's pretty old. I don't know what one would cost now."

"My camera cost three thousand and I thought I was being the last of the big spenders when I bought it. When did you buy yours?"

"This camera doesn't belong to me," I explained. "The van and all the equipment in it belong to the station. The program I work for gets to use it two days a week. We usually shoot on Mondays and Tuesdays so I'll take it back to the station tomorrow afternoon after I finish work at The Ranch."

"You only work two days a week?"

"I only work for 'A Day in the Lifestyle' two days a week, or sometimes three if Ella has lined up a really big project. The rest of the time I work on my own stuff."

"The nature films?"

"That's right. I meant it when I told you they take time. That fifteen-minute film on meadow voles that you saw took me two years to shoot and edit. 'Lifestyle' keeps me eating while I work."

"God, I wish you hadn't mentioned eating. I'm so hungry I could eat my shoes. If I'd known I was going to stay at The Ranch for dinner I'd have brought a sandwich along."

I felt much the same way myself. "How about a snack with your phone call?" I hoped I had something on hand besides peanut butter. We turned into my drive and parked the van in the garage. I collected the camera and we started toward the house.

The path was pitch black. I felt the whoosh of air from silent wings and ducked reflexively. Felix was not so lucky. His hat flew off into the darkness and he fell heavily to the ground. "Jesus Christ Almighty! What the hell was that?"

"I'm sorry. I should have warned you." I held out a hand to help him up. "Are you all right?"

"I think so." He climbed to his feet and brushed the leaves off his coat. "Aside from the fact that I'm probably having a heart attack."

"I really am sorry. I forgot to warn you."

"For God's sake, stop apologizing and just tell me what attacked me."

"An owl. A great horned owl. And he didn't attack you. He just wanted to knock your hat off. He was playing."

"Playing? What does he do when he's serious? Knock your head off?"

"I should have told you about him. You have every right to be angry." I did a bit more apologizing.

"I'm not angry," Felix said, a little more quietly. "I'm just a bit unnerved. I've never been an owl's plaything before. Is it a friend of yours?" he asked.

"In a way, I guess he is," I said. "I found him a couple of winters ago walking through my pasture in the middle of the day. His wing was broken. I took him to the vet and had the wing set and then I looked after him until it healed. It took him awhile to get strong enough to fly properly after his splint came off. He did most of his early flying practice in my barn. That's where he learned to knock off hats. It was his big thrill of the day, knocking off my hat when I came to feed him. He's never forgotten it." And neither have my neighbors. Felix was not the first person to be taken unaware by the big bird swooping out of the night on his silent wings.

"You mean he lives with you? You have a pet owl?"

"He doesn't live with me, he lives in the woods across the valley. And he isn't a pet. Definitely not. I don't keep pets. He's as wild as the day I first found him."

I had thrown my jacket over the hurt owl, bundled him inside it and carried him home. He hadn't protested much at the indignity of this treatment, but as I walked up the slope to the house, his sharp talons ripped through the jacket's leather and wrapped themselves around my hand. When I tried to pull away, the talons gripped even tighter. That was how we finished the trip. Finally, I'd had to prise each individual talon off my hand. Rescuing that bird was a painful experience.

"But he must be tame if he likes to play games with you and your hat," Felix said.

I shook my head. "He's a wild animal and I made sure he stayed that way." I had fixed the owl's wing and fed him for a few months but I never made an effort to tame him. In some fundamental way, taming him would have seemed self-indulgent, like taking advantage of his misfortune for my own pleasure. Besides, I think it is wrong to persuade a wild animal that not all humans are to be feared. "Knocking off hats is just an extension of his natural hunting behaviour," I explained. "And it's the only lasting effect of his stay in my barn."

"Do you have any more surprises lurking up your

garden path or is it safe for me to start my heart again?"
He began to look for his hat.

"No more surprises. But come to the house and get a
flashlight or you'll never find your hat."

I unlocked the back door and turned on a light. The
dog woke up, got out of his basket and stretched.

"If you don't keep pets, what's that?" Felix asked.

"He's not a pet, he's a watch-dog." The dog
meandered over to Felix, absent-mindedly licked his
proffered hand and continued past him out the open door.
All without a sound.

"Rowdy bugger, isn't he?"

"He's taken a vow of silence." I handed Felix a
flashlight and sent him in search of his hat.

CHAPTER 6

I rummaged through the cupboards and my sparsely furnished fridge and by the time Felix returned carrying his hat I had organized a plate of cheese and crackers and put the water on to boil for coffee. "Would you like a drink?" I asked. "Scotch? A glass of wine?"

"Scotch would do nicely. Thanks." He hung his coat and rumpled hat on a peg by the back entrance. "And your telephone, if I may."

I pointed him in the direction of the phone on my desk. I live in what used to be a three-bedroom bungalow. When Gavin and I moved in we knocked out most of the interior walls and converted the house into one large room. There's a bathroom and a tiny bedroom for guests separate from the main room but I do all of my living and much of my work in my one big space. I even have a very efficient small kitchen in one corner although I must admit that was largely Gavin's doing. The domestic arts are not my strong point. Nevertheless, I thought my plate of cheese and crackers looked quite respectable. The cheddar was well aged but not decrepit and the crackers were from an elegant box of English biscuits Cyrrie had given me. I'd even found a couple of apples that weren't too world-weary to appear in public.

"I'm afraid you're going to have quite a time persuading a tow truck to come all the way out here at night." I handed Felix his Scotch.

"I'm not even going to try." First he called the hospital

to check on two of his patients. He issued some brief instructions on their care and then dialed his answering service to collect his messages. Last, he called his wife, told her about the spareless flat tire, and asked her to drive out from Calgary to collect him. He did not seem to regard this as an unusual or unreasonable request and, judging from the brevity of the call, neither did she. Perhaps she had rescued him from the results of his absent-mindedness so often that she now regarded it as a normal part of life. Marriage does that to people. He put his hand over the mouthpiece of the phone. "How far from The Ranch to my car, would you say?"

"A couple of miles. But why don't you wait here? Much warmer than hanging around your car at this time of night."

"Thanks. It might take her a couple of hours to get here. You're sure you don't mind?"

I shook my head. "Tell your wife I'll leave the lights on by my front gate. There's a sign that says *Fairfax* tacked to one of the gate posts."

He delivered the message, said goodbye, and swivelled round in my desk chair to face the room. "Do you play?" He nodded in the direction of the grand piano which takes up far more space than it should in one corner.

"I'm strictly a Sunday amateur," I replied honestly and to my great regret.

"That, my dear Phoebe, is one hell of a piano for a Sunday amateur." It is a Steinway, lustrous black and full concert size.

"I inherited it from my Uncle Andrew. He played very well and since I was the only one in the family who could play at all he left it to me."

"It's a wonder the floor will support it." Felix wandered over to the piano and looked at the massive square legs.

"It wouldn't," I said. "I had to have the joists reinforced and some new posts installed in the basement." The bungalow is reasonably well built but even so the floor had not been up to bearing the weight of a nine-foot grand.

"May I hear what it sounds like?" he asked.

"Please do." I opened the lid of the keyboard for him. "It's all yours."

"Oh no, not me," he protested. "I can't even read music. Won't you play for me?"

"Sorry, but I never play for anyone but myself. Far too inhibited."

I was pleased when he didn't press. I really am strictly an amateur. Every winter I tackle a new Beethoven sonata and every spring I admit defeat. I enjoy the struggle enormously, but it is just for me. I do occasionally play for Cyrrie when he comes to visit. I get out Uncle Andrew's old books and play a little Cole Porter or Gershwin or some Noel Coward songs. It is good for both of us to hear them, Cyrrie because they are the songs he and Andrew grew up with and me because Uncle Andrew taught me how to play them. Although I am not half the musician he was, Andrew must have succeeded in teaching me something because now, on his wonderful old piano, even I sound pretty good to my Sunday self when I begin the beguine.

Felix played up and down the C major scale with one finger. I started to close the curtains on the two banks of six-foot windows that run the lengths of the bungalow's south and west walls. There are no trees in front of the windows and the view sweeps west across my pasture to the mountains. The dog pressed his nose silently against the glass of the patio door that interrupts the west windows and leads out on to a deck. I slid the door back and he sauntered in trailing his usual clouds of shedding hair. He flopped down by the desk and fell asleep instantly. I finished closing the curtains, collected the food and put it on the low table that sits between two easy chairs near the open fireplace. Felix joined me and we started in on the cheese and crackers. I had forgotten to provide napkins. How uncouth. No napkins, no fire in the grate, dog hair all over the carpet—my genteel hostess rating plummeted. "More Scotch?" I asked. A few belts of Famous Grouse and who cares about couth.

"I think I'd better put a layer of cheese down before I start on more Scotch. Heather's sashimi doesn't make much of a base for whisky."

I agreed. I already felt a little light headed on one glass of wine.

"I heard a rumour today that The Ranch is going to cancel the sashimi nights. Do you think there's any truth to it?" I asked. I knew Ben would be very upset if he lost The Ranch's contract. The Calgary restaurant trade is cutthroat competitive at the best of times and this was not the best of times. The city was in one of the lows on the economic roller coaster ride it delights in giving its small businesses. For Ben, The Ranch contract was a lucrative and stable constant in an often marginal and erratic business.

"I'd say the end of sashimi night was a certainty," Felix replied.

"But why? Ben's a great cook."

"And a friend of yours, isn't he?"

"We went to school together. We've kept in touch. But that doesn't mean I can't be objective about his talents and objectively speaking, he really is good at his job."

"If he weren't, The Ranch wouldn't have hired him."

"Then why cancel his contract? If the guests don't like sashimi then The Ranch should have Ben do a cooked Japanese meal. Japanese food is just as healthy and low calorie when it's hot and I think it tastes a lot better."

"There you go again, Phoebe, assuming that food at The Ranch has something to do with hunger and eating and nourishment." Felix bit into an apple. "Cancelling the sashimi nights has nothing to do with the food itself, it has to do with image. Japanese cuisine is not in keeping with the new image the company wants The Ranch to project. Oriental elegance is out."

"And what's in?" I asked.

"Clean air and clean water for starters," Felix said. "This is still a relatively pollution-free part of the world and The Ranch wants to capitalize on that. They want to emphasize the location. You know, all that nestled-in-the-pristine-wilderness-of-the-great-Canadian-West, sort of thing."

"What's it got to do with Ben?"

"Sashimi simply doesn't fit the western wilderness image. From now on at The Ranch it's back to the land and home-cooked country food. All very healthy and low cal, of course. The company's even bought itself a game ranch."

I wasn't surprised. Wild game ranches produce meat that is relatively low in cholesterol and calories. At the same time, it gives its mostly urban consumers the impression that they're living off nature. Broiled antelope. Now there's food that a good western image could really sink its health conscious teeth into. Actually, everything Felix said about The Ranch's new image made perfect sense. Its guests were a cosmopolitan crew. They came from cities all over North America and Europe. What appealed to them, particularly the Europeans, was The Ranch's unspoiled surroundings—water so pure they could drink it right from the stream and air so clean that simply breathing was a pleasure.

Felix finished the last of his drink. "I think I could

manage that second Scotch now."

"So sashimi is inappropriate to The Ranch's image." I poured the Scotch and refilled my wine glass. "Who decides what's appropriate?"

"At The Ranch, ultimately Phil Reilly I suppose," he replied.

"Not Dr. Morrison?"

"Heather is responsible for the health and medical programs. But Phil really runs the place. He's worked for the company for years. He's one of their top hotel men."

"Then what's he doing in a little backwater like this?"

"He had a massive heart attack a few years ago, shortly after his wife died. He's lucky to be alive. He recovered but not to the extent that he could take on the kind of work load he managed before his coronary. The Ranch had just opened and the company offered him the job of business manager."

I felt horribly guilty when I thought of how I had allowed Mr. Reilly and his damaged heart to help me carry the heavy camera gear. "So, instead of giving him the golden handshake they put him out to pasture here."

"Phil isn't out to pasture. Just the opposite. He's invaluable to the company. You see, The Ranch is really a pilot project. This type of health resort has the potential to produce enormous profits. You know the fees The Ranch charges. Think of the yearly gross they must add up to. The place is a gold mine and the company is planning on opening more of them in other parts of the world. There are two in the works for next year in Alaska and Australia and that's just the beginning. How they're developed depends on the policies Phil establishes at The Ranch. Who better to oversee a pilot project than a seasoned executive?"

"But I thought The Ranch was a big success," I said. "Why change the whole operation when it's only been in business a few years?"

"Because The Ranch can't run forever on the publicity it got from the Winter Olympics," Felix said.

According to Felix, the company had just begun developing its concept for a chain of health resorts when they purchased Mrs. Malifant's estate the year before the Calgary Olympics. Instead of waiting until their plans for the whole chain had been finalized they decided to rush ahead with a much more conventional concept and cash in on the world-wide interest generated by the games. The result was The Ranch. It played host to a prominent ski team during their last weeks of pre-Olympic training. The team won medals and the resulting hoopla featured prominently in The Ranch's advertising.

"You see, The Ranch was never intended to be an ordinary health resort," Felix explained. "So these changes aren't much of a surprise. The Ranch is really just catching up with itself. The whole thing's been good for Phil. He gets a light work-load and the company gets his years of experience and judgement. It's worked out well for both of them."

"It doesn't seem to have worked out quite so well for Ben," I said.

"That's no reflection on his ability as a chef. The sashimi nights are really Heather's baby. Phil thought they were a mistake from the first and Phil's the boss. He's a damn good one too. I wish we had a few hospital administrators like him."

"I'm working with him tomorrow morning," I said.

"Then you should have an excellent morning."

"You really like him, don't you?" It was difficult for me to reconcile Felix's Philip Reilly with the Philip Reilly who watched pornographic videos alone in his office.

"Yes I do. He's an interesting man—well-travelled, well-read. We often have coffee together after I'm finished for the afternoon."

The mention of coffee reminded me of the pot that now sat warming on the stove. I brought a tray with the coffee and cups and put it on the table between us. "Well, at least Byron should fit right in with The Ranch's new western image, lariats on his lapels and all."

"That jacket's something, isn't it?" Felix smiled and shook his head. "I told you the one I wore would pale by comparison. But you mustn't judge Byron by his dinner jackets. He's really very good at his job. The man knows horses and he knows the foothills."

Judging by the effect of my brief encounter with him earlier in the evening, horses and hills were not all Byron knew.

"He may be lacking a little polish," Felix continued, "But Byron looks and talks just the way the guests think a real cowboy should look and talk. You pay for a western image, you get Byron. He's actually ridden bucking broncos in the Calgary Stampede. That certainly impresses the guests."

It impressed me too. Byron came by his cowboy credentials honestly. The fact that it had taken him less than two minutes and one firm grip to the elbow to reduce me to a puddle of overactive hormones was an extra.

"Really, there's more to Byron than you might think," Felix said. "He's the one who got me interested in photography. It's his hobby too. Mostly still stuff though, not video. You should see some of his rodeo photos. They're remarkable."

"And what about you?" I asked. "What is it that you do at The Ranch, exactly?" I had listened to so many of Candi's interviews that I was starting to sound like her.

"Me? I lead group sessions on stress management. Two a week. Monday and Thursday afternoons from one-thirty to three-thirty."

"And that's all?" As I spoke, I realized how very rude I sounded. So did Felix. He started to laugh at my discomfort.

"Ah, Phoebe, you do need some educating in the fine art of health resortery. You see, I'm like the food, I'm there for The Ranch's image. My name and medical degrees look impressive on the letterhead. I'm good at what I do but what I do is of secondary importance."

"And that doesn't bother you?"

"Why should it? The guests are very pleasant to work with. I think they find the sessions helpful. And The Ranch pays me enormous sums of money."

"But doesn't it take too much time away from your real work?"

"Does 'A Day in the Lifestyle' take too much of your time away from your real work?" It was the gentlest of digs, and one I richly deserved.

"'A Day in the Lifestyle' pays my bills," I said, sanctimoniously.

"In a way, I suppose The Ranch pays some bills of mine, too." Felix finished the last of his drink. He shrugged dismissively and put the glass back on the tray. "Besides, I get to go swimming every time I go to The Ranch and swimming's good for my back. Psychiatrists are prone to back pain," he confided. "Comes from sitting on our backsides listening to sad stories all day."

"Then we have an occupational hazard in common. Television photographers get backaches too. Ours come from hefting heavy cameras on one shoulder day after day. One shoulder gets higher than the other after awhile. Give me until I'm forty and I'll probably look like Quasimodo."

Felix put his empty cup on the tray. "I would be very surprised if someone as beautiful as you could manage quite that great a transformation. You know you really do look lovely in that dress. I've never seen one quite like it before."

"It's an antique," I said. "I think it was made sometime in the thirties."

"Then we have something in common," he laughed. "So was I."

"More coffee?"

"No thanks. I'm sure it's one of the symptoms of acute middle-age but more than one cup of coffee after ten o'clock and I can't sleep." He looked at his watch. "I know I must be keeping you up. This is really very kind of you, Phoebe. I'm sorry to put you to all this trouble."

"No trouble at all." I collected the dishes and took them to the kitchen corner. "I was hungry too."

"People usually are after a meal at The Ranch," he said. "Our professional back problems aside, it really is too bad you didn't stay for a swim before dinner. That pool is a remarkable bit of design. I often wonder who built it."

"The lady who owned the estate before The Ranch took over had it built sometime in the twenties." I settled back in my chair. "One of her friends designed it. The tiles and the marble dolphins are all from Italy. The Malifant pool is part of local myth and legend. In our neighbourhood it's got the Hanging Gardens of Babylon beat all to hell."

"You know something of The Ranch's history?"

"I know the lady who owned it. Her name is Virginia Malifant. She's nearly ninety and lives in California now but until The Ranch bought her property she lived in the big house. My Uncle Andrew bought this place just after the Second World War so he and Mrs. Malifant were neighbours for nearly forty years. At least they were neighbours for summer holidays and weekends when Andrew could get away from his work in Calgary and stay out here. I've known Mrs. Malifant and her estate all my life."

"You were brought up by your uncle?"

"Nothing quite so Victorian. I have two perfectly good parents but I spent a lot of holidays out here with my Uncle Andrew and his friend Cyrrie. They liked me."

"Then the pool is nothing new for you. You'll have swum in it often."

"When I was a child, yes. But I haven't been in it for years. No one had until The Ranch took over. The pool needed repairs that Mrs. Malifant couldn't afford and it finally got too dilapidated to use."

Summer afternoons in Mrs. Malifant's pool with Uncle Andrew and Cyrrie were among the happiest and most vivid of my childhood memories. Even now the hum of insects on a hot July day can put me back in its cool water, floating on my back under the dome's open doors, listening to the honey bees feeding at the flowers on the slope.

"I haven't been in the pool for more than twenty years," I said. "Except for the morning I found the woman who killed herself." And now, because of that morning, Mrs. Malifant's beautiful pool and my memories of idyllic afternoons would be forever linked with images of death. "I had to jump in to get her out of the water." The room had grown cold. I got up from my chair and turned up the thermostat. I heard the furnace fan kick on. "Sorry I was such a bitch about that tonight." I found a sweatshirt and pulled it on over my bare shoulders.

"It was my fault, Phoebe. I could have picked a better time. You were in the middle of your work."

"I'm not working now if you still want to talk about it."

"You're sure you don't mind?"

"No, I'm not sure. But maybe that's why we should talk. I think I mind that I mind. Maybe talking to you will help that."

"Maybe it will help me, too," Felix said. "You see, Janet Benedict was a patient of mine. There's no way she should have killed herself. I don't understand what happened."

"I can't tell you what happened. All I did was find her body. She was dead before I got there."

"I know that. I read the police report." He shifted forward in his chair and looked at me. "But Phoebe, she shouldn't have died. Not that day, not that place, and not that way. I saw Janet two days before you found her. She was well and happy and making plans to go on a walking tour in France. I don't know of a single reason for her to kill herself."

"If she was a patient of yours she must have had some problems," I said.

"Of course she had problems. But she got over them. She had been ill and she recovered."

"The police report said she had a history of depression and that she had been drinking heavily."

"Yes, she did have a history of depression," he agreed. "But it was just that, past history. She was well when she died. I know she was well." He thumped the arm of his chair for emphasis.

"Look Felix, I don't think I can help you with this. I didn't know her, I just found her. What I said earlier is true, there's nothing I can tell you that I didn't tell the police."

"Please, I'd be grateful if you'd listen to what I have to say." He relaxed back in his chair. "You may even remember something the police didn't think was important. Besides, I'd like to tell you a little about her."

I wasn't sure I wanted to hear what he had to tell me. "What about medical confidentiality?" I said.

"After the police finished their investigation what

privacy did Janet have left?" He shrugged. "Her problems were made public property, even problems she didn't have. What I tell you won't violate a confidence that doesn't exist any more and I'd like to set the record straight, at least with you. The dead may have no right to privacy, but I think they have the right to a little truth."

According to the official record, Janet Benedict committed suicide while suffering from depression. Aside from her fatal mental illness, the report concluded that she had been generally healthy and in good physical condition. According to the pathologist, she had swallowed at least two dozen prescription pain killers and enough whisky to render someone twice her size unconscious. Despite this chemical arsenal she had aimed at herself, the actual cause of her death was drowning.

Felix's account of Janet Benedict differed from the official version on two points. First, according to Felix, she was not depressed. Second, she did not drink.

Janet Benedict had been referred to Felix by her family doctor about a year before her death. She was fifty-two years old, had been married to the same wealthy oil man for thirty years, and had two grown children. She was suffering from depression. Felix prescribed a course of anti-depressant medication and, over the course of frequent office visits, saw Janet's condition improve dramatically within weeks. She continued to see him regularly although much less frequently. Finally, after six months, she was able to stop taking the drug and only visit Felix once a month.

"Janet Benedict was one of my successes." The irony was impossible to miss. "The difference between the well Janet and the woman who dragged herself into my office the first time I saw her was so great you would hardly recognize them as the same person."

After six months of treatment, Janet was sleeping well,

eating well, feeling happy and back in control of her life. However, depression has physical effects as well as mental ones, Felix explained. Even though she was no longer depressed, Janet felt that she was still a little physically lethargic and definitely out of shape. By then, Felix had been working at The Ranch for some time and he suggested that she might benefit from a couple of weeks of Dr. Morrison's diet and fitness regimen. It certainly couldn't hurt her, he thought, to get out in the foothills air and do some strenuous physical exercise. Besides, Janet loved horses and the out-of-doors. The Ranch was just the place.

"So you sent her off to summer camp."

"Exactly," Felix smiled. "Except it was November."

"And did it work?"

"Splendidly. She came back from The Ranch looking as fit and healthy as it is possible for a fifty-two year old woman to look. As a matter-of-fact, she looked ten years younger. The Ranch could have used her as an advertisement."

"What happened?"

"I don't know. She came to see me for the last time in January. She seemed very well and said she felt well. There was no reason for her to keep on seeing me. The next time I saw her was by chance at a symphony concert last April, two days before she died. That's when she told me she was going walking in France. Phoebe, I know Janet didn't kill herself. I'm sure of it."

If Felix took it this hard every time he lost a patient, I wondered how he managed to keep on being a doctor. "They found a bottle of pills and a bottle of whisky beside the pool with her fingerprints on them," I said. "How could that have been an accident?"

"It wasn't an accident," he said. "Janet Benedict was murdered."

It was a real conversation stopper. I think my jaw probably dropped. It should have. The idea of murder was preposterous. I simply couldn't think of anything to say. I wondered why Felix found it impossible to admit that a patient of his had committed suicide. It couldn't have been the first time it had happened. The silence grew awkward. Felix got up and began to walk back and forth in front of the fireplace.

"Those pills," he said. "There was no label on the bottle and the police were never able to determine where they came from. I certainly didn't prescribe that crap for Janet and neither did her GP. And another thing, she hardly ever drank. Maybe an occasional glass of wine with dinner but that's it. Cheap rye was hardly Janet's style."

It was pretty flimsy stuff to invent a murder out of, I thought. Everyone who's ever had a toothache has had a prescription for pain killers and the stylishness of the booze you use to wash them down probably isn't your first concern when you're drinking your farewell toast to the world.

"Felix, people kill themselves. You must have had other patients who committed suicide, why not Janet Benedict? Couldn't you simply have made a mistake about her?"

"Give me a little credit for experience, Phoebe. I've been in this business a long time. I've seen hundreds of depressed patients, most of them a lot sicker than Janet and, God knows, I've made my share of mistakes. It's possible that Janet was one of them, but I don't think so. Everything I know tells me she didn't commit suicide."

"How can you be so sure? A bottle of pills and some cheap whisky are pretty thin murder evidence."

"They're small parts of a whole picture that just doesn't make sense," he said. "You see, Phoebe, the way a person chooses to commit suicide is a product of their personality. Within a certain range, the methods are fairly predictable. I suppose you could say that people kill themselves in character. That's what disturbs me about Janet's death. It was totally out of character. I knew Janet. I knew her well enough to know that if she had committed suicide she would have left a note. She loved her children. She wouldn't have left them with no explanation, no goodbyes. And she wouldn't have killed herself in such a horrible, messy way. Drowning yourself is a pretty grim endeavour. It's also miserable for the person who finds you and Janet would have thought of that too. She wouldn't have put anyone through what you went through that morning. Not intentionally. And why would she drive all the way to The Ranch?" He stopped pacing and looked at me. "None of it makes any sense, Phoebe. At least it makes no sense if you knew Janet."

"Just because suicide doesn't make sense to you, doesn't mean she was murdered." From suicide to murder was too big a leap for my imagination.

"If it wasn't suicide and it wasn't an accident, what else could it be?"

"Have you told the police what you think?"

"Yes, and they think the same as you do. That I'm an egomaniac doctor who would rather make accusations of murder than admit I'd made a mistake about one of my patients."

"I didn't say that."

"No, but you think it. And I can't say that I blame you. I suppose it looks that way. You didn't know Janet."

"For what it's worth, the fact that she didn't leave a note has always bothered me too," I said. But murder? "Felix, I'm sorry." I didn't know what else to say.

"I read in the police report how you tried to save her even though you knew she was dead. When I met you today at the pool I wanted you to know about Janet. I suppose I thought I owed you that for trying so hard to help her." He rumpled his hair and shook his head. "God, I'm behaving like an idiot! Come on Phoebe, let's have that second cup of coffee and talk about something sensible like lenses and f-stops."

I heard a car turn in to my drive. The dog's ears perked up in his sleep.

"That is a very subtle watch-dog you have, Miss Fairfax."

"He never causes unnecessary commotion, Dr. Sanders," I replied archly. "Sufficient to the situation, that's his motto."

Felix went to the door and collected his coat and hat. I followed him and reached for my jacket. "No, no. Don't come out with me. There's no need for you to get cold," he protested. "I'll find my own way and I promise I won't put my hat on until I'm safely past your owl and in the car." He buttoned up his coat. "And thank you, Phoebe. I'm very grateful to my flat tire." He took my hand in his for a moment. "Thanks for listening." He kissed me lightly on the forehead, then opened the door and walked toward the lights of the waiting car.

I closed the door behind him and listened until I heard the car door slam. Then I turned off the outdoor lights, put the glasses and plates in the dishwasher and got ready for bed. Bed in my one-room house is a queen-sized sofa bed that faces the bank of windows. I drew open the drapes, collected my pillows and goose down duvet from the closet, opened the bed and climbed in. I couldn't sleep. I lay staring at my eyelids for fifteen minutes before I gave up and reached for a book.

Experienced insomniacs, old pros in the waking game, probably keep copies of *Moby Dick* and other sure-fire soporifics on hand for these occasions. However, I'm a rank amateur and insomnia is such a rarity for me that I foolishly started on Stephen J. Gould's latest collection of essays. It was nearly three before I could tear myself away and put the book down. Finally, I switched off the light and lay gazing out the window at the stars. I started to count them, my surrogate sheep. I began with Orion's belt. I was asleep before I reached his dagger.

CHAPTER 7

I overslept so this time it wasn't me who found the body. I was at home safe in my bed when one of The Ranch cooks discovered the corpse on a path near the pool. It was shortly before six. The cook had been on his way to the house to begin preparing breakfast. Breakfast was late that morning.

So was I. By the time I showered and dressed it was nearly eight o'clock. The dog accompanied me to the garage and watched while I loaded the camera and my work-bag into the back of the van. He hopped into the passenger seat and we drove to the gate together, a distance of some twenty-five yards. He made this journey with me every working morning. I stopped by my mailbox to let him out and check for messages from Tom.

This morning's missive read, "Tomorrow hunting corral Tom," a reminder that the big game hunting season was about to begin in the forest reserve. For the next weeks Elvira and Pete would be denied the freedom of the pasture and confined to the corral near the barn. Despite the *No Hunting* signs posted all through our district, many of my neighbours had had livestock killed by hunters who were either so stupid or so drunk that they did not know where or at what they were aiming their high-powered rifles. One horse had been shot in the mistaken belief that it was a moose. The poor beast was wearing a saddle and bridle at the time. Elvira and Pete were not totally safe even in the corral but it was the best I could do short of keeping them in the barn all day.

The morning was bright, still, and cold, the frost thick on the hills. The steering wheel numbed my fingers and I wished that my gloves were on my hands and not tucked away in my work-bag. I turned on the van's heater, got a blast of cold air over my legs, and huddled deeper into my down-filled coat. By mid-day it would probably be warm enough to work in shirt sleeves but even summer mornings in the foothills are chilly and it was now nearly November. Faint stirrings of warm air began to waft from the heater just as I arrived at The Ranch.

A police car blocked the approach to the gate. I stopped in front of it and six feet four of RCMP constable emerged. "Are you Phoebe Fairfax?"

"Yes. What's wrong?"

"May I see your driver's licence please, Miss Fairfax."

I fished my work-bag out of the back of the van and produced the licence. "What's happened, Constable?"

"Thank you." He returned my licence. He was impassively polite and totally unforthcoming. "You're expected up at the house. Constable Lindt will meet you at the front door."

"Please, what's going on?"

"I'll radio ahead to Constable Lindt now." He opened the gate, moved his car from in front of it and motioned me through. I saw him speaking into his radio. I continued down the drive until I rounded a curve and was out of his sight. Then I stopped the van and got the camera out of the back. I loaded a video tape into it and rested it on the passenger seat within easy reach. Rule of life: never pass through a police road block with an unloaded camera. I continued slowly up the drive and, as soon as I had a clear view of the house, I pulled over and took a wide shot through the van's open window.

An ambulance, an RCMP van, and two squad cars

filled the driveway in front of the steps. Just as I was about to turn off the camera, two Mounties came around the side of the house. They were followed by a man in a brown overcoat and a couple of ambulance attendants pushing a stretcher with a neatly draped bundle strapped on its bed. I kept the tape rolling. None of them noticed me. Their attention was focused on the stretcher. They watched as the attendants lifted it into the back of the ambulance and drove past me toward the gate. No lights flashed. No sirens blared. The scene was almost identical to the morning of Janet Benedict's death. The sensation of *deja vu* was so powerful I began to feel slightly sick.

The man in the brown overcoat talked for a few moments more with the police and then set off in the direction of the visitor's parking lot. By now both the police officers had noticed me. One of them walked toward the van. I opened the camera and tossed the tape I had just used into my work-bag. I hastily reloaded with a fresh tape and was still clutching the camera when Constable Lindt barked at me through the window.

"Miss Fairfax? I'll need to see your driver's licence." Constable Lindt was dark haired, pretty, and very young. Her fine featured face was set in what she no doubt regarded as a sternly authoritative expression. She probably practiced in front of a mirror.

"The officer at the gate already checked it."

"Your driver's licence." Constable Lindt held out a graceful, gloved hand and, after much fumbling with the camera and work-bag, I gave her my licence. She alternated peering at the photo and then at me for a full thirty seconds. I half expected her to demand fingerprints or, at the very least, a sample signature. She passed the licence back and ordered me to park in the spot vacated by the ambulance. The edge of belligerence in Constable Lindt's orders made me suspect she was fresh from

Mountie school and this was her first job. Perhaps she was so uncertain of her own authority that she was afraid civility would be mistaken for weakness.

"Before you park, Miss Fairfax, give me the tape from that camera."

"Why?"

"Just give me the tape."

"But, Constable, it's not illegal to take pictures."

"Miss Fairfax, give me the tape. It will be returned to you."

I protested a little more before I opened the camera and handed her the blank tape. "When do I get it back?"

"When we're finished with it."

Which wouldn't be before the six o'clock news, I thought. I pulled into the ambulance's spot, collected the camera and my work-bag and stood beside the van.

"Put the camera away. You won't need it this morning."

"The camera goes where I go."

"You won't be taking any pictures here." Constable Lindt had progressed from rude to down right surly. "Put the camera back in the van."

"No." I am as willing as the next woman to make allowances for inexperience, but there are limits. I was beginning to get very tired of Constable Lindt.

"Put the camera in the van, Miss Fairfax. Now." She practically stamped her foot at me.

"Constable, this camera is an expensive piece of equipment. The television station it belongs to wouldn't appreciate it if I made a habit of leaving it lying around. The camera goes where I go. Be reasonable."

"Are you refusing to obey the direct order of a police officer?"

"I'm sure Miss Fairfax would never even consider it. Would you, Miss Fairfax?" A tall man in a well-cut suit, an overcoat draped over his shoulders, came down the stairs. "Thank you, Constable." He dismissed the glowering Lindt. "It is good to see you again, Miss Fairfax." We shook hands.

"Inspector Debarets, I'm glad you're here." He was the senior RCMP officer who had come to take charge on the morning of the drowning. "What's happened?"

"Would you come for a short stroll with me, Miss Fairfax. I need a breath of fresh air to clear my mind. Shall we walk?"

"I'll just put the camera in the van and be right with you."

Constable Lindt's glare implied that boiling oil would be too good for me. "Sir, I think you should have this." She handed Inspector Debarets the confiscated video tape. "It's from Miss Fairfax's camera. She took it just before you came. While the doctor was taking the body away."

"Thank you, Constable." He took the tape.

"Whose body, Inspector? What's happened?" He took no notice of my questions and we set off in the general direction of the stables.

"A very zealous young officer, Constable Lindt." Inspector Debarets was from Montreal and, although his English was impeccable, he spoke with a slight trace of a French accent. "What's really on this tape, Miss Fairfax?"

"Nothing," I answered. "It's a blank." With Inspector Debarets, honesty was the only policy.

"Zealous, but still a little naive I think." He smiled and handed me the tape.

"Please, Inspector, won't you tell me what's happened? Who's dead?"

No one ignores questions better than a policeman, especially if the questions come from someone connected with the news media. It was as if I hadn't spoken.

"Beautiful place this, isn't it? I remember from the

last time we met that you live not far from here yourself, don't you, Miss Fairfax? Do you have as good a view of the Rockies?"

"Has there been an accident?"

"I've lived in Alberta for almost six years now and I am very attached to this country. I am due to be transferred soon but I do not want to leave. These foothills get under your skin, don't they? The skiing's not so bad either."

I gave up. We walked along the path to the swimming pool. We passed a few of The Ranch guests heading to the dining-room for breakfast.

"How well do you remember our last meeting, Miss Fairfax?"

"Too well."

"Yes, it was not a pleasant morning. Such a lovely woman. Such a very sad death." The sun had begun to melt the frost that sparkled on the pool's glass dome. Another uniformed constable stood outside a roped-off area a few yards from the pool. Behind the barrier, a police forensic team busied itself with the tools of its grim trade.

"It is a little odd that we should meet here again under such similar circumstances, don't you think?" he said.

"If you'd tell me what the circumstances are then maybe I could answer your question. Has someone else drowned?"

"No, no one has drowned." He stopped and turned to face me. "Please, Miss Fairfax, I am not being coy with you. I simply would like to ask you some questions before I tell you what has happened here. That way your answers will be without prejudice. You are very valuable to me because you are an excellent witness. You couldn't have given me a clearer picture of what you observed in that pool last spring if you had filmed it all with your camera."

"It's part of my job. If you want to photograph things you have to look at them first."

We stopped at the corral fence and watched Byron and two wranglers grooming the trail ponies. Byron waved from across the corral. This morning, his formal finery had been replaced by jeans, a checked shirt, and a down-filled vest in a shade of fluorescent orange bright enough to lacerate your eyelids. However, the vivid vest was not simply another of Byron's bold fashion statements. I had one much like it myself at home. Everyone who goes near the forest reserve in hunting season has one like it. The vests lessen the chance of being mistaken for a moose. I waved back.

"You know the cowboy?" the inspector asked.

"Byron Wilke. He ate at our table last night. The 'A Day in the Lifestyle' crew were guests here at dinner. Byron and I spoke for a minute or two afterward." I felt my face redden a little at the memory of that brief but impressive conversation.

Inspector Debarets shivered slightly and pulled his coat a little closer round him. He looked at his watch. "Shall we return to the house?"

"Whatever happened, it's bad, isn't it, Inspector?"

"It's as bad as my job gets, Miss Fairfax," he replied. "It's murder."

Inspector Debarets had commandeered Dr. Morrison's third-floor office. We sat in the comfortable chairs in front of her desk. Another plainclothes officer with a notebook sat at the desk. The inspector turned on a tape recorder and began his questions. None of them gave me the slightest clue as to what had happened. He took me through the whole day, right from my arrival at The Ranch to my Scotch and cheese with Felix. Some parts we went through twice.

"What time did you pick Dr. Sanders up?"

"After ten-thirty, before eleven. I'm not sure exactly."

"And when did he leave?"

"His wife picked him up about one."

"Did you speak with her?"

"No. She didn't get out of the car and I didn't leave the house."

"Then you didn't see her?"

"No."

"What did you and Dr. Sanders do during the time you were together?"

"We had a bite to eat and we talked."

"What did you talk about?" The inspector's relentless questions gradually divided and subdivided the details of my day.

"The Ranch, mostly."

"What about The Ranch?" Each reply prompted another question. I told him about the company's plans for The Ranch, about the other health resorts they hoped to open, and about the imminent cancellation of Ben's contract.

"We also talked about Janet Benedict. Felix Sanders was her psychiatrist."

"Yes. I spoke with him myself last spring when we were investigating Mrs. Benedict's death. What did Dr. Sanders say about her?"

"He thinks she was murdered," I said. Inspector Debarets' face remained impassive.

"Did he give you his reasons?" he asked.

"Yes." I recounted the details. "He also says that he talked to the police but that you didn't take him seriously."

"He did talk to the police, Miss Fairfax. He talked to me and what he said made a great deal of sense. I assure you I took him very seriously indeed." He turned off the tape recorder and nodded to the officer at the desk who immediately put down his pen. "There is not a doubt in my mind. Janet Benedict was murdered."

That wasn't what I had expected to hear. It took me a moment to regain my balance. "Then why did the police report say she committed suicide? Why aren't you out looking for her murderer?"

"Because there was sufficient evidence to make suicide the only logical conclusion for a coroner and I have no hard evidence of murder," he said. "All I have is what Dr. Sanders has, my years of experience that tell me this suicide feels wrong. I have a feeling, a very strong feeling, but nothing more."

"So someone is going to get away with murder."

He ignored my remark. "The police cannot investigate feelings, Miss Fairfax. We need evidence." He turned the tape recorder back on and the other policeman picked up his pen.

"What did you do after Dr. Sanders left?"

"I went to bed and slept until just before eight this morning."

The questions stopped there. I was surprised he didn't ask me what I had dreamed about.

"If you remember anything else, no matter how irrelevant and trivial it may seem to you, please call me."

"Inspector, you know everything I saw and did yesterday. There's nothing more to tell." I felt tired and hungry. It was after ten and I hadn't had so much as a cup of coffee. Maybe Mr. Reilly would stand me lunch in lieu of our lost breakfast.

"I would also like to view the tapes that you took yesterday. Do you have them with you?"

"Sorry. Ella Baxter, 'Lifestyle's' producer, took them with her last night. They're probably at the station."

"I shall send an officer to collect them. Perhaps you would tell Miss Baxter to have them ready." I could imagine what kind of response that would get from Ella.

Her program lost forever in a police file.

"I had an appointment with Mr. Reilly to finish my work here today," I said. "Will that be possible?"

The inspector took a large brown envelope from the desk and extracted a stack of polaroid photos.

"I'm very sorry, Miss Fairfax," he said, "But you will not be working here today. And not with Philip Reilly." He passed the photographs to me.

They were shots of Mr. Reilly's body taken from every angle possible. He lay face down on the path, his arms flung out in front of him and his head resting awkwardly on a large gnarled tree root. The handle of Ben's sashimi knife protruded from between his shoulders. Its blade was so long that although it had pierced Mr. Reilly's heart, a good six inches of cold blue steel were visible above the bloody folds of Byron's jacket.

I gave the photos back to the inspector. "You don't think Ben Sugamoto did this?"

"At the moment we do not know who murdered Philip Reilly."

"Just because it's Ben's knife doesn't mean anything. He left his knife on the kitchen counter while he went out to have a cigarette and take some sashimi scraps to the barn cats. Anyone could have taken it."

Inspector Debarets did not reply. He turned off the tape recorder and re-wound the tape.

"May I go now?"

"Yes, of course." He got up from his chair. "I think we're finished with you for today, Miss Fairfax, but you will probably have to answer more questions later. Just like last time." He opened the door for me. "If you wish you may use the phone out here to call Miss Baxter about that video tape."

We stepped into the outer office. Dr. Morrison sat in a straight-backed chair staring out one of the dormer windows. Constable Lindt stood in front of a closed door on the opposite side of the room. The yellow police tapes sealing the door told me that it led to Mr. Reilly's office. A woman in a red blazer and a tweed skirt sat at a desk weeping quietly. She didn't sob. The tears simply welled up in her eyes and rolled down her cheeks. Her face looked every day of its sixty years.

"Dr. Morrison, would you come with me please." Now it was the doctor's turn to experience Inspector Debarets' relentless questions. She nodded a curt hello in my direction. I could hardly blame her for not being overjoyed to see me. Phoebe Fairfax, photographer and harbinger of bad public relations. I had visited The Ranch twice in six months and both times someone turned up dead. The inspector followed Dr. Morrison into her office and closed the door behind them.

There hardly seemed to be any point in asking the woman at the desk if she were all right when she so clearly wasn't. "May I use your telephone?" I said instead. She reached out and pushed it across the desk toward me.

"You're Phoebe Fairfax," she stated. "He had an appointment with you this morning. He was looking forward to it. He liked you." The tears still flowed. "I'm Margaret Sabbatini. I'm his secretary. That is, I was his secretary." She corrected herself in a perfectly steady voice oddly at variance with the weeping.

"I liked him too, Mrs. Sabbatini. I'm sorry."

"Oh, don't worry. The police will get her. She won't get away with it." I must have looked blank. "Her. God's gift to medicine." Mrs. Sabbatini nodded in the direction of Dr. Morrison's office. "Not that throwing her in jail will bring poor Philip back." She spoke in a totally matter-of-fact manner while the tears dripped off her face. It was creepy.

"Can I get you anything, Mrs. Sabbatini?"

"Maybe punishing her won't bring Philip back, but at least she won't get away with murdering him, will she?" The calm voice continued. "That will be some comfort, don't you think?"

What I thought was that Mrs. Sabbatini had flipped her neatly coiffed grey lid. "Would you like some coffee?" I asked.

"She knew that Philip wanted to fire her, you know. The way she wanted to run The Ranch it would soon have had no customers at all."

"A glass of water maybe?"

"He would have fired her already if Mr. Pepper hadn't interfered. But really," she confided in the same tranquil tones, "It was only a matter of time and she knew it." Her tears continued to stream.

"Mr. Pepper. You mean the Reg Pepper who's a guest here?" I asked.

"Yes. But he isn't just a guest," she replied. "He's an executive with the company. He does Philip's old job. The one Philip had before his heart attack." I didn't know the human eye could produce such a volume of fluid. "Philip wasn't well, you know. How could she attack a man with a heart condition?"

I didn't even try to answer that one. Instead, I decided to phone Ella. "Please excuse me for a moment, Mrs. Sabbatini. I have to make a call." Her calm, dispassionate voice continued to ramble on while I dialed the station.

"Hello, Phoebe. Finished the shot list already?" Ella sounded pleased and cheerful and sane. That wouldn't last long. I told her the news, including the bit about the tape. She reacted exactly as I expected. "But they'll keep it for months," she raged. "We're going to fight this. We'll get the station's lawyers right on it."

"Ella, get real," I said. "The station might—and that's a very big might—fight this if it was footage for a hard news story. But can you honestly see them doing it for 'A Day in the Lifestyle?' And even if they did, the tapes would be out of your hands. All it would mean is that a bunch of lawyers would have them instead of the police."

"Then you tell me how I'm supposed to put together a program out of tapes I can't keep?" Ella shrieked down the wire.

"Copy them," I said. "Look. Inspector Debarets hasn't said we can't broadcast that footage. All he's said is that he wants to have a look at it. If he really thought he was going to find anything on that tape he wouldn't have told me to phone you. He'd just have sent someone around to get it. He's giving you time to have the tapes duped."

"Oh no, she could never have duped Philip." Mrs. Sabbatini spoke in my left ear. "He was far too clever for her. She could never have pulled the wool over Philip's eyes."

"But what if he does find something?" Ella shouted in my right ear. "What happens to the tape then?" My circuits started to scramble.

"Who knows?" I said. "Cross that bridge when you come to it. He's a reasonable man." I looked across the desk at Mrs. Sabbatini. "Are you sure you wouldn't like a cup of coffee?"

"He was far too reasonable a man, if you ask me," Mrs. Sabbatini said. "Maybe if he hadn't been so reasonable with her he'd still be alive."

"What do you mean, do I want a cup of coffee?" Ella bellowed down the line. "Are you going to finish the interior shots today or is that all screwed up too?"

"For God's sake Ella, a man has been murdered. The place is crawling with police. It's not exactly business as usual around here. Of course I'm not going to get your damn shots."

"Not shot. No no no. She didn't shoot him. She stabbed him. She stabbed him in the heart with that funny cook's fish knife," Mrs. Sabbatini explained carefully.

"Then when will you be back at the station?" Ella asked.

"They still need me for some more questions here," I lied. "I'll probably have to hang around for awhile."

"We don't hang people any more in Canada," Mrs. Sabbatini said. "It's really such a shame."

"Ella will you tell News that I have some footage of the police taking the body away? It's nothing great but I'll have it there in time to be edited for six o'clock. See you later." I hung up before either Mrs. Sabbatini or Ella could ring her side of our conversational triangle again.

"Thanks." I pushed the phone back to Mrs. Sabbatini.

"I haven't told you anything you won't soon be hearing from the police," she said. "He's probably arresting her now." She looked at the door to Dr. Morrison's office. Her tears had not abated in the least.

"You're sure I can't get you anything?" I asked.

She shook her head.

"I have to leave now. Will you be all right?"

"I thought you wanted to use the phone," she said.

"That's okay. I'll make my call later."

"Are you leaving, Miss Fairfax?" Constable Lindt asked. She muttered something into her walkie-talkie and a minute later another uniformed officer appeared at the door. He escorted me in silence down to the van. The tall constable at the gate was still on duty. He moved the police car again to let me out. I saw him talking on his radio while he watched me drive off down the grid road.

CHAPTER 8

I stopped at my place to phone Cyrrie and invite myself for lunch. A large green florist's box protruded from my mailbox. The dog sat underneath it. I collected them both and drove to the house. The flowers were from Felix, two dozen long-stemmed red roses, along with a note that said, "To Phoebe, With my thanks, Felix." Two dozen roses seemed a pretty extravagant thank you for a little Scotch and a chunk of cheddar. Maybe he felt uncomfortable about telling me his suspicions regarding Janet Benedict's death, and the roses were an apology. If so, they were quite an apology. I put the flowers in a vase and admired them while I checked my answering machine for messages.

The first was from Felix, thanking me again for aiding the stranded traveller and asking for some help with a project for his photography class. The next voice on the line was Ben's.

"Hello, Phoeb. This is Ben. Something terrible's happened." The words came in a rush. "Reilly was stabbed last night with my sashimi knife. They're gonna think I did it." There was a long pause. I thought maybe he'd hung up but the tape was still rolling. Finally his voice came back on. "He's dead, Phoeb." Another pause. "For God's sake, please come home and answer your phone." This time he did hang up.

I dialed his home number. There was no answer so I called the restaurant. His wife answered.

"Oh, Phoebe, I don't know where he is." Marianne was close to tears. "The police have been here all morning. Two of them are sitting at a table eating lunch right now. They say they just want to ask him some questions but I know they're going to arrest him."

"Have you called Stan?" I asked. Ben's brother Stan is a lawyer.

"Yes," she said. "But what can Stan do? It was Ben's knife that killed the man."

"Look Marianne, I saw Ben leave his knife on a kitchen counter last night before he went outside to have a cigarette. Anyone could have taken it. Just because it was Ben's knife doesn't mean a thing." I tried to sound reassuring.

"You don't understand, Phoebe." She struggled to control her voice. "He didn't tell anyone his knife was missing."

It took a minute to sink in and when it did, I didn't like the feeling. Ben would never have left The Ranch without his knife any more than I would have left without my camera. "He must have mentioned something to Marge and Carter before they drove home," I said. "He was late meeting them at the van. Maybe he was looking for his knife then. He must have told them about it."

"He knew where his knife was," Marianne said. She started to cry.

It took another ten minutes of disjointed conversation to patch together the bare outline of Marianne's story. According to her, Ben had finished his second cigarette and was on his way back from the stable to the kitchen to collect his apron and knife and go home. He found his sashimi knife sooner than he expected, sticking out of Mr. Reilly's back. He panicked. He threw up behind a tree. Then he ran. He met Marge and Carter in the guest parking lot and the three of them drove back to Calgary.

He spent the night pacing the floor while Marianne begged him to call the police. At about six, he left the house to buy cigarettes. She hadn't seen him since.

"Why didn't he call the police?" I asked.

"He was afraid because he'd had an argument with Mr. Reilly just before dinner and he knew one of The Ranch doctors had overheard. They were going to cancel his contract, Phoebe."

Not for the first time I wondered how an intelligent adult male could behave with such incredible stupidity. They were going to cancel more than Ben's contract now. "Have you any idea where he could have gone, Marianne?"

"No. I thought you might know."

"He left a message on my machine but no number."

"Phoebe, I don't know what to do."

"Ben isn't an idiot," I said without much conviction. "I'm sure he'll come home when he's had a chance to think things over. Where's Stan?"

"He had to be in court this morning but he said he'd come over as soon as he was done."

"Good. I'm going to be at Cyrrie's for awhile and then at the station. If you need me, call Cyrrie. He'll make sure I get the message."

"Thanks Phoebe," she said, her voice almost under control again.

"And Marianne, don't imagine things to worry about. The policeman in charge of this case is smart and he's fair. He doesn't go around arresting innocent people." I hoped I was right.

I phoned Cyrrie and he promised me lunch. I grabbed an apple, collected the dog, and an hour and a half later we pulled up in front of Cyrrie's house in Calgary. He sat on his front steps waiting for us, reading the *Herald* in the afternoon sun. Cyrrie is the dog's favourite person. He

goes on a canine emotional binge every time they meet.
He tore up the walk like a puppy and fell in a great heap of
wriggling fur at Cyrrie's feet, his huge paws flailing the
air.

"You and that dog are a disgrace." I gave Cyrrie a
kiss. I have known him all my life and, although his hair
is thinning and more than a little grey now that he is
seventy, he never seems to age. He is still as trim and
spruce as the young man who smiles from the photo taken
over forty years ago on the day he and Uncle Andrew
moved into this house.

"My dear, you've got that forlorn look. What's the
matter?" He put his arm around my shoulders and we
went inside. "Do hurry up, Bertie." He held the door open
for the dog who had nearly recovered from his emotional
excesses and trotted in behind us.

Cyrrie led the way to the kitchen where he had set two
places at a butcher block work island that doubled as the
kitchen table. The sun streamed through a skylight
directly above.

"What's happened?" he asked. "I thought you were
supposed to be out working at Virginia Malifant's old
place today."

"I was," I said. "But The Ranch's business manager
was murdered last night."

"Murdered?"

"Stabbed to death," I said.

"Where did it happen?"

"At The Ranch. On one of those paths just down from
the pool."

"A murder at Virginia's. Who'd ever believe it?"
Cyrrie shook his head. "Have the police caught the person
who did it?"

"They haven't arrested anyone yet."

"Do they know who did it?"

"I'm not sure," I said. "I spent most of the morning answering questions for them but they didn't tell me much. They weren't exactly what you'd call forthcoming."

"Some health resort. First that woman you found. Now a murder. That place is lethal." He paused. "Phoebe, it wasn't you who . . ."

"No. Not me. Not this time," I said. "One of the cooks found him." Cyrrie looked relieved.

"Did you know the man?"

"A little. We were going to work together this morning. He invited me for breakfast."

"And I'll bet you haven't eaten a thing today, have you?"

"I had an apple on my way into town."

"An apple. It's almost one o'clock. No wonder you look dreadful." He pulled one of the high wooden stools out from the island. "Pour us both some wine and then sit down. Lunch will be along when I've dressed the salad."

"I haven't told you the worst of it." I handed him his glass of wine.

"I didn't think it was possible to get worse than murder."

"It is." I told him about the sashimi knife and Ben's argument with Mr. Reilly and his panic when he saw the body. "The police say they only want to talk to him but even Marianne doesn't know where he is."

"How could Ben be such a damn fool?" Cyrrie said, worry and anger competing for top place in his voice. Cyrrie had known Ben almost as long as I had. When we were high school kids, Ben often came with me on my visits to Cyrrie and Andrew. Ben claimed they had civilized us both. Cyrrie had given Ben his first cooking lessons. "Do you have any idea where he might have gone?"

"None at all. Maybe I should have stayed at home and

waited for him to call again."

"Don't be ridiculous," he said. "Ben doesn't need his hand held. He needs his arse kicked."

"Don't shout at me. I'm not the one who ran away. I've spent the whole bloody morning cooped up with a mob of Mounties." I could feel tears start.

Cyrrie put his arm around me. "My dearest girl, I'm not shouting at you. You know that," he said gently. "And you also know that Ben's not a stupid person. He'll turn up as soon as he's had a chance to calm down a little and think." He tried to comfort me just as I had tried to comfort Marianne.

"I used that exact line on Marianne," I said. "Do you really believe it?"

"Of course I do," he said, so staunchly that I began to think it just might be true. He handed me a Kleenex from a box on the counter. "And right now what you need is some food and no more talk about this until after you've eaten. Really Phoebe, you're looking far too thin these days."

"Fashionably thin," I said, and blew my nose.

"Foolishly thin," Cyrrie countered.

"You can never be too rich or too thin," I quoted.

"Oh yes you can, and that ridiculous woman was both." He put on a large white apron. "Sit," he ordered, and both the dog and I obeyed.

Sometimes it feels very good to be looked after. The wine tasted cold and crisp and the room was filled with wonderful warm cooking smells. Two ovens flanked a range top and a vented barbecue grill. Businesslike pots and utensils hung from a rack overhead. I watched Cyrrie dress the salad. His movements when he works in the kitchen are deft and quick, just like Ben's. Lunch was mushroom quiche and a romaine salad with his own garlic-laced dressing. I tasted my first forkful of quiche.

"This is good but it isn't yours, is it?"

"Simon the Pieman's," he replied. "Just a touch heavy-handed with the pastry, don't you think?" Cyrrie is a serious cook. "But next to mine, theirs is best." Although not a modest one.

The dog sat at Cyrrie's feet, his eyes glued to the quiche and his salivary glands out of control. "Bertie, that drooling is disgusting. Go lie down somewhere," Cyrrie ordered. The dog flopped obediently at his feet. His slobbery chin rested on one of Cyrrie's immaculately polished moccasin loafers.

I laughed. "I've told you that you shouldn't let him hang around the table while we're eating."

"Don't be such a killjoy, Phoebe. Dog spit's good for the leather." He surreptitiously slipped the dog a bit of pastry. "What word of your parents?"

"I had a letter last week. They're still in Hawaii. Australia for Christmas they hope." My father is a retired banker. He and my mother spend their summers in Calgary and their winters wandering to various warm bits of the world.

"It's their wedding anniversary next week," Cyrrie reminded. "Let's wire them some flowers. Forty years is an occasion. Andrew and I celebrated for a week."

Cyrrie is English. He and Uncle Andrew met and fell in love in London during the Second World War. Uncle Andrew was a pilot in the Royal Canadian Air Force, stationed near London. When the war ended and it was time for him to come home, Cyrrie came too. He sometimes refers to himself as a war bride. He and Andrew bought their house together long before anyone had even thought of the gay rights movement. For years the whole family carefully maintained—and probably even believed—the polite fiction that they were just two young bachelors sharing digs until the right girls came along.

However, after they had been together for forty years, even the dimmest of my aunts must have got the message. In any case, by the time I was born, Cyrrie was as much a part of our family as any of our more conventional uncles.

"Seconds?" he asked as I finished the last of my quiche.

"No thanks. This was delicious."

"Another drop of the Italian wine lake?" He held up the bottle. I shook my head. "Good, isn't it?" He poured an inch more into his own glass. "And what's even better, it's cheap." I had my doubts about that. Cyrrie's notion of cheap still has a cork in the bottle. Screw tops are beyond his experience and I don't think he even knows that wine in cardboard cartons exists.

He cleared the plates away and ground the beans for coffee. "Go find yourself a comfortable chair and we'll have our coffee there."

I wandered out to the living-room and looked out the big picture window. Cyrrie's house stands on the brow of a hill on the north side of the Bow River valley just above the city centre. The large living-room window faces west to one of the best views of the mountains Calgary offers. The city sprawls below. Andrew's piano used to sit in front of the window. Cyrrie's big brass kaleidoscope now stands in its place, firmly mounted on a sturdy oak tripod. With its gleaming machined casings and precision-crafted optics it looks like an old-fashioned telescope.

"What's new with the view?" I asked as he brought in the coffee tray.

"It's going through one of its blue periods," he replied. I aimed the scope at the skyline, put my eye to the lens and peered into the prisms. The mountains formed a jagged circle around fractured office towers and countless shades of sky blue shafted through the whole cubist's dream. Cyrrie's kaleidoscope is to those cardboard tubes of your childhood what a Mozart symphony is to a kazoo.

"You should let me get you a cine head for this tripod," I said. "Then you could pan along the mountains. The movement would make wonderful patterns."

"My dear, I don't think I'm up to quite that much wonder. The thing makes me dizzy now." He poured the coffee and we sat and sipped in silence for a few minutes.

"I almost forgot to tell you," I said. "I wore the Molyneux last night. It's the nicest dress I've ever had. It felt wonderful."

"My dearest Phoebe, calling that Molyneux a dress is like calling an ocean liner a boat. The *Queen Elizabeth* is a ship. The Molyneux is a gown."

"Give up, Cyrrie," I laughed, "I just ain't got no couth." I looked at my watch. "I guess I should get the van back to the station soon. It's almost two-thirty and I have some stuff to be edited for the six o'clock news."

"Finish your coffee."

"I told Marianne she could phone here if she needed anything. I said you'd pass on the message."

"When will you be back for Bertie?" he asked. The dog was asleep at his feet. He spends most of his time in town with Cyrrie. He raised an ear at the mention of his name.

"About six, maybe a little before. And, please, don't give him too many funny things to eat," I added, knowing full well that the bag of dry dog food I keep at Cyrrie's would go untouched, as always. "He may look like a wolf but he actually has a very delicate digestive system."

"Will you stay for dinner before you drive back?" he asked.

"I'd like that. Thanks."

Traffic was light so I took the scenic route to the station, down Tenth Street past Riley Park and along the river. It was a beautiful afternoon and joggers ranged in packs along the riverside paths.

I met one of the newsmen in the station parking lot and he offered to help me carry the equipment in from the van. I was surprised. Newsmen aren't famous for their accommodating manners and this one was a particularly offensive example of the breed.

"Hear you got some footage on that murder for us, Phoebe." Now I knew why the egotistical little snot had condescended to tote my light cases. He'd probably been waiting for me.

"In the bag, David." I slung my work-bag on my shoulder and grabbed the camera with one hand and the tripod with the other. On the way in he tried to grill me about what I had seen and heard at The Ranch. I wished I had carried the gear myself.

"This murder your story, David?" I asked. David is a blatant claim jumper if the story is juicy enough.

"Cheryl's actually," he admitted.

"Then I'll wait and tell it to Cheryl." He'd have dropped the lights and left me standing if we hadn't already reached the photography department. As it was he huffed off without bothering to say goodbye.

I stowed the gear in the equipment room and continued down the hall to the technical services office. The station's chief technician is a good friend. In his spare time, Larry keeps the cameras and editing equipment I use at home for my own work in good repair. Except for some preliminary stuff that I use a little home-market video camera for, I shoot all of my own work on sixteen millimetre film. I have a very fancy new Arriflex camera, a second-hand clockwork Bolex, and a Moviola editing bench. Without Larry I'd have big problems when things go wrong with them. The lens turret on the Bolex had been sticking a little and he'd promised to have a look at it.

"How's the Bolex?" I asked.

"All fixed," he said. "I finished it last night. This thing is built like a tank." He brought the camera in its case out from under his desk.

The battered old Bolex was the first film camera I ever owned and, if I were only allowed a single camera, it would be the one I'd pick. It's probably the most reliable camera ever built. When its sleek modern competitors have drained their batteries or seized up in the cold, the Bolex's Swiss-made mechanical innards just keep chugging the film on through.

In daily television, however, film cameras are a thing of the past. What used to be filmed is now recorded electronically on videotape. All my work for the station is done on video. Tape is cheap, quick, and reusable. By comparison, film is expensive, slow, and a one shot deal. But, it is also very beautiful. Every second, twenty-four frames of film pass through the camera's gate. Each frame holds one clear, discreet little picture. As individual brush strokes build a painting, these tiny still photos build a film. Processed and printed, sorted and cut, re-arranged and spliced, the little pictures trick the human eye and form images that seem to move.

I thanked Larry and went on to the newsroom where I stopped to deliver the tape of Mr. Reilly's body being removed from The Ranch. Cheryl asked me a lot of questions which I answered as well as I could while carefully avoiding any mention of Ben or his knife. Then I wandered on in search of Ella. She wasn't in her office but her computer was running so I knew she was still in the building. I sat down to wait. She came in a couple of minutes later with a smile on her face and a large bouquet of flowers in her arms. It was a formal florist's arrangement in a vase, but all spring flowers and really very pretty. It certainly was "Lifestyle's" day for flowers.

"Secret admirer?" I asked. Ella blushed right down to

her immaculate cream silk collar.

"Just a thank you from The Ranch," she lied.

"Well, I guess Marty Bradshaw does work at The Ranch," I conceded. "But whatever can he be thanking you for, Ella?"

"Knock it off and mind your own business, Phoebe."

"Candi says you're in love with him."

"Candi's an idiot."

"Ah, Ella, love at first sight. You mad, impetuous, romantic fool, you."

Ella started to growl so I quit. She put the flowers on a table in front of the window and slipped the little card that came with them under her desk blotter.

"I don't suppose you managed to get any work done today," she said.

"Why Ella, you speak as if I'd let a little thing like murder stand in the way of my duty." Now it was my turn to growl. "Of course I didn't get any work done. I told you the place was crawling with police."

"You certainly do have the knack, don't you?" she said.

"What knack?"

"First a suicide now a murder. What's next, Phoebe? Plague, famine, pestilence, maybe a little war?"

"For God's sake Ella, it's not my fault that someone murdered Mr. Reilly. I don't ask for these things to happen."

"Any idea when they'll let you go back and get those interiors?"

"Later in the week maybe. You'll have to check with the police. Have they picked up yesterday's tapes yet?"

"Not yet. We've almost finished dubbing them. They're really good." At least Ella knows quality when she sees it. "Want to go down to editing and have a look?"

We arrived at editing just in time to watch Reg, clad in

his green sweats, struggle his way into the saddle. He'd attracted quite an audience.

"Great stuff, Phoebe," said Derek, the chief video editor. "Who's the porker in the pixie suit?"

A shout of laughter went up at a particularly unflattering shot of Reg's posterior poised over the saddle. "Way to go, Chubby Cheeks!"

"Who's the overweight elf?" The news editor wandered in to investigate the source of the laughter.

I began to feel a little defensive on Reg's behalf. Most of the men who were standing laughing at him weren't exactly threats to Arnold Schwarzenegger and, in Derek's case, it was an instance of the pot calling the paunch plump.

"That fat elf just happens to be one of the top executives in the company that owns The Ranch." I flaunted the one nugget of real information I had gleaned from Margaret Sabbatini's ravings.

"Reg?" Ella said, plainly not believing me.

"Reg," I repeated firmly.

Candi wafted in. The men at the station are not quite so susceptible to her charms as strangers. Constant proximity has inured them a little, built up their Candi antibodies as it were. Some of them can actually breathe normally when she's around.

"Hey, there's Reg," Candi waved at the screen. "Isn't he a cutie?"

Reg finally made it into the saddle. Next, dappled light played over the dappled rear of Byron's Appaloosa mare and the trail ride disappeared into the woods. That was the last shot on the tape and really a lovely piece of camera work.

"Hot damn, I'm good," I announced to the room which ignored me except for one Philistine in the cheap seats who gave me a very loud raspberry.

"That's it, Ella. All done." Derek put the duplicate tape in its case.

"Ella Baxter, please contact the front desk." The nasal Voice of Doom, otherwise known as Marcia the Receptionist, boomed over the intercom. "Ella Baxter. There is an RCMP officer waiting for you."

"Just in time. Thanks Derek." Ella took the tape.

"Not the police again. How many times you been arrested for it this year, Ella?"

"The Mounties are gonna throw away the key on you if you keep this up." The assembled adolescents were having a field day with Marcia's announcement.

"We just can't keep passing the hat for your bail, Ella. You gotta give it up and get yourself a real job."

Ella ignored them. "I'll see you two in my office in five minutes," she said to Candi and me. "We've got to discuss how we're going to work around this delay." She walked to the door where she stopped and turned to face the room. "I know you're right, guys, and I really am going to quit," she announced. "Just as soon as I make enough money to pay for your hair transplants." She left before any of them could get off a topper. Candi and I wandered down the corridor to wait for her in her office.

"Hey, great flowers." Candi looked closely at Ella's bouquet. "I wonder who sent them. Maybe there's a card."

"I think they're from Marty. She stuck the card under her blotter," I added without thinking. "Candi! That's Ella's private correspondence."

"Don't be such a party pooper, Phoebe. Everyone knows that flower messages are like postcards. I mean they're practically public property." She read the card, smiled, and slipped it back under the blotter.

"Well?" I said.

"Well what?"

"Well what does it say?"

"But Phoebe, that's Ella's private correspondence. I wouldn't want it on your conscience that you'd read Ella's private note from Marty." From time to time I find the urge to throttle Candi so strong that I can truly sympathize with Ella.

"Candi," I said steadily. "What does the note say?"

She caught my tone. "It says 'To a wonderful lady and a wonderful beginning. Marty.' Isn't that romantic, Phoebe? He seems like a real nice man, doesn't he?"

"Boy," I corrected. "He's younger than you are. He's probably ten years younger than Ella."

"Well what difference does that make if they're in love? If Ella was the man and Marty was the woman you wouldn't even think about it. For someone who's always on about equal rights for women you can say some real unequal kinds of things, Phoebe."

It's very irritating when Candi is right.

"I mean that doctor we ate with last night is way older than you are but I'll bet you never even noticed that when you were goofing around with him before dinner. He must be over fifty so if its dumb for Ella to fall for Marty when she's only ten years older than him, then it's double dumb for Felix Sanders to fall for you. And I'll bet you he's married so you'd better watch out."

"You should write romance novels, Candi. You've got the imagination for it."

"You can laugh all you like, Phoebe but . . ."

I was spared more of Candi's lecture by Ella's reappearance. .

"The police want to talk to you and me tomorrow morning, Candi," she said. "They want us at the station by ten-thirty."

"Not Phoebe, too?"

"They questioned Phoebe today. That's why we still

have half the 'Lifestyle' taping left to do. By the way," she said to me, "You can finish those interiors on Friday morning. It's okay with the police and there's a camera available."

"What about The Ranch? Are you sure it's okay with them? Mr. Reilly was supposed to take me around. I don't think they're just going to give me the master key and let me go to it."

"Right. I'll take care of it. Be at The Ranch at nine and someone will meet you."

"Isn't it awful about Mr. Reilly," Candi said. "He was such a nice man. But then, when you get right down to it, all the other people we met yesterday seemed pretty nice too, didn't they? Even Reg's wife wasn't all that bad."

"Could we skip the personality assessments, Candi. It's getting late," Ella said.

"What I'm trying to say," Candi persisted, "Is that it's very weird to think that it's probably one of those nice people who murdered Mr. Reilly. I mean, we actually met a murderer and didn't know it. Murder's not exactly something you think of everyday people doing, is it? Especially people you like."

"Maybe someone you didn't like did it," Ella said, rather nastily I thought. "Tell us, Candi, was there anyone at The Ranch you didn't like?" As always, the sarcasm was lost on Candi.

"I told you, I thought they were all very nice," she said. "Except maybe the cowboy in the funny clothes. I didn't like him much."

"Byron? He hardly said two words all night," I said. "What's not to like?"

"He gave me the creeps, the way he looked at me."

"Candi, everything with a Y chromosome looks at you that way." You'd think she'd be used to it by now.

"You can make fun of me if you like, Phoebe, but that

guy is a creep."

I smiled to myself. What we have here, I thought, is not opposites attracting but likeness repelling. Two north poles competing for the same magnet. It seemed that Candi and Byron, the sexual spellbinders, were not simply immune to each other's magic but actively repulsed by it. Candi had not warmed to the glimpse of herself that she caught in Byron, her masculine mirror image.

"Now, if we're finished with the important stuff, maybe we could move on?" Ella's sarcasms are not lost on me. I just find them irritating. It was nearly four-thirty by the time she finished droning on about the difficulties and delays that Mr. Reilly's murder had caused "A Day in the Lifestyle" and how she proposed to deal with them. For a bright lady, Ella can be a real drag.

"Want to go somewhere for a drink?" Candi asked after we left Ella's office. "It's a bit early but we deserve it after that. Can't she just drive you to drink some days?"

"Bottle of gin and a straw," I agreed. "But I can't today. Sorry." Candi looked disappointed. "Are you coming out to my place this Saturday?" I asked. On weekends, Candi often helps me with my work. She's a surprisingly competent assistant and she keeps my shot lists and location notes in better shape than I do. Right now I'm teaching her how to do sound.

"One o'clock again?" she asked.

"Twelve if it's a nice day," I said. "I'll make us a picnic lunch."

"But Phoebe, you always make the lunch," Candi protested. "I'm starting to feel guilty. Let me bring the trail mix this time."

CHAPTER 9

I collected my car from the station lot, pulled out into the rush hour traffic and went looking for Ben. I thought I'd try a few of the places we used to go when we were kids and the world and algebra class were too much with us. Calgary has all sorts of green places tucked away close to the centre of the city and Ben and I had played truant at most of them. I liked the illusion of being out in the country and the feeling of freedom it gave me. I was big on nature poets in those days. Ben was big on anywhere he could smoke. I wondered if he had felt the need of a little Wordsworthian idyll today. I'd follow the butts.

I drove east down Ninth Avenue to the Inglewood Bird Sanctuary. If you don't look up at the office towers looming five minutes away, you'd swear the bird sanctuary was in the heart of the country not the heart of the city. There were no other cars in the parking lot but I decided to check the footpaths anyway. I jogged past Colonel Walker's old red brick house and went once around the path that loops through the park along the river bank. Just past the footbridge a couple of Canada geese tried to mug me for a grain handout. They waddled along the trail behind me honking and hissing, birdy thugs with black hoods and spread wings. The path was a mess. Loose as a goose is not just an idle expression. Further along I met a flock of mallards and a dozen more geese who obviously hadn't got the message about flying south, but no Ben.

Minus the birds, it was the same story at Reader's

Rock Garden but at least the path there was shorter and cleaner. The garden is built into a hillside very near the Calgary Stampede grounds. It overlooks the Saddledome and the race track. I stood for a moment at the top of the hill and looked down past the bare trees to the scene of Elvira's many triumphs. The horses were trotting toward the starting gate for the first race. In the slanting rays of the late afternoon sun, the jockeys' silks looked even brighter than usual. I hadn't been to the track since Elvira won the Alberta Derby, the year Uncle Andrew died. I walked back through the empty garden down the hill to the car.

Thanks to the downtown traffic, I was still in the car for the six o'clock news. I turned up the radio. The murder was the lead story, short on fact but long on sensation. According to the report, there had been no arrest as yet in connection with last night's brutal knife murder at a luxury health resort south of town. However, the police had released the name of the murdered man. A fifteen-second biography of Mr. Reilly followed. They padded the rest of the item with a lot of background on The Ranch and its wealthy customers. Money and murder are an unbeatable combination. Dr. Morrison couldn't hush this one up.

It was almost dark when I parked near St. Barnabas church and walked through Riley Park's west gate, past the empty wading pool and on to the cricket pitch. I stood in the middle of the pitch and listened to the sound of the traffic on Tenth Street. Car lights flickered beyond the park's east railing. Still no Ben. I felt cold and a little lonely. I gave up and went back to the car.

It was after seven and dark when I drove up the hill to Cyrrie's. The Sugamoto's Catering van was parked in front of his house. I found Ben sitting in the kitchen eating a plate of Cyrrie's chicken stew.

"Where the hell have you been, you idiot? Marianne's worried sick about you."

"Keep your shirt on, Phoeb." Ben was very subdued.

"Keep my shirt on! The police are looking for you, you know. The RCMP no less. I've driven half of Calgary looking for you myself and you tell me to keep my shirt on!" The dog ambled over and licked my left hand. Cyrrie put a large dry vermouth in my right.

"We've phoned Stanley," Cyrrie said. "He's meeting Benjamin here and then they're going to the police together."

"And Marianne," Ben added, "I phoned Marianne too." He looked exhausted. "Do you think they'll arrest me, Phoeb?"

"Of course they won't arrest you." I hoped I sounded more convinced than I felt. "You haven't committed a crime. Not unless rank stupidity has become a criminal offense. Where have you been all day?"

"I drove up to Lake Louise and had breakfast at the Chateau. Then I just sort of wandered around near the lake. Me and about five hundred Japanese tourists. I fit right in." His eyes were bleary from lack of sleep. "Hey Phoeb, did you know that all the signs at the Chateau are bilingual now—English and Japanese?"

"For God's sake Ben, Mr. Reilly's been murdered, the police are looking for you, and you're giving me a tourist report." I wanted to shake him.

"I just thought it was sort of interesting."

"Don't badger the man, Phoebe," Cyrrie said softly. "He really has been through enough. A little more cacciatore, Benjamin?"

"No thanks, Cyrrie. That was great. As usual."

"You drove to Lake Louise and back in your van?" I asked in disbelief. Ben's van has Sugamoto's Catering written on it in red letters about a foot high. I was amazed that the Mounties hadn't managed to get their flamboyantly labelled man.

"Yeah. And then I came to Cyrrie's and we decided it was best for me to go to the police so we called Stan."

"Did you think of calling the police? Maybe they'd like to know where you are too."

"Everything's under control, Phoebe," Cyrrie said. "Just sit down and drink your vermouth." The front door bell rang. "I'll bet that's Stanley now." He went to answer the door. The dog padded along behind him.

"Phoeb, I'm sorry," Ben said. "I know I've been an idiot. You're right to be angry."

"I'm not angry, and you don't have to be sorry. I guess we've all been so worried about you that nobody's thinking straight."

"Cyrrie's thinking is just fine," Ben said. "That's why I came here. You know Cyrrie's going to tell you the truth."

"Did he?"

"Told me I'd been a real asshole and made me phone Marianne and Stan and the police. In that order."

"He really called you an asshole? Cyrrie?" I laughed in spite of myself. It was totally out of character. Cyrrie is the politest person I know. He even apologizes to the dog when he trips over him.

"Guess he figured it was the only word for the occasion and he's right," Ben said. "I am an asshole. At least I behaved like one. I think I must have gone hysterical or something. It was really weird, Phoeb. I can't explain it. I've never felt a feeling like that before. Sort of sick and scared and high all at the same time. I saw my knife sticking out of Reilly and all I could do was puke and run." He looked at me. "If they do arrest me, will you and Cyrrie look in on Marianne and the kids once in awhile?"

"The police are not going to arrest you, Ben. You haven't done anything."

"That's not what it looks like. You see, I had one hell of a fight with Reilly before dinner last night. We got pretty loud. At least I got loud," he corrected. "Reilly didn't, but I know people heard me yelling at him."

"Was that when you caught him watching the porno movie?"

"Yeah. But the fight didn't have anything to do with that." Ben got up and put his empty plate in the sink. "He was going to can the sashimi nights, Phoeb. The bastard didn't even give me a reason. Just no more sashimi at The Ranch after my contract runs out in December. That was it."

"They're going to change a lot of stuff at The Ranch," I said. "Cancelling your sashimi nights is just part of it."

"You know something I don't?"

"They're going after a whole new image," I said. "Back to the old western wilderness—country food, living with nature, that sort of stuff. You just got caught with an image problem."

"I didn't know about any of that. All Reilly told me was no more Sugamoto's Catering and that was it. No reason, no explanation." I had the feeling that Ben had flown into a rage before Mr. Reilly had time to offer reasons and explanations. "Where'd you find out all this stuff?" he asked.

"Felix Sanders," I said.

"He's the one who heard me yelling at Reilly."

"Felix?"

"Yeah. His office is just down the hall from Reilly's. He was there when I got the boot."

"Felix didn't say anything about a fight. He just told me about some of the changes that are coming at The Ranch."

"When was this?"

"Last night," I said. "After dinner. He stopped at my place for coffee."

"When did you two get to be such good friends? I didn't know you'd even met the guy before yesterday," Ben said. "Watch it, Phoeb, I think he's married."

I ignored him. First Candi, now Ben. One cup of coffee and they had us launched on a full-scale affair. "Felix says the company's even bought a game ranch."

"So they're going into game. I knew the trendy bastards would do something like that," Ben said in disgust. "Bambi burgers. Shit."

"Relax, Ben. Those Bambi burgers put you right in with God knows how many other people who might lose their jobs because of Mr. Reilly's plans. Maybe even Dr. Morrison. If you're a suspect at all, you're sure not the only one. They're not going to arrest you."

"Just keep on believing that, Phoeb," he said as Cyrrie and Stan came into the kitchen. Stan and Ben are so alike they could almost be twins but the similarity stops at their looks. Stan is a couple of years younger than Ben but he was born middle-aged and reading a law book. To Stan, everything is serious. Tonight he looked particularly sombre and it wasn't just his dark blue three-piece suit.

"Hello, Phoebe," he said. "Good to see you." He didn't waste either greetings or pleasantries on his brother. "Ben, how could you be so goddamn dumb?"

"Nice to see you too, Stan," Ben said.

"Don't you realize what kind of trouble you could be in?"

"For God's sake, I didn't kill the guy."

"I know you didn't."

"Well that's something."

"But you left him lying where you found him with your knife sticking out of his back. How did you know for certain that he was dead? What if he was still alive when you found him and you left him to die? Did you think of that?"

"You're a real treat, Stan. You're just what I need right now."

"You think I'm bad. Wait until the police get through with you."

"He was dead. He was dead when I found him."

"And when did you graduate from medical school?" Stan looked at his watch.

"Got any other happy lawyer stuff you'd like to tell me?" Ben asked.

"Can't you take anything seriously?"

"I'm serious about this," Ben replied. "And I'm scared. So maybe instead of giving me this shit you could tell me why they're not going to lock me up tonight."

"Let's go," Stan said. He checked his watch again.

"That's it? Let's go. You don't want to know what happened?"

"You can tell me in the car on the way to the police station. Come on. Let's go." Stan looked at his watch for the third time in under a minute.

"What about my van?"

"Leave it here. Nothing will happen to it in front of Cyrrie's. Let's go," Stan insisted.

Cyrrie and the dog saw them out.

"Stan was pretty rough on Ben," I said as Cyrrie came back into the kitchen. "I've never heard him talk like that before."

"Stanley is very worried," Cyrrie said. "He's afraid for Ben. It makes him sound irritable."

"That was irritable? As in Attila the Hun got a little irritable every now and then?"

Cyrrie didn't answer. He took placemats from the drawer and began to set two places at the counter for dinner. I drank the last of my vermouth.

"I hadn't thought of that," I said. "I mean that Ben might have left Mr. Reilly to die."

"I know you hadn't," he said. "Neither had Ben." But Cyrrie had.

"Oh God, Cyrrie. What an absolutely horrible mess this is."

"My dearest girl, a human being was robbed of his life last night. You are caught in the aftermath of murder most foul. What else did you expect?"

"But Ben didn't kill him. So I thought if he went to the police then everything would be all right. What do you think they'll charge him with?"

"I don't know," said Cyrrie. "Probably nothing right now."

"If Mr. Reilly was still alive when Ben found him, can they charge him with something?"

"I don't think so," Cyrrie said. "I don't believe the law requires you to be a Good Samaritan. But that doesn't change the fact that Ben ran away. For all he knew Mr. Reilly was still alive and he left him to die. That won't ever be all right. It's something Ben will have to live with for the rest of his life."

"Reilly was dead," I said. "Inspector Debarets showed me some photos of the body. He was dead when Ben found him."

"I hope you're right," Cyrrie said. "And for the rest of this evening the subject is closed. There's nothing more we can do for Ben right now. So we're going to have a pleasant meal together and talk of other things." He brought a bowl of salad, a jar of dressing, and the salad forks and set them in front of me. "Toss."

I poured a little of the dressing on to the lettuce and followed orders. "Cyrrie?"

"Present and listening." He added a little salt to a large

pot of boiling water and dropped in two handfuls of fresh pasta.

"Inspector Debarets thinks that Janet Benedict was murdered too. So does the doctor I met at The Ranch yesterday. Felix Sanders. He's The Ranch psychiatrist. He was her doctor."

"Do you believe them?" He peered under the noodle pot and adjusted the gas flame.

"I don't know what to believe," I said.

"Did they tell you why they think she'd been murdered?"

"That's the problem. Neither of them has any real reasons." I told him about my conversation with Felix and about the inspector's remarks during our interview that morning. "All they have are feelings, a hunch that something about her death isn't right."

"Do you think they could be right?"

"Well, they each came to the same conclusion independently and both of them are pretty bright men. They're good at their jobs. I've been on the receiving end of Debarets' questions enough to know that, and Felix must be good, too, or The Ranch would never have hired him. I like them both. They're not a couple of flakes. They're both intelligent, rational, reasonable men."

"Then I guess you have to take their opinions seriously."

"But the case is closed. The verdict was suicide. If they're right, then someone is going to get away with murder."

"Someone won't get away with it twice," Cyrrie said. "Not if your inspector is as good a policeman as you say he is."

"You think the murders are connected?"

"It would be a very unlikely coincidence for a place like The Ranch to have two murders in six months unless they were tied together in some way. The police will discover the connection. Sooner or later."

"You have lot of faith in the police. Why will they be able to catch Mr. Reilly's killer when they can't even prove Janet Benedict was murdered?"

"Because this time the murderer didn't make any effort to be subtle. Maybe he didn't have time or maybe he was so sure of himself after his last triumph that he didn't bother. This time he'll get caught." Cyrrie sat down on the stool next to mine.

"Look at it this way," he said. "A dead body with a Japanese cooking knife stuck in it is not exactly an everyday find. Especially at a place like The Ranch. It's obvious that Mr. Reilly's murder was not a random killing. It's a murder with a motive. So ask yourself, how many people could have had reasons for wanting him dead? I don't expect you'll find the landscape littered with suspects. There just can't be all that many possibilities for the police to explore. For all we know there may even be a witness or a piece of damning forensic evidence. It was a pretty blatant crime after all. But even without that, I'm willing to bet that this time the Mounties will get their man and, when they do, they'll find the connection to Janet Benedict. The murderer won't get away with it twice."

"I still think you have too much faith in the police."

"It's got nothing to do with faith," he said. "I simply know that the police success rate on crimes like Mr. Reilly's murder is very high. Think of the way they work on things like this, my dear. Think of the resources they have. I don't have faith in the police so much as I have faith in time and detail and infinite patience."

A little water boiled over the edge of the noodle pot and sizzled as it hit the stove. Cyrrie got up and stirred the pot. "Dinner is ready," he said. "And we really have talked too much about murder. No more of it tonight.

Taboo. It's time to pour the wine." He strained the noodles in a large stainless steel colander and put them in a bowl which he handed to me with a flourish. "Tonight's menu features chicken cacciatore with fettucini, a mixed salad with house dressing, and the same hooch you had for lunch."

"Two great meals in one day. My stomach will be getting ideas above its station." I put some noodles on both our plates.

"You mean it might start to expect something radical like proper food at regular intervals? That would never do, would it? You might have to learn to cook." He brought the pot of cacciatore and set it between us on the counter.

"I cook all the time," I said. Cyrrie started to laugh. "Well, quite often." He laughed even harder. The dog's tail thumped an accompaniment. The traitor. "More than twice a week." Cyrrie wiped his eyes, steadied his hand and served the cacciatore.

Really, I don't know why men are so obsessed with food. They're worse than baby birds. Or house guests. They're always thinking about their next meal. At least my ex-husband was. We used to split the household chores. One week Gavin cooked and I cleaned up, the next week we reversed the process. The cook always did the grocery shopping. I swear Gavin spent hours making his grocery lists and planning his week's meals. He'd rush home from work and start messing around in the kitchen as soon as he got in the door. He even began to collect cookbooks. Personally, I regard most cookbooks as a form of imaginative fiction. But not Gavin. Give him a pig's foot and a bottle of beer and he'd start looking for recipes in Julia Child. We'd have a week of stir-fried this and clay-baked that and souffléd the other and then it would be my turn. And what's wrong with a pot of chile that lasts four days? That's what I'd like to know. People can't be expected to drop what they're doing just so they can start cooking a meal they're not even hungry for and probably forgot to buy anyway. It isn't reasonable. But Gavin wasn't a reasonable man. He even liked doing the shopping. Can you imagine? My idea of hell is being chained to a shopping cart and doomed to push it forever round and round the aisles of the Supermarket of the Damned. Which, by the way, has no racks full of tabloids near the checkout stand, this being my one salvation in the grocery store.

"Very good cacciatore," I said, which was pretty generous of me I thought, considering the recent aspersions cast on my domestic probity.

"Thank you, my dear. I'll give you the recipe." Another snort of laughter.

"Really, Cyrrie. I'm a very respectable cook."

"And so you are. I've had some dandy scrambled eggs at your house."

Obviously the conversation needed a new direction. "Has *The Blood-Horse* started to come yet?" *The Blood-Horse* is the weekly bible of the thoroughbred breeding industry. If you want to know who's who in the world of equine aristocrats *The Blood-Horse* is the oracle to consult. I bought Cyrrie a subscription for his birthday.

"Yes. It started several weeks ago. Very handsome magazine. Thank you," he said.

"Have you found a suitable stud for Elvira?"

"Not yet. I've been rather busy and it's going to take some study."

"You haven't even looked at the magazine yet, have you?"

"It's not the kind of project you want to rush. More salad?"

"Cyrrie, Elvira is seven years old. She ran her last race at three. She's done nothing but roam around my pasture eating her head off for four years. It's time to breed her. Either that or sell her to someone who will. Her racing years are done. It's not right to waste her best breeding years too."

"Don't nag so, Phoebe. Of course, you're right. I'm going to start soon. We can't do anything before spring anyway."

"But if you want to be certain of getting a booking with a good stallion you know you have to decide as early as possible. It may already be too late for next season. And what about all the shipping arrangements? Cyrrie, you've got to start now." But I knew he wouldn't. His heart is no longer with the horses. Cyrrie's interest in their little stable seemed to have died along with Uncle Andrew.

Before Elvira, the Blithe Spirits Stable owned three horses, two honest geldings who earned their oats every summer at the track, and one filly whose promising career had been cut short by a training accident. Cyrrie and Uncle Andrew bred the filly to a respectable local stud and the serendipitous result was Elvira, every horse owner's dream. Elvira made her debut at the track in May of her three-year-old year and, except for one race in which she lost a shoe and only managed a third, she was first across the finish line every time she ran. Elvira cleaned up.

It was one of the happiest summers I can remember. Perhaps the lovely expression *halcyon days* would not be out of place, because in my memory it was a time of sunlight and serenity. Gavin and I were newly married and very much in love. Our drab days and cold silences were still in the future. Andrew and Cyrrie played hosts at what seemed like a whole summer of celebrations. Every race of Elvira's was an excuse to get the family and all our friends together to cheer her down the stretch and afterwards, to toast her victory with a party at Ben Sugamoto's restaurant. That summer Elvira made all of us winners. She capped the season with a two-length triumph in the Alberta Derby. Even my brothers came home for that one. It was the last time we were all together. Two months later, Uncle Andrew died.

That winter, Cyrrie sold the Blithe Spirits horses. All but Elvira. After Andrew's death, he lost interest in the stable and in just about everything else. Time helped but even four years later he still had not completely recovered from his loss. Perhaps he never would. He was still the same Cyrrie, as much fun to be with and as kind as ever but something was missing. I thought perhaps if I could prod him into taking an interest in Elvira again it might help.

"I really will get busy on it soon," Cyrrie said. He tried to muster a little conviction for my benefit.

"Remember we can check it all out on computer too," I said. "Did you get a chance to look at that stuff I sent you about data bases for horse breeders?"

"Phoebe, please give it a rest. I know what you're trying to do and I'm very grateful that you care. But sometimes you push a little too hard. Give it a rest."

"I'm sorry. It's just that I worry about you."

"I worry about you too," he said.

"Please, no more about my not eating properly."

"I worry that you've turned into too much of a loner. It isn't healthy for you. Ever since you and Gavin split up, it almost seems like you've cut yourself off from people. What are you afraid of?"

"I'm not afraid of anything. It's just that my work is kind of solitary. Nature photography isn't exactly a group activity. But I'm not a loner. I see people socially all the time. It's only Tuesday and this is the second time I've been into town for dinner this week.

"Both times with me."

"So, you're people."

"I'm a seventy year old retired stockbroker who's known you since the day you were born. I'm not a social life. I'm your old uncle."

We finally agreed to stop improving each others lives for the remainder of the evening. I helped him clean up the kitchen and load the dishwasher. We decided to phone my parents and spent the next ten minutes trying to figure out what time it was in Hawaii. We did a lot of dithering with degrees of longitude and juggling of daylight and standard time zones before we finally remembered we could simply ask the operator.

"I'm old. I'm allowed to be forgetful. What's your excuse?" Cyrrie laughed. We tried my parents but they were not in their hotel room. "Want to watch the news?" He switched on the television and we settled in for an assortment of mayhem and madness chosen largely at random by the CBC. I dozed off.

"You should go to bed, Phoebe." Cyrrie's voice woke me. "You look exhausted. Are you sure I can't persuade you to stay the night? Your room is always ready."

"Thanks but I should go home. I want to start work early tomorrow. The work print for some of the beaver pond footage came last week and I haven't had a chance to look at it yet."

I loaded the dog and a care package of the leftover cacciatore into the car and set off on the drive home. I keep a supply of tapes and talking books to entertain me on the way. If you spend as much time driving as I do, a good car stereo is a necessity, not a luxury.

The night was cold with a feeling of snow in the air. Clouds hung low and the blustery little wind had a bitter edge to it. I cranked the heater up to high and loaded a Blossom Dearie tape into the deck. Soon we were a warm island of sound, me and Blossom and the dog. Blossom launched into "I Like You, You're Nice." The song reminded me of Felix. Then it happened. The outward sign of a canine digestive system in deep inner distress wafted nastily from the back seat. I pulled over to the curb and looked back at the dog. He peered over his shoulder.

"Don't bother looking for the culprit. We both know who did it. There's only you."

He hung his great head in shame. His huge ears lay plastered close to his skull.

"How could you? It's that damn leftover quiche, isn't it?"

He gave his tail an ingratiating twitch or two. I rolled down all the windows and then got out the old parka I carry in the trunk and put it on. I zipped it up to the neck and buttoned the hood. Before I put my gloves back on I turned off the tape.

"You don't deserve to listen to Blossom," I said. "Blossom doesn't even let people smoke when she sings at her cabarets."

We started on our way again. The cold wind roared through the car dispersing the miasma. I entertained myself for the whole blood-freezing, bone-chilling trip plotting my revenge on Cyrrie. I settled for sending him and the dog off on a little drive together with the car windows sealed shut.

CHAPTER 10

I was surprised not to see snow on the ground when I woke up Wednesday morning but the clouds had dispersed overnight and the sky was clear with the promise of another in our string of perfect autumn days. I helped Tom feed and groom the horses. We put some extra hay in the corral to make up for the grass they would miss grazing while the pasture was off limits. Back at the house I made a pot of coffee and loaded a reel of the work print on to the editing bench. Then the phone rang. The RCMP requested the pleasure of my company at their Calgary office. Just a few things to sign and a few more questions to answer. Any time before twelve would do.

This time I talked to the quiet officer who had taken notes in Dr. Morrison's office. He fired off a barrage of questions about Felix and Byron. The questions made sense, I suppose, if you assumed that the murderer had made a mistake and stabbed the wrong person. After all, the path was very dark and Mr. Reilly had been wearing Byron's jacket, the same jacket Felix had worn for most of the evening.

I did a little grocery shopping before I left Calgary and drove home. It was such a beautiful afternoon that I couldn't make myself go back inside the house to work. Instead, the dog and I went for a walk along the stream that is the west boundary of my property. We got home around six. I gave him his dinner, put mine in the microwave oven to thaw and sat down at my desk to play back the messages on my answering machine. The first was from Felix. More thanks for my hospitality and another request for some help with a project for his class. He would call again later. The next beep brought Ella confirming a Friday morning finish to the "Lifestyle" taping at The Ranch. Dr. Morrison would meet me at nine and do the escort honours herself. I'll bet the doctor was thrilled at the prospect of playing minder to the harbinger of doom. The thrill was mutual.

Ben brought the messages to a close. He sounded much better. His voice was firm and there were none of the long panicky pauses that marked his last message.

"I'm a free man, Phoeb. For now, anyway. Call me when you get home. I'm at the restaurant." He hung up.

I dialed the restaurant. Marianne answered. We talked for a minute or two. Like Ben, she sounded much stronger, much more in control than she had yesterday.

"And thanks for everything, Phoebe. We're very grateful to you."

"But Marianne, I didn't do anything."

"You were there when we needed you. Cyrrie too. That's enough."

"Cyrrie's always there when you need him." I wasn't as certain about me.

"Ben says you and Cyrrie are coming for dinner this week. When shall I write your reservation in?"

"Sometime later in the week," I said. "I'll give you a call when I've checked with Cyrrie."

"You know if I let you do that you'll get busy working on something and forget. I've written you down for Saturday at seven and I'll phone Cyrrie. Okay?"

"Marianne, you're worse than my mother," I laughed. "I'll see you Saturday."

I heard restaurant kitchen sounds in the background while I waited for her to call Ben to the phone. A door closed, the sounds stopped, and Ben came on the line.

"I told you they wouldn't arrest you," I said.

"They'd like to. I think I'm their best bet so far. Anyway, I'm sure as hell the odds-on favourite."

"If they had enough evidence to arrest you they'd have done it by now."

"They're working on it."

"What did Inspector Debarets say?"

"What didn't he say? He kept Stan and me there until four in the morning asking me questions." The inspector had asked, re-asked, rephrased, and repeated until finally the police knew more about the previous thirty hours of Ben's life than Ben knew himself. They let him go with the promise of more questions to come. He had gone home to bed and slept until five o'clock in the afternoon.

"Have you called Cyrrie?" I asked. "He was pretty worried."

"Right after I left the message on your machine. To tell you the truth Phoeb, I'm pretty worried myself. Unless someone confesses I figure it's just a matter of time before they arrest me."

"You're innocent."

"And so are you for thinking that matters. I don't look very innocent. Reilly and I had that fight before dinner. It was my knife that killed him. I ran away."

"There you go, giving yourself the starring role," I said. "You keep thinking you're the only person with a motive. Did you ever consider the possibility that Mr. Reilly wasn't even the right victim? It was dark that night. He was wearing Byron's jacket. Felix Sanders wore it too. Maybe the murderer was after one of them."

"Who've you been talking to this time, Phoeb?"

I told him about the questions the police had asked me about Byron and Felix. "Who knows, it's possible Mr. Reilly was into something besides managing The Ranch.

Could be his murder has absolutely nothing to do with The Ranch. There's a ton of stuff we don't know Ben, so don't go arresting yourself."

"Maybe you're right." He didn't sound convinced. "But I won't feel off the hook until they catch whoever did it."

"They will," I said. "Believe it. Inspector Debarets is the best." I seemed to have caught a little of Cyrrie's faith in the police.

After dinner I loaded the editing bench again and actually managed to do a little work despite more telephone calls. The first was from my parents in Hawaii enlisting my aid in their plot to get Cyrrie to join them in Australia for Christmas. Even their voices sounded tanned and relaxed. The last call was from Felix. He phoned from the hospital a little after ten.

"Hello. Is that the fabulous Phoebe Fairfax, famous photographer?" He ran the words together quickly, like a tongue twister.

"It is," I replied. "And could that be the fabulous Phoebe Fairfax famous photographer's fun friend Felix phoning?"

"I think you won that one," he said.

"Want to make it best of three?"

"Thanks, but I'll pass. I know when I'm beaten."

"Did your answering service give you my message about the flowers?" I asked. "They're very beautiful and I'm enjoying them."

"I got your message and thanks again for rescuing a stranded traveller."

"You mentioned that you want some help with a project for Jerry's class."

"Not to business so soon, Phoebe," he said. "It's been a long day. Let me enjoy hearing your voice for a few more minutes. How's your watch-dog? How's your owl?

How are you?"

"They're both fine and I'm fed-up with answering questions for the police."

"Me too," he said. "I spent most of yesterday evening at the police station. How long did they keep you?"

I told him. "They even asked me questions about you and Byron. They think it's possible the murderer mistook Mr. Reilly for one of you."

"Ah, yes the famous blue jacket. They were on at me about that too," he said. "Do I have any enemies? Disgruntled patients? Jealous husbands? They got me feeling quite paranoid before they were through."

"Could they be right?" I asked. "Do you think whoever did it might have made a mistake?"

"You're such a comfort, Phoebe."

"Sorry," I said. "I guess that was pretty tactless."

"Concerned for my welfare or just curious?" he asked.

"Both."

"You needn't be concerned. I lead a blameless and innocent life. I'm so damn dull that no one could possibly want to do away with me."

"Are the police finished with you?" I asked.

"Lord no. More questions and signing things tomorrow."

"Same for Ben," I said. "Candi and Ella had their sessions this morning."

"It's the same for everyone who was at The Ranch the night Phil was murdered."

"Even the guests?" I asked. Dr. Morrison would be somewhere west of hysteria at the thought of the Mounties grilling The Ranch's guests.

"Even the guests," he replied. "Although maybe not quite so many questions for them as for those of us who knew Phil or worked with him. Poor old Phil," he added. "Well, at least it was quick."

"Do you think so?"

"If that knife got him right in the heart then it was probably all over in a matter of minutes. He'd likely have been unconscious for most of it. I hope."

"I know he was your friend, Felix. I'm very sorry."

"So am I, Phoebe. So am I. He was a good man. There should be more of us to mourn him."

"What about his family?" I asked.

"Phil was a widower. No children. His entire family is two nephews and a brother-in-law in California he hadn't seen for ten years."

"Friends?"

"I suppose he had lots of business friends," Felix replied. "But he's been at The Ranch and away from the business mainstream since his heart attack. I guess I was his best friend around here these past few years."

"What about Mrs. Sabbatini?"

"Margaret Sabbatini too," he agreed. "She fussed over him and mothered him. Sometimes she drove Phil crazy but she meant well."

"I met her the morning he died. She seemed very upset." I told him about the river of tears and the matter-of-fact voice. I left out the accusations. "Do you think she was in love with him?"

"Probably," he said.

"Is there a Mr. Sabbatini in the picture?"

"Very much," Felix said. "I met him at The Ranch a few times when he came to pick Margaret up from work. She seemed very attached to him. But then it's certainly possible to love two people at the same time. People do it every day."

"So I've heard," I said. "But if you're married to one of them, that could make for a real mess."

"People in love don't tend to be tidy. Love's a messy emotion, don't you think?"

"Tell me about this assignment for your film class."

"There's a hint if ever I heard one," he said. "Never let it be said that Felix Sanders couldn't take a hint. Especially one from both barrels at close range."

"Sorry. Subtlety isn't one of my strong suits," I said.

"Consider the subject closed. Love is no longer on today's discussion list."

"So what do you need my help with?"

Felix outlined his class project. It was a typical Jerry O'Neil assignment designed to teach his students how to plan shots in sequence. They were required to produce a three-minute video, no editing allowed, in which they described an environment as completely as they could. The tape must be ready for final viewing right from the camera. Good news pros learn to do this very early in their careers. Most amateurs never do.

"I thought I'd use the area around the stream that runs through The Ranch. I like it there. What do you think?"

"Sounds good to me. It's a very pretty stream. Follow it for a couple of miles and you get to my place. What shot will you start with?" I asked.

"That's my first question. The second is what do I do after that?"

"I can see you're really into this assignment."

"Don't laugh. For all you know I might be a brilliant undiscovered talent and you could discover me. How would you like to be my mentor for a few hours some sunny afternoon?"

"You mean come with you and hold your stop-watch?"

"Not exactly. I think you might have to start by telling me where to point my lens. I asked Jerry O'Neil and he says you're very generous about finding time to help beginners. And good at it too. I'd be learning from an expert."

"Did Jerry tell you to try flattery?"

"Do you think I'm overdoing it?" he laughed.

"Perhaps a touch but who's complaining. Maybe we could arrange to meet for a couple of hours one afternoon next week."

Arranging an afternoon when both of us were free proved something of a problem but we finally agreed to meet at The Ranch on Sunday afternoon. Felix would okay our expedition over The Ranch's private property with Dr. Morrison.

I felt lazy and relaxed after I finished talking with Felix and decided it was too late to do any more work. I turned on the television and watched the news. There was nothing new about the murder but the story was sufficiently sensational that the news department had rehashed yesterday's mix of fact and speculation and made it the second item in the line-up. They even replayed my footage of Mr. Reilly's body being removed and managed to eke the whole thing out to two minutes by adding some general views of The Ranch and the swimming pool that they must have filched from Ella's "Lifestyle" tapes.

The next morning I loaded a reel of film on to the editing bench and a stack of disks on to the CD player. This year I'm working my way through Mahler. I managed a whole morning at the Moviola without interruptions. I stopped for lunch around one, grabbed an apple for myself, filled my pocket with carrots for the horses, and strolled out to the corral. I sat on the fence enjoying the warmth of the midday sun. There wouldn't be many more days of sitting outside in shirtsleeves. For the Alberta foothills in late October, this Indian summer weather was a case of living on borrowed time. Our first blizzard was long overdue.

The horses were bored with life near the barn. Elvira tried to keep Pete away from the carrots but, while she was busy being superior and standoffish and very much the temperamental Thoroughbred, he managed to squeeze himself in on the fence next to me and collect his share. They both followed me as far as the corral would allow when I walked back to the house to resume work. Elvira actually unbent enough to whinny after me when I left, graciously indicating that she regarded even my lacklustre company as a degree less tedious than the four fenced sides of the corral.

At a quarter to four, Reg called to remind me of our tea date. I had totally forgotten it was Thursday. I changed out of my jeans into a skirt and sweater and, still wondering why he wanted to talk to me, I grabbed my purse and left the house. I caught up with him about a mile past The Ranch trudging south on the gravel road. I stopped the car, leaned over and opened the passenger door for him. He eyed my conservative clothes as he settled in and fastened his seat belt.

"I hope it's okay for me to be dressed like this." He wore The Ranch's bright green sweat suit. "I didn't have time to change."

In other words, he'd snuck off. Deanne probably thought he was with Byron riding down woodland trails on his way to becoming lean and fit. Instead, here he was with me, sitting in a car on his way to a roomful of tea and calories.

"You look just fine, Reg," I assured him. "It's a very informal place. They'll probably recognize your outfit but they'll never tell. Your secret's safe at the Prince of Wales Teahouse."

I hadn't been to the Teahouse for a couple of months. It's one of my standby places for entertaining visitors and usually makes a big hit, especially with fans of home baking and the Royal Family. It's located on a ranch that once belonged to Edward, Prince of Wales, Duke of Windsor and, for eleven uncrowned months in 1936, King

Edward VIII. In 1919 the Prince travelled to Canada on a state visit. He fell in love with the Alberta foothills and bought himself a ranch which he owned and operated from 1919 until 1962. In those forty-three years, he only managed to visit his EP Ranch six times.

I suspect the present owners got so fed-up with tourists wandering through their pastures and knocking at their door in search of royal history that they decided to open the Teahouse in self-defence. It occupies what was once the Prince's ranch house and most of the unpretentious furnishings in it are original. There, for five dollars a person, you get Canadian history, the Royal Family, an unsurpassed view of the Rocky Mountains, a pot of tea, and as much of the superb fresh baking as you care to eat at the buffet-style afternoon tea. I figured it was just the place for someone who'd spent a week at The Ranch. Especially a someone shaped like Reg.

While we drove we talked about the weather, Reg's riding, my photography, last Monday's dinner, anything but Mr. Reilly's murder. Reg didn't even mention why it was he wanted to see me. We seemed to have a tacit agreement that the big topics should be left until after tea. Maybe Reg figured he needed to load in a few calories before he tackled the tough stuff. He could have tackled the Stampeders' entire defensive squad on the calories lined up at the Teahouse that afternoon.

His eyes widened in delight as he took in the sight of a large table covered with home made scones, butter tarts, all manner of cookies, and a large Prince of Wales cake. The cake reigned over the rest of the table in brown-sugared splendour, each raisin-laden slice such stuff as dieters' dreams are made on.

"Do you know how many times I've stayed at The Ranch in the last few years? How could I not know this place existed?" Reg filled his plate with scones and jam.

"No Prince of Wales cake?" I put a slice on my own plate.

"The scones are appetizers," he explained. "After my main course, I'll have the cake for dessert." He broke open a scone and slathered it with butter and jam. "Ah, Phoebe, so much for sashimi and salads." He smiled contentedly and licked some stray jam off his fingers. "There's no calorie like an empty calorie."

The room was large with a high-beamed ceiling and dark wood floors. We sat at a table near a huge fire place with the initials EP set into its stones. For an afternoon so late in the season, a surprising number of the other tables were occupied. Probably, most of our fellow tea drinkers had taken advantage of the fine weather to drive out from Calgary on a last autumn excursion to the hills. The blue-rinse brigade was there in force along with a few tables of younger women with their pre-school age children. Reg was the only adult male in the place. He didn't seem to mind in the least. A waitress brought us a large brown pot of tea and two old-fashioned flowery cups and saucers. I poured the tea and watched Reg attack his scones. When they had disappeared he sat back and drank some tea.

"Those scones are real filling," he remarked in some dismay.

"Maybe you're just out of training," I suggested.

"You're right," he agreed. "I'll bet it's those dinky little meals at The Ranch. They probably shrink your stomach. I guess I'll have to skip the main course and move right on to dessert." He returned to the buffet and collected a large slice of Prince of Wales cake. "Why do they call this place the Prince of Wales?" he asked. "He sleep here or something?"

"He owned it and we're sitting in his ranch house. Or what's left of it." Part of the house had been too dilapidated to restore. Only the section built for the

Prince, a large living-room, a dining-room, and a sun porch, remained. "See the initials in the fireplace?" I pointed. "EP, that's for Edward Prince. It was his brand."

"This his recipe?" Reg asked with his mouth full of cake.

"Baked up a batch every morning before he headed out to punch cattle."

"Wear his crown while he worked, you suppose?"

"Absolutely. Just tucked it up under his ten-gallon hat and away he went. They have pictures to prove it." I pointed to the old photographs that hung around the room.

Reg finished the last of his cake and got up to look at the photographs near our table. Some were of the prince and his guests, but many were portraits of prize livestock. "Looks like the man was a serious rancher," Reg said.

"He was," I said. "Part of his reason for buying a ranch out here was so he'd have a place where he could help to improve the breeds of livestock in western Canada. He imported some top stock from his holdings in England—Thoroughbred horses, prize cattle, even some Dartmoor ponies."

Reg gazed for some time at a casual photo of the Prince and Mrs. Simpson, by then the Duke and Duchess of Windsor, taken on a visit to The Ranch in the early forties. They stood in front of the house, dressed in their fashionably cut tweeds and surrounded by a pack of little dogs. "He has sad eyes," Reg said. "Do you think he ever regretted marrying her?"

"Probably," I said. "Most married people regret it at least once in a marriage. I don't see why he'd be any different."

Reg smiled. "You're a cynic, Phoebe. Are you a married cynic?"

"Once. For a few years. But right now I'm a single cynic."

"Wallis Warfield Simpson. She was from Baltimore, you know. So's my wife. Deanne even looks a little like the Duchess did in this picture, don't you think?"

As a matter-of-fact, I thought Deanne looked very much like the Duchess. Fashionable, brittle, and bitchy. But, I didn't think that was quite what Reg wanted to hear. He sat down and drank the last of his tea.

"You haven't finished your cake, Phoebe," he said. "Maybe you need a few more meals at The Ranch to give you the proper attitude to food."

"It's getting late, Reg," I said. "Maybe you should tell me what it was you wanted to talk to me about."

"Right." He sat back in his chair and looked at me. "First I should probably tell you that I'm not just a guest at The Ranch."

"I know that," I said. "Margaret Sabbatini told me."

"What did she say?"

"That you work for the company that owns The Ranch. That you do Mr. Reilly's old job. The one he had before his heart attack."

"I'm in charge of hotels and resorts. That includes places like The Ranch. We're a pretty diverse operation. Right now I'm planning a series of new projects with Phil. At least I was." He swirled the remains of the tea around in the pot and poured a few leafy dregs into his cup.

"You want some more hot water?" I asked.

He shook his head. "I usually visit The Ranch for a day or two every couple of months to meet with Phil. This time my wife decided that a week as guests would be good for both of us so she came with me. I'm supposed to be combining business with a little vacation. Deanne's enjoying herself but I can tell you The Ranch sure isn't my idea of a holiday. Especially now."

"Because of Mr. Reilly?" I asked.

"Phil was more than just a business associate. He was

a friend. I guess you could call him my mentor. He recommended me for this job. I owe him a lot."

"I only met him the two times I worked at The Ranch but I liked him too," I said. "He was very kind to me, especially last spring when I really needed some kindness."

"Was that when you found Janet Benedict's body in the pool?"

"Yes, it was." I wasn't surprised that Reg knew about my connection with Janet Benedict. As the company's executive in charge, he would be familiar with all The Ranch's business.

"I recognized your name from the police report when we met at dinner on Monday," he said. "That's really why I wanted to talk with you today. Do you mind if I ask you some questions about that morning?"

"You know, Reg, I'm thinking of writing a press release about discovering Janet Benedict's body. That way I'd have a handout for everyone who wanted to talk to me about her. The last few days that seems to be just about everyone I meet."

He looked a little startled. "Who else has been asking about her?"

"Felix Sanders for one."

"Sanders was her doctor," he said. "What did he want?"

"He doesn't think she committed suicide," I answered. "He thinks she was murdered." I expected this would be a shocker but Reg didn't even look mildly surprised. He merely nodded.

"For what it's worth, I agree with him," he said.

"You mean you actually think she was murdered?"

"Yeah, Janet was murdered," he replied matter-of-factly. "She was murdered just like poor old Phil, only she died one hell of a lot grimmer death. I keep thinking there has to be a connection. The night he died, Phil wanted to talk to me about Janet. He told me that he'd discovered something that might explain her death. I was supposed to meet him in his office after my bridge game. He never came." Reg shrugged. "I guess you can't call that much of a connection."

"Did you tell the police about it?"

"Yeah, but they didn't seem very impressed." He sat back in his chair and looked at me. "What do you think, Phoebe? You found her. You must have an opinion. Do you honestly think her death looked like suicide?"

Until this week I had been reasonably sure that Janet Benedict had killed herself. Now that I had heard from Reg and Felix and Inspector Debarets, I wasn't so certain. "I don't know what suicide is supposed to look like," I said. "According to the police she killed herself and for now that will have to do. If you've read their report then you know as much as I do."

"That police report was pretty sparse reading," he said. "I was hoping you could tell me something more, that maybe you'd noticed something that wasn't in the report."

"Honestly, Reg, if I said anything more I'd only be guessing. I found her body. That's it." I had never seen Janet Benedict alive but lately I'd met so many people who wanted to talk to me about her that I felt we were getting to be old friends.

"You'd have liked her," Reg said. "I got to know her while she was a guest at The Ranch last year." He smiled to himself. "Janet was terrific—beautiful, smart, sophisticated, funny. Almost as good on a horse as Byron. I've never met anyone so full of life."

"Deanne with you on that trip?" I asked.

"You're sharp, Phoebe," he said. "And you're right. I suppose I was a little in love with Janet. She was very easy to be a little in love with. Getting the call from Phil about her death was a real shock. I'd been to The Ranch on business again a couple of days before. Janet and I had dinner together in Calgary the evening I left. I don't care what the police report said, a woman like that with so much to live for, she wouldn't kill herself. Especially not that way."

"Where was Mr. Benedict while you were out wining and dining his wife?"

"It wasn't like that," he shook his head. "It wasn't like that at all. You see, Janet and her husband led independent lives. They still lived in the same house, but that's about it. I think they liked each other all right, but their children were grown, their interests were different, and they mostly went their separate ways." Reg looked like it was an arrangement he might yearn for from time to time. "Janet was free to see who she pleased, whenever she pleased."

"I really am sorry I can't help you, Reg."

"That's okay, Phoebe. I just had to be sure." We sat in silence for a minute. "Two violent deaths in less than a year. That's some health resort we're running." He echoed Cyrrie's sentiments.

"If Mr. Reilly was murdered, could it have been because of the changes you're planning at The Ranch?" I asked.

"I doubt it. Phil's murder won't make any difference to the those plans. They're all in place ready to go ahead."

"So sashimi nights are a thing of the past?"

"How do you know that?"

"Ben Sugamoto told me. He's a friend of mine. He thinks the police suspect him of killing Mr. Reilly in a rage over his cancelled contract."

"For a chef, he has a great imagination," Reg said.

"What about Dr. Morrison?"

"What about Heather?"

"Are you cancelling her contract too?"

"I don't want to be rude, Phoebe, but that's not really any of your business, is it?"

"Reg, you hauled me away from my work in the middle of the afternoon to ask me a lot of stuff that wasn't any of your business. Instead of telling you where to put your damn questions like I probably should, I did my best. It's not my fault I didn't know the answers. It's your tough luck. And now I think you owe me a question or two of my own."

"Wow, I thought us Americans were the pushy ones," he said, a little taken aback. "You Canadians are supposed to be real polite."

"One of my grandmothers was from Denver."

"That explains it," Reg laughed.

"Yeah," I agreed. "Bad blood. Now what about Dr. Morrison?"

"As far as the company's concerned, Heather's job is hers for as long as she wants it. Whether she'll still want it after the changes go through is up to her. You see, Phoebe, what the company is offering at The Ranch is really an image package but Heather doesn't see it that way. She believes that what we're doing is delivering a kind of preventive health care."

"You mean she really believes all that stuff she spouts? New ways of wellness. Getting in touch with simplicity. She's actually sincere about it?"

"Passionately," Reg said. "I think that's why she's probably going to have some difficulty accepting the innovations at The Ranch. My guess is that Heather will resign."

"You mean she might figure doctoring an image package isn't quite what she went to medical school for."

"Don't sound so disapproving," he said. "Image is what sells things. The world is full of equivalent products. What makes people choose one identical car over another?

Image. The Ranch is a good health resort but it's no better than a hundred others you can choose from. Health is a saturated market. If you want to make money in this business you can't simply follow trends, you've got to set them. And that's what we're going to do at The Ranch. We're going to set the trend for health resorts for the next twenty years."

Although The Ranch had done well since the day it opened, the company was looking ahead. It was after long term success and both Reg and Phil Reilly agreed that the conventional health resort was not the way to go. There were already too many places where people could go to exercise and lose weight and learn about the latest food fads. But how many of those resorts were in a part of the world still pollution-free enough to boast about it? Reg and Mr. Reilly planned to make clean water and clean air the latest thing in health resort chic.

"A healthy body in a healthy world," I said.

"Exactly," Reg agreed without a hint of irony. "There's nothing wrong with that, is there? At The Ranch we're going to put most of our emphasis on the out-of-doors. Step up the trail rides and that sort of stuff. We'll build a lodge back in the hills that you can only reach by horseback. We'll copter in food and maintenance staff and a couple of chefs and the guests can go there on overnight camp outs."

"Nothing like roughing it."

"Right. We're changing the food, of course. The new menu will be based on wild game." Reg warmed to his topic. "We'll keep a lot of the same exercise and massage programs like every other health resort has but we're going to downplay them. You won't have to starve and exercise until you drop at the new Ranch. You'll get healthier by just living there for a week or two breathing the air."

"So you figure you can sell air?"

"When was the last time you tried breathing in Manhattan?" Reg asked. "And New York's a day in the country compared to some of those cities in Europe and Japan. Sure, we can sell air."

And in a world up to its arm pits in filth he probably could. The best things in life aren't free any more. Pure air and clean water are fast becoming rarer than fine wine or Russian caviar. Soon only the very rich will be able to afford them.

"We might even tell our guests about the Prince of Wales Teahouse too. It's a real interesting place, Phoebe. Thanks for bringing me here. First time I've felt full for a week." Reg looked around the now empty room. The waitress had long since removed the tea buffet and tidied the other tables. She hovered near the cash register. "I guess we should go. The lady looks like she wants to lock up." He left a generous tip on the table and paid for our teas.

I dropped Reg off near The Ranch and continued on to my place. The dog was waiting for me in his usual spot under the mailbox. The box's flag was up and inside I found a note from Felix scribbled on a sheet torn from his prescription pad.

"Stopped by to see you on my way back to town but you are not here. Sorry I missed you. Will phone. Yours, Felix. P.S. Your watch-dog is very good at his job. He wouldn't let me past the gate today."

CHAPTER 11

"I think you'd get a much better picture if I opened the drapes." Dr. Morrison sounded just like Ella. If anything her helpful suggestions were even more irritating. At least Ella had some clue about cameras.

"These shots have to match the ones I took in this room before dinner on Monday," I explained. "It was dark then. The drapes were closed. We used artificial light. If we open the drapes now and let the sunlight in, then the shots won't match." I completed a close-up of the fireplace tiles and crossed it off the list on my clipboard.

So far, my Friday morning hadn't exactly been what you'd call a real sparkler. I'd had to drag myself out of bed at four-thirty in order to drive to Calgary, pick up the van and camera equipment at the station, and get back out to The Ranch by nine to meet Dr. Morrison. She was late. She kept me waiting for over an hour. I passed the time in The Ranch's library. Its shelves were filled not with books but with videotapes. Each tape was carefully labelled with a colourful identification sticker that had the title of the movie plus The Ranch's mailing address printed on it. The collection would have done credit to a small video store and the golden oldies section was one of the best I'd seen. A few beleaguered books huddled together in one corner behind a library cart that held a VCR and a television set. I was starting in to enjoy a browse through the Cary Grant movies when Mrs. Sabbatini bustled in with coffee for two.

She didn't recognize me. Mrs. Sabbatini had been so out of it at our previous meeting that she seemed to have completely forgotten I'd ever been in her office. She'd stopped weeping but her conversation still had an odd edge to it. Nothing as bizarre as last time, but still a little off kilter. She put the coffee tray on the writing table in the centre of the room.

"Do sit and be comfortable, Miss Fairfax." She pointed to one of the huge wing back leather chairs near the table. "My name is Margaret Sabbatini. I'm Dr. Morrison's secretary. She'll be with you as soon as she gets off the phone. Cream and sugar?"

"Black please." I accepted a cup and sat obediently in the chair.

"I was Philip Reilly's secretary too." Her eyes got a little dewy at the mention of his name but, much to my relief, she managed not to stage a repeat of Tuesday's flood. "Philip spoke very highly of you, Miss Fairfax. He thought you handled yourself so professionally on the morning of that unpleasantness last spring." She poured herself some coffee and sat in the chair next to mine. "I know you'll want to come to his funeral service. I'm in the middle of planning it right now. It's on Monday afternoon and your name's going to be on the guest list." She simpered and tapped me lightly on the arm.

I made some non-committal noises back but it didn't matter much. Mrs. Sabbatini was off and running again. I heard all about the plans for Mr. Reilly's funeral. She described the coffin that she'd chosen for him in minute detail, right down to the bronze handles and the shade of the blue satin lining.

"We're having it in the pioneer church at Millarville, of course. Philip was a great supporter. He loved that church. They'll use the old order of service, not that modern junk. Philip loved the old Anglican service.

Shakespeare's plays, the *Bible* and *The Book Of Common Prayer*—the three greatest achievements of the English language according to Philip. He detested the new order of service." Mrs. Sabbatini put her coffee cup back on the tray. "Not that Philip was against change. Far from it. He was very progressive. Far more progressive than some others around here I could mention." She hitched her chair a little closer to mine. "The police found one of her contact lenses not ten feet from Philip's body."

"You mean Dr. Morrison's contact lens?"

"She told the police that she'd lost it months ago. Does she really think anyone's going to believe that?" Mrs. Sabbatini cast a furtive little glance at the door as if she and I were intimately involved in some sort of conspiracy. "She thinks nobody else knows about the lens but her and the police. What a laugh. You can't keep a secret like that at a place like this." She leaned closer and put her hand on my arm. "It's only a matter of time now, Miss Fairfax, and I pray every day that the police are quick. Philip won't rest properly until his murderer is brought to justice." Maybe I hadn't seen Mrs. Sabbatini at her best but, frankly, sanity didn't seem to be her strong suit. I even began to feel sorry for Dr. Morrison which was quite something considering that it was thanks to her that I was Mrs. Sabbatini's captive audience.

"You certainly have a fine collection of video tapes at The Ranch." I got up from my chair and walked over to the shelves. Anything to get away from that hand on my arm.

"Each of the guest cabins has a VCR," she said. "The staff lounges have them too. The library's movies are very popular. We have a lot of self-help videos too but no one ever watches them. I guess that isn't too surprising. Philip predicted that's what would happen but she insisted on ordering them."

"Who's in charge of choosing your movies?" I asked, searching desperately for a topic to take her mind off Mr. Reilly. "They've done a terrific job."

"Philip, of course."

"When do you think we'll get our first blizzard?" I was a desperate woman. "We should have had one by now, don't you think?"

"Philip always said that the weather in the foothills . . ." Mrs. Sabbatini babbled on. I gave up and waited for Dr. Morrison to rescue me.

It was after ten when she finally emerged from her office, her ear all sweaty from important phone calls and her head full of ideas for shots I should take of The Ranch. She didn't apologize for keeping me waiting but at least she got me out of Mrs. Sabbatini's clutches. She also condescended to carry the tripod. Neither of us mentioned Mr. Reilly's murder although with everyone else at The Ranch it was topic number one. By eleven-thirty we'd managed to finish a guest cabin and were back at the house working our way through the living-room. We were only half finished Ella's list and already I was on the brink of braining the doctor with my clipboard.

"You mean you're not going to bother photographing the view of the mountains that you get out these windows, Miss Fairfax? The guests all love this view. It's the best thing about the living-room."

With great restraint I put the clipboard on the floor.

"Just let me finish this last fireplace shot and then we'll open the drapes and do the view." I knew Ella wouldn't use any shots that were not on her list but at least it would shut Dr. Morrison up. I'd been using this ploy on her for most of the morning. For every legitimate shot of Ella's, I took another to placate Cecil B. de Morrison. I figured it wasted less time to take the doctor's extra shots than it did to explain why we couldn't use them. Life's short, tape's cheap, and everyone's a director.

"Miss Fairfax, why don't you stand back against the wall opposite the windows. Then, if you aim your camera from there, the mountains will look like they're a series of pictures framed by the windows. Won't that be beautiful?"

"Right." The doctor's idea wasn't half bad aside from some monumental problems with light contrast and depth of field. "Open the drapes and let's try it."

Dr. Morrison touched a button, the heavy drapes parted on silent runners, and the late morning sun poured through the windows. The light transformed the room. It danced through the dust motes and gave the place the same feeling that meadowlarks give to a summer morning. I hauled the camera on its tripod over to the wall opposite the windows. By the time I'd stopped down the lens and focused on the mountains the doctor had come up with an even more elaborate scheme for the shot.

"Let's take the camera off the tripod, Miss Fairfax. You can rest it on your shoulder like you did Monday night. Then you'll walk toward the windows with it. Very slowly. Like this." Dr. Morrison began a stately, gliding walk. Her right hand supported an imaginary camera above her shoulder. Her left floated free in great explanatory swoops. "You see, you start out with the camera looking across the living-room to the windows. Then, as you walk, you slowly get closer and closer and closer to the windows." She hardly even missed a beat when she tripped over the rug. "Finally you're standing right in front of the glass and you're focused sharp on the mountains." She gave her phantom lens a twist and turned to face me. "What do you think?"

I started to laugh. I couldn't help myself. Dr. Morrison had just invented the dolly shot. Make no mistake, this lady was ready for Hollywood. "Not bad," I said. "But we're going to have to do something to keep the movement really smooth. We'll need a set of tracks to run the camera along, or at least a good dolly. Then if we can get a focus puller and enough lights to blow every fuse in the foothills, we'll be all set."

"I think you're making this far too complicated." She seemed a little hurt. "What we need is simplicity. Now, Miss Fairfax, forget the heavy hardware. What's the very simplest way we can do this?"

"How about I grow three extra hands and wear a pair of roller skates? You can push."

This time Dr. Morrison laughed too. It was startling. I'd never even seen her smile before. At least not a smile with any genuine feeling behind it. This was a new Dr. Morrison. Laughter changed her the way opening the curtains had changed the room.

"I guess I got a little carried away," she admitted. "But it was a great idea, wasn't it?"

"Actually, if we'd tried earlier when the sun was still low we might even have pulled it off. The picture frame idea I mean, not the moving shot." The doctor was beginning to seem almost human.

"Tell me truthfully, Miss Fairfax," she said. "Are my suggestions helpful? You seemed a little irritated a couple of times."

"Some of your ideas aren't bad at all." I found myself overwhelmed by a nauseating wave of tact. "They're just a little impractical."

"How long have you been a photographer?"

"Almost as long as I can remember. My parents gave me my first camera when I was five."

"I mean this kind of photography," she said. "Television work."

"I did volunteer work for community TV when I was in high school. I got my first professional job right after I graduated from university. I've worked for the same station ever since. That's over eight years now."

"Felix Sanders says you're a very highly thought of nature photographer. One of the best in Canada. You win awards." She hesitated for a moment, searching for the tactful phrase. "So why do you work for 'A Day in the Lifestyle?'" She didn't find it. "This can't be very meaningful work for you."

"It means I can pay my bills," I said. I resisted getting in a few digs about doctors who found meaning running over-priced havens for hypochondriacs with fat phobias. After all, she was trying to be nice. "This is how I earn my living. Making the kind of nature documentaries I do is a terrific get poor quick scheme. 'Lifestyle' gives me a little security. Are you interested in photography?" We'd talked about me long enough.

"I'd never thought about it until this morning," Dr. Morrison said.

"You seem to have an eye for composition. You'd probably have made a pretty good photographer." And that was true as well as tactful. "You should try it sometime."

"Like Felix, you mean."

"Video photography is easy to get into now that the cameras are so cheap and so good."

"I understand you and Felix are making a video of The Ranch's stream this Sunday."

"He's taking a photography class from a friend of mine and I agreed to help him with an assignment. Why don't you come with us? I have a camera you could use."

"I'm not a dabbler, Miss Fairfax. I don't have time for hobbies and I'm not in need of occupational therapy." Dr. Morrison's curtain swept shut again. "Are you going to be finished in here soon?" She looked at her watch. "This is taking much longer than I expected."

I'm not nearly as good a silent screamer as Ella, but

the shriek I suppressed could have filled the Saddledome. "Then perhaps we should stick to the shots that are on my list."

"We'll have to wait until after lunch to do any more. I always eat with the guests." Lucky them. "Would you like some lunch? I believe the staff dining-room is serving spaghetti today. I have a meeting first thing this afternoon so we'll start work again at three. You can wait for me in my outer office."

My Glasgow grannie had a name for women like Dr. Morrison. No matter what their age, they were *auld besoms*. My Denver grandma would have called her a snooty bitch. At this rate, by the time we finished, my whole day would be shot. "There's really no need for you to do this yourself, Dr. Morrison. I'm sure one of your staff who isn't as busy as you could manage quite adequately."

"Even a local program like 'A Day in the Lifestyle' is important to The Ranch, Miss Fairfax. Especially considering what's been happening around here lately. If you don't mind, I'd just as soon make sure it's done properly." Dr. Morrison dumped me and my equipment at the door of the staff dining-room and took herself off to share platters of plant life with the guests.

The staff dining-room was already crowded. It was a good deal less glamourous than its guest counterpart. The guests enjoyed a view of the Rockies while they ate. The staff looked at the garbage bins behind the kitchen. Here, the table cloths were checked cotton, the flatware stainless, the napkins paper, and the waiters absent. Nevertheless, the room was comfortable and homey and actually a much more cheerful place to eat than the formal splendour down the hall. One of the assistant cooks dished out the lunch from a large hatch that opened into the kitchen.

I joined the line in front of the hatch and while I waited

for my food I watched the waiters in the kitchen loading trays with the guests' lunch. Herbed falafel on a bed of alfalfa sprouts. It looked like the dog had been eating grass. The staff spaghetti was a big step up. The sauce was some vegetable concoction with lots of mushrooms. It smelled wonderful and I suddenly realized how hungry I was. The cook placed a bowl of salad beside the pasta and handed me my tray.

"Miss Phoebe." Byron called from across the room where he was sitting with Marty Bradshaw. "Over here." He pointed with his fork to an empty chair at their table. Byron wore jeans and another of his checked shirts. Perhaps he reserved his more outrageous outfits strictly for formal occasions because I'd never seen him in the diurnal equivalent of his evening clothes. Only the bright blue bandanna knotted around his neck hinted at his peacock penchants. It also emphasized the blue of his eyes. "This is a real nice surprise, Miss Phoebe." He gave me one of his knee watering smiles before he went back to work on his mound of spaghetti.

"Please Byron," I said. "Just Phoebe." I felt an answering smile spread across my own face. It didn't please me much. I've seen the goofy grins most men wear around Candi. It wasn't flattering to think of myself as the female form of those poor idiots.

"Ella told me you'd be here today," Marty said. "But I thought you were supposed to finish up this morning."

"I was," I said. "But Dr. Morrison's taking me around while I shoot interiors and she was late. We're only about half finished. Phone calls and meetings."

"More like the police." Byron rested from his luncheon labours for a moment. "That's who she's been meeting with this week. Every time she turns around there's another cop waiting for her. They got her jumpier than a cat in a roomful of rocking chairs."

Marty put his fork down and applauded. "One of your all time best," he said. Byron acknowledged the praise with a grin and small nod of his head. "Byron practices folksy sayings in his spare time. He thinks they beef up his cowboy image with the guests. Unfortunately, he's right." It sounded to me like Byron's folksy sayings were the verbal version of his dinner jackets.

"I do not practice," Byron protested with a good natured laugh. "I don't need to. I'm a genuine cowboy from High River, Alberta and proud of it. Where you from, Phoebe?"

"I was born in Calgary."

"Then I guess you and me are gonna have to make some allowances for Marty here," he said. "The poor guy's from Toronto so he's even more ignorant about Alberta than most other folks. I'm trying to educate him about the west but I swear it's like trying to teach a brick to tap dance." Maybe the guest dining-room had inhibited him on sashimi night because here in the staff eatery Byron was a talker. "Besides what I said is true," he continued. "Morrison has been real twitchy all week."

"Maybe she's worried about her contact lens." I told them Mrs. Sabbatini's story.

"Phoebe, you gotta know that sometimes Margaret Sabbatini is a little . . ." Byron tapped his head significantly.

"Besides, in Dr. Morrison's case, one lost contact doesn't mean much," said Marty. "She's always losing her lenses. For a super-organized lady she's a real slob about her contacts. It's actually kind of a joke around The Ranch. I'd be surprised if there were any place around here you couldn't find one of Dr. Morrison's lenses."

"That's true," Byron agreed. "She kinda sheds them like scales. But I still think she's acting pretty spooked for somebody who's got nothing to hide."

"Well, maybe you're right," Marty said, "But she's not the only one. Everyone's been edgy this week. You look around and there's a Mountie asking you another bunch of questions. Even the guests got questioned."

"Did any of them leave?" I asked.

"Only two," Marty said. "I don't think the murder bothered the rest of them very much. They were shocked at first but none of them really knew Phil Reilly so that faded pretty fast. Now some of them even seem to be finding it interesting. Sort of like one of those murder mystery weekends you can go to at fancy hotels."

"I never answered so many questions before in my whole life," said Byron.

"Same here," I agreed.

"This is the second time for you, isn't it?" he said. "They must've asked you a lot of questions about that lady you found who drowned herself. Kinda weird that you were here for both of them."

"Guess I'm just lucky."

"Do you think they're gonna catch whoever did it?"

"I have no idea."

"I hope they do and real soon." Byron spoke with some feeling. "Poor old Ben Sugamoto's in deep shit right now just because it was his knife and he had a fight with Reilly before dinner. The sooner they catch whoever did it the sooner Ben gets off the hook. It's stupid. I know Ben. He's out here every week. He's a real good guy. He's no more of a murderer than me or Marty here."

"Thanks, Byron," I said. "Ben's a friend of mine, too. I'll tell him what you said. He could use a vote of confidence right now. How do you know about his fight with Mr. Reilly?"

"I was there. At least I was in Doc Sanders' office giving him my extra dinner jacket when Ben lit into Reilly. I never seen him but I sure heard him. Reilly was going to cancel Ben's contract and Ben was real mad."

"The police asked me a lot of questions about you and Felix Sanders," I said. "They think maybe the murderer was after one of you and got Mr. Reilly by mistake because of your jacket."

"Maybe I got a couple of enemies but none so bad they'd like to see me dead," Byron said.

"Only half the husbands between here and the Montana border," Marty laughed. "It's a miracle none of them have come gunning for you before."

"Don't you listen to this clown, Phoebe. I don't know about the doc, but no one thought it was me in that jacket. If the murderer made a mistake, I guarantee he wasn't aiming to kill me."

"Phil Reilly was a good guy," Marty said. "And I hope they catch whoever murdered him. But can we please talk about something else? This is all we've talked about out here since it happened. It kind of gets to you after awhile."

"Sorry, Marty," Byron said. "I didn't know it was getting you down. Say, what're you taking pictures of today, Phoebe?" It wasn't subtle, but it got the job done. I was all for a change of topic myself.

"So far, the inside of one guest cottage and some close-ups of the living-room fireplace. I'm meeting Dr. Morrison again at three to do the rest of the house. And that's it."

"You mean you're not going to take any pictures down at the stable?" Byron asked.

"It's not on my list," I said.

"You should at least take a look at the stable," Byron said. "It's something else. You shouldn't miss it out of your program." Another director. "If you don't have to be back at work until three then why don't you bring your camera and I'll show you around after lunch?" At least

Byron would be a lot more fun to focus on than Dr. Morrison.

"Thanks, Byron," I said. "I'd like to have a look around." I hadn't been inside the stable since I used to play there on rainy days as a child.

"So Dr. Morrison's giving you the guided tour herself," Marty said. "If you rate the personal treatment from Mama Doc you must be an important lady, Phoebe. What are you doing eating in here with the help?"

"I got above myself. I told Dr. Morrison she should take up a hobby."

"A hobby, eh? That's pretty serious stuff. I'd say you're probably lucky you got lunch at all."

"I'll tell you what hobby that lady needs," Byron grinned. "What she needs is a real good regular . . ." A warning look from Marty stemmed the flow of Byron's prescriptive observations.

"Well, you may have to eat with the hired help but I guarantee you the food's better in here," Marty said.

"They always have great desserts on Fridays." Byron smiled at me over his rapidly receding plate of pasta. This time I tried not to smile back. I didn't succeed.

"Can I get you something to drink?" Marty asked.

"Finish your lunch," I said. "I'd like a cup of coffee after I've eaten but there's no hurry."

"Guess I'm ready for seconds." Byron twirled the last strands of spaghetti around his fork, dispatched them tidily and went back to the hatch to collect more food. I noticed that he walked with a slight limp.

"Did Byron hurt his leg?" I asked.

"Not recently," Marty said. "That's an old injury. He smashed it up in a rodeo accident a few years ago. Got his leg caught between a bronc and the bucking chute and broke it in three places. I think it still hurts him pretty badly some days."

That explained why Byron was no longer a rodeo cowboy. But even with the limp he was still the best looking man in a room full of good looking men. Individually, The Ranch staff were handsome men. Collectively they were devastating, and they'd all collected for lunch. It's hard to eat and stare at the same time so I gave up on the food and just stared. Byron started back to our table. Somehow he even made the limp look sexy.

"Admiring the view?" Marty smiled.

I focussed my attention back on my lunch. I hoped I wasn't blushing.

"I brought you guys dessert." Byron carried three dishes of apple crisp on his tray along with his second load of spaghetti. "Hope you like apples, Phoebe." He put a pitcher of cream beside the desserts. Obviously, cholesterol levels were not a big concern on this side of the kitchen.

"How long since you've been swimming?" Marty asked.

"Must've been Sunday, I guess," Byron replied.

"You've got to do those exercises the physiotherapist showed you every day or they won't do any good," Marty said. "You're walking all stiff again. You have to swim every day."

"I know," Byron said. "And I tried. But every time you went anywhere around here this week there was some cop hanging around."

"They're finished this afternoon. That's the word from Dr. Morrison. So you're in that pool tonight for sure."

"Will you be there?" Byron asked.

"I've got this weekend off," Marty said. "Ella's taking me to a play in Calgary. Shakespeare."

"Watch it, Marty," Byron said. "They start getting you cultured then you know they're thinking serious."

After lunch I walked to the stable with Byron. We

took the same path that Mr. Reilly had walked on the night of his murder. The police and their yellow barricade tapes were gone. Nothing remained to mark the spot.

"You're real sure you don't want to take any pictures?" Byron asked again. I'd left the camera equipment back at the house. "If you change your mind I'll be glad to help you carry your camera stuff."

"Thanks, Byron. But my producer wouldn't use the shots anyway."

The stable's big front door was open. We stood for a moment looking down the row of a dozen stalls, six to each side of the wide central corridor. Every stall had its own window placed very high in the wall, well out of the horses' reach. Rays of sunlight shafted though the hay dust down to the scrupulously clean floor. A couple of the stalls were occupied. Long, whiskery noses poked curiously over the half doors.

"You're from Calgary so you might have heard of this place," Byron said. "It's real famous around here. Some old lady owned it before The Ranch. They say she kept polo ponies in here once, a long time ago. Nice to be rich, I guess."

"She didn't stay rich," I said. "That's why she had to sell the place." I explained my connection with Mrs. Malifant and her estate to Byron. "I used to come down here and play in the stables when I got bored with the grownups' talk. But there weren't any horses. They'd all been sold by then."

"My folks used to bring us out here for a Sunday drive sometimes but the closest I ever got was the road," Byron said. "We'd stop and have a look and try guessing what it was like inside a mansion. You were a real lucky kid, Phoebe."

"There was an old side saddle in the tack room. Mrs. Malifant used to let me put it on a fence rail and pretend I was riding a real horse. I wonder what ever happened to it?"

Byron took out a key and unlocked the tack room door. He pointed to one of the upper pegs near the back. There was the side saddle, its leather dust-free and polished to a warm lustre. "I found it junked in a corner when I first come to work here. It's a funny old thing but I figured it was worth a clean. Don't know why. No one ever uses it. I guess I just liked it for some reason."

I rubbed my hand over the soft leather of the leg post. "It looks beautiful. Far better than I remember."

"Want to go for a ride on it again?" Byron asked. "Only this time I'll put a real horse under it for you."

"Thanks but I'd probably kill myself before I got out of the corral."

One wall of the tack room was covered with black and white photographs. Most of them were action shots of rodeo events. They were good, but the shots of the rodeo people, the clowns and the cowboys and the anxious women watching them, were even better. "Felix Sanders told me you do some photography," I said. "Are these yours?" Byron nodded. "You're good."

"Thanks," he said. "Coming from a real photographer like you that means something."

"Do you do your own printing, too?"

"Yeah, upstairs in my bathroom. It's pretty crude but I manage. You really like my pictures?"

"Yes, I do. Very much." It was obvious that the photographs had been taken by someone who loved his subjects. There were none of the art school mannerisms that beg the viewer to notice the cleverness of the photographer. Here, the animals, the people, the action, claimed our attention completely. "Have you ever shown these anywhere?"

"A newspaper in Calgary printed one once. This one

of the bull rider's wife. She's watching him ride." He pointed to a close-up of a young woman sitting hunched over in a lawn chair, one arm clenched across her middle. Her other hand grasped her hair, her pale knuckles revealing the pressure of her grip. Her arm partly shaded her eyes as if she could neither bear to look nor look away. "My sister sent it to them. They printed it for free, too."

"I'll bet they did," I said.

"I got lots more upstairs in my apartment. You want to see them?"

I have lived enough of my life around fanatic photographers to know that when one of them inveigles a woman up to his apartment to look at his prints, what she ends up doing is looking at his prints. Byron was a fanatic photographer. The Byron of the bedroom eyes seemed to have been put on hold for the moment. The only part of me this Byron wanted to take advantage of was my photographic expertise. Actually, I think I was a little disappointed. I suspect that if he had made a pass at me that afternoon I probably would have gone to bed with him. No, that's not true. I don't suspect, I know. One crinkly blue-eyed smile and I would have jumped right in with no probably about it.

But Byron was too busy arranging his photographs to make a pass and, what was worse, I found myself starting to like the guy. Nothing sullies a nice pure lust more than liking. As soon as you start to like someone, out goes casual sex and up looms complicated sex, more commonly known as a relationship. Besides, Byron probably had platoons of women willing, able and eager to have sex with him at a moment's notice. I've never been much on losing myself in a crowd. Not even when I'm eating sour grapes.

Byron installed me in a chair in the snug three-room apartment he occupied over the stable. Unlike the rest of the staff, who shared spacious apartments in their own building, Byron lived alone. "If you don't count the horses, that is," he said. "They're why I have to live down here. There's usually one of them in for stall rest for something or other. And when a horse has colic and has to be walked all night I'm real glad I live over the store." Mounds of photographs lay strewn across the coffee table in front of me.

"What kind of camera do you use?" I asked.

"I got a new one last year," he said. "Hang on a minute. I'll go get it." He disappeared into the bedroom which gave me a chance to sit back for a moment and take a breather from the photographs. The living-room was simply furnished with a couple of easy chairs and the coffee table. A small television set sat on a bookcase along with a VCR and half a dozen tapes. Each of the tapes bore one of the bright Ranch labels. Clearly, Byron was not a faithful returner of his library materials. He reappeared before I had a chance to check out his taste in movies.

"Here it is." He put a large metal camera case on the coffee table and snapped open the lid to reveal two Hasselblad bodies and four lenses. A Hasselblad is the Rolls Royce of cameras. It is probably the most beautifully made still camera ever manufactured. It is certainly one of the most expensive. And here were two of them along with every pricey accessory bell and whistle imaginable. It was like the company's catalogue had come to life on Byron's coffee table. I was amazed.

"You knock off the Hasselblad factory or something?"

"It looks like it, doesn't it? I can tell you this stuff sure set me back a paycheque or two or five or ten," Byron laughed. "But just look what it can do. See this?" He picked up one of the prints. "I took this with my old camera. Now look at this one with the Blad. There's a hell of a difference, eh?" We were off to the photographs again.

By the time I remembered to look at my watch it was nearly three. "I have to go or I'll be late for the mad doctor."

"And I got a trail ride at three-thirty," Byron said. "What'll we do about the pictures? I don't have time to pick them out now." I had promised to take a selection of his work to show a friend of mine who owns an art gallery in Calgary.

"I'll be back here Sunday afternoon," I said. "You can give them to me then. Or if you aren't going to be around on Sunday just leave them in my mailbox. I only live a couple of miles north of The Ranch."

"You mean we're neighbours?" He held out his hands and pulled me up from the chair. The physical contact had the same effect on me that it had that night beside the van, but this time I knew he felt it too. We stood very close, our bodies almost touching. "Neighbours." The blue eyes smiled down at me. "Now that has some real nice possibilities, don't it?"

Despite our damaging camaraderie over the photographs, at that moment I thought it might still be possible to rescue pure lechery and have a wonderfully meaningless relationship with Byron. But lust is a delicate thing, especially for women. It can't be hurried. We require at least two minutes and my time was up. I was already late for work with Dr. Morrison.

By the time I reached the house and collected the gear it was a few minutes after three. As she promised, the doctor met me in her outer office.

"I've been standing here waiting for you for over four and a half minutes, Miss Fairfax." She tapped her wristwatch. "At this rate we'll never finish your work."

CHAPTER 12

The shrieks of a thousand half-crazed tea kettles shattered the Saturday morning peace. Another calliope concert had begun. The dog shivered in misery under my desk as a chorus of "She'll Be Comin Round the Mountain" screamed across the pasture and careened through the hills. I swear the sound waves rippled the surface of the coffee in my cup.

Jack is no musician so his repertoire is, to put it kindly, somewhat limited. The pieces he plays on Saturday mornings all come from a children's piano book I gave him entitled *Campfire Favorites For Little Hands*. It is about as inspired as it sounds. After Jack drives those six white horses round their mountain and through the consciousness of every living creature from here to the Calgary suburbs, he moves on to demolish Daisy and her bicycle built for two. This is followed by "K-K-K-Katy," "Oh Susanna," and "When the Saints Go Marchin' In." Then the whole cycle starts again.

"God, Phoebe. Can't we get him another song book?" Barbara asked. "I'm so sick of 'Comin Round the Mountain' I could scream." Barbara is Jack's wife and Tom's mother. She spends Saturday mornings at my house, a refugee from her husband's hobby. She always brings a plate of fresh baked muffins and we pass the time eating them and drinking coffee and gossiping in very loud voices.

"Scream away," I said. "No one will notice. You'll

blend right in. Besides, Jack doesn't need a new book. There are dozens more songs in the one he's got. He just hasn't bothered to learn any of them."

"He wants to know if you'll play for him next Saturday," Barbara said. "Tom is off to some hockey do in Calgary so Jack's on his own."

The Saturday calliope concerts are a combined father and son effort. While Jack sits at the keyboard, Tom runs the mechanics of the operation and keeps the boiler stoked and the steam pressure up. Jack loves playing his five campfire songs and when Tom's absence forces him to take over the steam engineering himself, he doesn't ask just anyone to substitute for him at the keyboard. In Jack's eyes it is a privilege, an honour that he does not bestow lightly. If I'm around, the honour is generally mine.

I have to admit that at first I was excited by the prospect of being the one who got to make all that noise. I'd been waiting my chance, following Jack's progress as he rebuilt the tarnished whistles and cracked keys back into a functioning instrument, all glittering brass and polished ebony. It took him months. He'd even had a special wagon built that he'd designed to hold the finished calliope. It was painted in the best gaudy circus style and the name *Phoenix* marched in flashy gilt letters down either side.

In the summer, the calliope is the entertainment highlight at our local fairs and rodeos. For the rest of the year it lives under lock and key in an old log barn about fifty yards from Jack's house. The barn, with its great thick walls and one tiny window, is a relic from the days of the foothills' homesteaders and the calliope on its wagon pretty well fills its small interior. Nevertheless, there's still room for the instrument's necessities—a water tank, a wood bin, and a small furnace. This last keeps the barn's temperature at an even seventy two degrees all winter which Jack says is very important because cold does funny things to the whistles. Even so, on all but the worst winter Saturdays, Jack and Tom open the barn's big plank doors, hitch the wagon shank to their old pick-up truck, and pull the Phoenix outside for its concert.

The first time I sat behind the keyboard, I was enchanted by the hiss of the steam and the brassy sparkle of the rows of whistles. The old instrument conjured up images of circus parades I'd never seen, imagined memories of elephants and clowns and beautiful ladies on white horses. Then my fingers touched the keys and my romantic fantasies evaporated along with the cloud of steam from the first note I played.

For listeners at a safe distance, the sound of the Phoenix's whistles echoing through the hills is pure distilled fun. For the chump at the keyboard, it's a misery. First, the sheer volume of the noise shakes your innards and numbs your ears. The set of ear protectors, the same kind that people who work around jet aircraft wear, doesn't even begin to block the blast. Then, the great clouds of steam from the whistles condense and turn into hot rain. Five minutes and you're soaked to the skin. Combine this with the radiant heat from the boiler and its fire and you begin to understand how boiled lobsters feel. But, truthfully, it's the boiler itself that worries me the most. I'm convinced that someday Jack will get so caught up in the fun of the moment that he won't notice the needle on its pressure gauge creeping into the red. I expect to be the first Canadian woman to ride a steam calliope into low earth orbit.

"Ask Jack to call me later in the week," I said. "I think I might have to work next Saturday."

"You should be so lucky," Barbara laughed.

"No really," I protested. "If the weather holds, I want to spend the weekend out at the beaver dam."

"How's the film coming?" Barbara nodded in the direction of the editing bench where I'd been working just before she knocked on my door.

"Slower than I'd like, but that's pretty usual. Candi and I are going out to the dam again this afternoon but I don't expect I'll do any filming. It's more to give Candi some practice with the tape recorder. She's getting pretty good at sound."

"Tom says the two of you were working at The Ranch when that man was murdered. What a terrible thing. It's all everyone's been talking about this week." Barbara filled me in on the neighbourhood theories regarding Mr. Reilly's death. I rely on her to keep me up-to-date on all the neighbourhood news and gossip. Apparently our local murder, the first anyone could remember in years, had created quite a sensation. "Do you think the Mounties know who did it?"

We discussed the murder for a little while, but talking at that volume is tiring so we took a breather for a few minutes and listened to the saints go marchin' in.

"What are you up to this weekend?" I asked during one of the short lulls between pieces.

"Karen's home for the weekend," Barbara replied. Karen is Barbara and Jack's daughter. She is in her first year at university, studying drama. "She's brought a friend with her. Moira. Very arty number. The pair of them were still asleep when I left the house but good luck to them with this racket."

As if on cue, two faces peered in the door from my deck. I slid the door open and Karen and Moira ran in followed by a blast of "Comin Round the Mountain." I managed to slam the door behind them before the six white horses could whoop through the room.

"We were still asleep when Dad started in on the calliope," Karen said. They collapsed on the couch. "This is Moira." Moira nodded weakly in my direction. Her first encounter with the calliope had left her a little frazzled. "Moira, this is our neighbour, Phoebe Fairfax."

"Moira and Karen are doing a play together," Barbara explained.

"We open on Wednesday but we have this weekend off. We're supposed to rest," Karen said. "At least until Monday night. That's dress rehearsal. I'm working backstage. Moira has a part."

"What play?" I asked.

"*Hedda Gabler*," Moira answered. "It's by the Norwegian playwright Henrik Ibsen." She neglected to mention the dates of his birth and death.

Good old Hedda Gabler. Scandinavia's melancholic Annie Oakley. The hapless victim of generations of amateur actresses. The gallant survivor of countless college productions. "Are you playing Hedda?" I asked.

"Oh no," Moira looked shocked. "First year students don't get leads." I was suitably admonished. I went to fetch the coffee and two more cups.

"There's an animal in here." Moira sniffed the air suspiciously.

"It's just poor Bertie," Karen said. The dog raised his ears at the sound of his name but he didn't budge from his refuge under my desk. "You don't much like Dad's music, do you Bertie?" Karen knelt beside the desk and stroked his head.

"Would you mind putting him outside?" Moira asked. "I'm allergic to dogs." She coughed slightly by way of proof. ' i'm afraid I can't even stay in the same room with them without wheezing."

"Bertie can't go out right now," Karen said. "He's frightened of the noise."

"It's okay," I said. "I'll put him in the basement."

"Would you?" said Moira. "I adore animals. I seem to

have this special rapport with them. But when you're in theatre you have to be so very, very careful of your voice." She coughed again.

I hooked my hand through the dog's collar and hauled him to the basement door. He glowered reproachfully at Moira and then disappeared down the stairs.

"That's so much better," Moira said. "I truly do appreciate it." The coffee and muffins seemed to be reviving her. "What a charming, charming house this is." She got up from the couch and began to roam the room like a restless understudy surveying a new set. "And what a wonderful view you have." She spoke this last to the windows, keeping her back to the audience while she acted up a storm with her shoulders. "It's the kind of sight that nourishes my soul."

"Another muffin?" I asked.

"Thank you, Phoebe." She turned to face the room. "Phoebe, Phoebe. How lucky you are to have such a beautiful, beautiful name." Words came in pairs to Moira's lips. She sent them fluttering off two by two, like verbal pigeons destined for some lexical Noah's ark. "Did your parents name you for Phebe the shepherdess in Shakespeare's *As You Like It*? I think she's such a darling." For some folk, a university education in the dramatic arts is not a wholesome experience.

"I'm called after my mother's favourite aunt. Great Aunt Phoebe. She's dead," I added for no particular reason.

"How fortunate she left you her lovely, lovely name. I would imagine you must be very grateful to her."

"I'm grateful her name wasn't Euphemia."

"We've been invited to the dress rehearsal of the girls' play." Barbara sailed us past the squall she sensed looming on the conversational horizon. "We're driving to Edmonton Monday afternoon and we won't be home until

Tuesday night."

"Tom too?" I asked, thinking ahead to the care and feeding of the horses.

"Tom can't miss school," Barbara answered. "He's staying with a friend in Calgary."

"School my eye," Karen said. "He's staying in Calgary so he can go to a hockey game. Quel philistine."

"Right," I agreed. "That boy wouldn't recognize an Ibsen if he stepped in it."

The calliope began to sound a little spluttery and a lot flatter. This is a sure sign that the steam pressure and the concert are both running down.

"Well, that's that for another week," Barbara said. "It's safe to go home now. Thanks for the haven, Phoebe. Come on girls." She herded them to the door before Moira had time to improvise a dramatic exit.

"Good luck with *Hedda Gabler*," I said. The pair of them looked at me in horror. "Sorry," I apologized, "I meant break a leg."

"Don't give me ideas," Barbara muttered.

After the Phoenix's din, the house seemed unnaturally quiet. The clink of china as I cleared away the coffee cups was like bird song after a thunderstorm. I opened the door to the basement for the dog but he didn't appear until he heard Candi knock on the back door. Then he bounded up the stairs and flung himself at her feet. Even male animals go a little mooney over Candi.

"Didn't the calliope sound terrific this morning?" Candi is one of the Phoenix's biggest fans. "And does that sound ever carry. I swear I could hear it as I was driving past Spruce Meadows. You know, we should have Jack on 'Lifestyle' some day. I mean Ella's always looking for people to come on and talk about art and antiques and music and stuff like that. Well, the Phoenix has got it all. Here's lunch." She held up a plastic bag of trail mix. "I got the kind with lots of raisins."

One of the drawbacks of my film work is loneliness. I enjoy being by myself but sometimes even I get a little tired of the long hours of solitary waiting the work requires. Having Candi for company is a pleasant change even though I can't quite understand why she's chosen to spend so many of her Saturdays helping me lug camera equipment over the hills. I stuffed the trail mix and a couple of cans of Coke into my vest pockets. This was the first weekend of the deer hunting season so both of us wore our bright orange vests. Even so I was a little edgy.

I shut the patio door on the dog. He pressed his nose to the glass and wagged his tail ingratiatingly. "You can't come with us today, you idiot. Some near-sighted hunter will think you're a deer and blow you away." Like the horses', the dog's activities are greatly restricted during hunting season. Besides, he's really not the ideal companion to have along when you're doing your best to blend into the landscape and be an unobtrusive observer. Dogs don't have a flair for stealth.

I carried the camera and the microphone case while Candi managed a set of earphones and twenty pounds of tape recorder. It's only a few miles from my place to the beaver pond's sheltered valley but they're mostly uphill miles and the gear starts to feel pretty heavy by the end of the trek. However, the place is so perfect that the reward is more than worth the effort.

A spring fed pond backs up from the dam the beavers have built at the valley's mouth. The slopes of the hills on either side are covered in an equal mix of spruce and poplar. Thanks to the restless teeth of the residents, the poplars near the water's edge are beginning to look a little sparse. Still, the big lodge bespeaks prosperity. It is obvious that the place is inhabited by beavers of means, rodents of wealth and property. The dam is wide and in excellent repair and the pond behind it so clear you can watch rainbow trout dozing near its sun-dappled bottom.

We chatted while I helped Candi set up the recorder and mike. There wasn't much point in maintaining silence. Beavers are nocturnal creatures so the likelihood of our voices disturbing one about his beaver business in the middle of a sunny day was remote. For the next hour, Candi practised with the tape recorder while I sat on a sunny log and tried to decide on the best location for the blind I planned to build so I could photograph inside the lodge. I'd hoped to have the blind in place before winter in order to get some footage of the birth of the beaver kits, but I had run out of time. That would have to wait until next year.

Candi took off the earphones and sat down beside me on the log. She leaned forward, rested the tape recorder on the ground and slipped its wide leather strap off over her head. "That thing weighs a ton after awhile." She rotated her shoulders and rubbed the back of her neck. I opened the Cokes and put the trail mix between us on the log. "Come up with anything for the blind?" She nibbled a handful of nuts and raisins.

"I think I know where to put it but it's too late for this year. No time," I said.

"If it wasn't for 'Lifestyle' you'd have the time," Candi said. This was one of her favourite topics. In Candi's opinion, I should not be working for "A Day in the Lifestyle." I should be out spending months in exotic wilderness locations shooting movies so marvelous that National Geographic will be sick with envy. Money, it seems, is no object.

"If I didn't work for 'Lifestyle' I couldn't afford to build a blind or buy the film to shoot from it." I knew my part of our script.

"Phoebe, you know that's just an excuse," Candi said.

"By now your old films should be making enough money to support the new ones you're working on. The real truth is that you're totally hopeless at selling yourself." Sometimes she sounded a lot like Cyrrie. "What you need is a good business manager." This was a new tack.

"Are you volunteering?"

"Don't laugh." She looked hurt. "I couldn't do a much worse job of it than you're doing right now. I'm not a total airhead, you know."

"I'm sorry," I apologized. "I didn't mean to imply that you couldn't do it. It's just that I've never thought of you as the business type, that's all."

"That's okay, Phoebe," she said. "I guess sometimes I'm a little too sensitive about people thinking that I'm dumb. Because they do, you know." Candi was right about that. People don't tend to regard her as the brightest candle on the cake. "Especially men," she continued. "They're the worst. Men never really talk to me. All they ever do is say silly stuff they think is dumb enough for me to understand while they try to get me into bed. Men never want to get to know the real me."

"And you're complaining?" I said. The men I meet always want to get to know me. They're hopeless romantics. They all want what they refer to as a *real relationship*. This is an ominous phrase. It means that when you're not having profoundly meaningful sex, you're supposed to have profoundly meaningful talks. Or, more to the point, you're supposed to listen while they talk. Endlessly. You're actually expected to be interested in why their first marriage failed and the existential angst they suffer as computer programmers. I ask you, is a nice little roll in the hay really worth all that? In my books, the ideal man for an idle evening is one who wines you and dines you and entertains you with frivolous chat until he takes you home to your place. There, he shuts up and proceeds to make equally frivolous love to you. Afterwards, just as you are drifting off into a lovely night's sleep, he gets dressed and tiptoes out carrying his shoes. Next morning, you awake refreshed and delightfully alone instead of beside a stubbly face that wants to make love, or even worse, conversation, before you've had your first cup of coffee. Just where are all Candi's single-minded sex fanatics when you need them? Maybe you have to look like her to find them. Or maybe the men who want to sweep Candi into bed are the same men who want to discuss their ex-wives with me. Now there's a depressing thought.

"You'd complain too if no one ever took you seriously," Candi said. "Especially if you were supposed to be a television interviewer."

"Maybe it's an advantage there," I said. "People aren't expecting tough questions from you so they don't have their guard up. You take them by surprise."

"Tell that to Ella," Candi said. "She hates the way I interview."

"I'm telling it to you," I said. "I think 'Lifestyle' is lucky to have you." And I did. For me, Candi's wacky interviews are the program's one redeeming feature. Plus my photography, of course. "You see, Ella's problem is that she's very conventional. She'd like you to be a Pamela Wallin clone. But why should you? There are a zillion Pamlettes in Canadian television. There's only one Candi Sinclair. You're unique. Cyrrie thinks you're the most entertaining interviewer in Calgary."

"Really?" Candi said. "You're not just saying that to make me feel better?"

"Of course I'm saying it to make you feel better, but it also happens to be true." Cyrrie never misses "A Day in the Lifestyle." At first it was mostly to watch my photography but soon he got hooked on Candi's interviews. By its very nature, "A Day in the Lifestyle" attracts more than its fair share of pompous idiots as guests. To Cyrrie's great delight, most of them manage to slip on at least one of the interrogative banana peels Candi scatters through every program and the more pretentious they are the harder they fall. Cyrrie waits for it. He was going to love the Dr. Morrison interview. "He's especially looking forward to the program on The Ranch. He was a good friend of the lady who used to own it."

"Tell Cyrrie he might have to wait for that one," Candi said. "Ella is having a hard time getting permission from the police to use the tape you shot. The stuff besides the interview I mean. She's thinking of re-scheduling the broadcast to next spring. We probably won't even be able to play it then unless they've caught the murderer."

"Then the whole thing will be out of date," I said. "They're planning some big changes at The Ranch in the next few months. Even your interview with Dr. Morrison could be totally irrelevant if she's not managing director any more." I told Candi about the new plans for The Ranch.

"I sure didn't hear anything about changes," Candi said. "Does Ella know?"

"I don't think so," I said. "Dr. Morrison was Ella's contact person at The Ranch and apparently she doesn't approve of the new plans. They were Mr. Reilly's idea. And Reg Pepper's. He thinks Dr. Morrison might quit before all this new stuff happens."

"I don't think she's looking for another job. At least she didn't mention it to me," Candi said. "But if she is, she sure won't have any trouble finding one. Dr. Morrison could get a job anywhere. Did you know that she graduated top of her class from medical school? She worked at some pretty fancy places before she went to The Ranch. She was even offered a job at that place that's kind of like the Mayo Clinic only it's in California or somewhere."

"How do you know all this?" I asked.

"Because she told me," Candi said. "Remember, I'm an interviewer. At least you just said I was. People are supposed to tell me things."

"When did you talk to her?"

"We had a lot of time between our 'Lifestyle,' interview and that sashimi dinner. We talked then."

"You mean she actually spoke to you after that interview?"

"Of course she spoke to me. Why wouldn't she?" Candi was genuinely puzzled. "Heather's a real nice person."

I squashed my Coke can and put it back in my pocket. Candi placed hers on a rock and jumped on it, telescoping it to a neat inch high cylinder. She handed it to me along with the trail mix. We hadn't made much of a dint in the bag. Lunch for next week. It followed the Coke cans into my pocket.

"It's cold." I zipped up my vest. The sky had clouded over while we sat drinking our Cokes.

"I heard the weather report this morning. We're supposed to get snow this weekend," Candi said.

"I hope it holds off until Monday. I'm supposed to meet Felix Sanders out at The Ranch tomorrow afternoon and help him with an assignment for his photography class. I could do without getting snowed on."

"Phoebe, I'm pretty sure he's married." Candi sounded worried.

"How can you tell?" I laughed. "Do married men have some sort of identifying mark that I've missed all these years?"

"Married looks married. I can just tell," she maintained stolidly. "And what's more, married and out for a little fling on the side looks like Felix Sanders."

"Well, you don't need to worry because I'm not planning on being Felix's little fling. There's absolutely nothing romantic about this. I'm simply helping the man with a class assignment. I'm doing it more as a favour to Jerry O'Neil than anything else."

Candi shook her head and gave me a look that had born yesterday written all over it. "I'll bet you twenty dollars he makes a pass at you tomorrow."

"You're on," I said. "I'll collect my winnings on Monday." A gust of cold wind swept down the valley. "Let's go home. There's not much more we can do out here this afternoon." I was at a low point on this film—the point where I begin to think the whole thing is a dumb idea and I should never have started to work on it. It happens to me on every film. Why had I chosen to work on nocturnal creatures, especially nocturnal creatures who spend the better part of their lives under water?

We had just packed up the gear when Candi put a silent hand on my arm and pointed to the pond. A large beaver swam in the direction of the dam. The ripples from his wake trailed out over the surface of the water. He climbed on to the dam and began an orderly and methodical inspection. "It's the alpha beaver," I whispered.

"Hello Alfred," Candi whispered too, but I could hear the excitement in her voice. "I didn't know you'd given the beavers names. When did you do that?"

"Not Alfred," I said. "Alpha. As in alpha, beta, gamma, delta. You know, the Greek alphabet."

"Why did you name him after a foreign alphabet letter?" Candi asked. "This big guy has always been Clyde to me."

"I haven't named him," I said. "Alpha's not a name. It's just another way of saying head beaver."

"Then let's call him Clyde. Isn't he gorgeous, Phoebe? I'll bet he'd let us come right up to him if we worked at it. Pretty soon he wouldn't even be one bit afraid of us."

"You know we can't do that," I said. "These aren't cuddly toys that move, they're wild animals. We want them to stay afraid. We wouldn't be doing this guy any favours if we taught him not to fear human beings." Candi looked crushed. "You know as well as I do that there are people who would shoot him just for target practice."

"I know you're right," she said. "But what harm could it do to give him a name? Just between us. So we know who we're talking about. What difference does it make if we call him Clyde or Alfred or Alpha?"

"If you give creatures names, you get attached to them," I said.

"Well I am attached to them," Candi said. "I've spent so many Saturday afternoons out here watching them that it would be pretty strange if I wasn't. You practically lived out here for most of the summer, so don't try to tell me you don't love them too." The beaver slid into the water and his sleek mahogany bulk disappeared beneath the surface. "So long, Clyde. See you next week."

By the time we arrived back at the house, the sun was shining again. There's a saying around here to the effect that if you don't like the foothills weather wait five minutes and it will change. Like many folk sayings, this one earned cliché status by being true. There wasn't a cloud in the sky when the dog rushed to the door to greet us. Maybe Candi's weather report had been wrong. Then again, give it five.

"What are you doing tonight?" Candi asked. "Want to go to a movie or something?"

"Cyrrie and I are going to Sugamoto's restaurant for dinner. Why don't you come with us. I'm meeting him there at seven."

"That'd be great. I haven't seen Cyrrie for ages."

By the time I arrived at the restaurant at ten past seven, Candi and Cyrrie were comfortably ensconced at a table sipping warm sake. The restaurant was full but Ben and Marianne managed to find time to join us for a few minutes. The murder was still uppermost in their minds which wasn't too surprising.

"Here's to freedom." Ben lifted his sake cup. "Mine."

"I wonder if they're close to making an arrest?" I said.

"As long as its not me," Ben said.

"It won't be, Benjamin," Cyrrie said. "Remember, you're innocent."

"Everyone who believes that is probably sitting at this table," Ben said.

"That's not true," I said. "I was at The Ranch yesterday. Everyone out there knows you're innocent too. Byron practically wrote you a character reference." I knew it sounded pretty lame.

"If Byron had been at the stable where he was supposed to be when I took the sashimi scraps to the barn cats I wouldn't be in this mess. I'd have an alibi."

"I don't think we should talk about this any more tonight," Marianne interrupted firmly. "For one evening we should try to forget. You're our guests tonight and you're here to enjoy yourselves."

"Marianne, how many times must I remind you that you're running a restaurant not a soup kitchen," Cyrrie said. "We're paying for our dinners and that's that." Cyrrie and I fought this one out with the Sugamotos every time we came to the restaurant. I figured the battle honours were about even.

"Don't worry, Cyrrie. Everything's been taken care of," Ben said. "Phoebe's paying for tonight's dinner. Or at least she will on Monday."

"What's Monday?" I asked. "Isn't that your night at

The Ranch?"

"Not any more it isn't," Ben said. "Dr. Morrison sent me a cheque and told me not to bother working out the last of my contract.

"I'm sorry, Ben," I said.

"Don't be. The contract was a goner anyway so what does it matter."

"Monday is Lisa's birthday," Marianne said. "We're having some of her school friends over for a party."

"It's the kid's tenth and she's having a small soirée to celebrate the double digits," Ben said. "Would you come and shoot a little videotape of the party, Phoeb? It's nothing fancy. Just eats and a little whooping it up. You don't have to dress. What do you say? Tonight's dinner for the kid's party video. Fair exchange?"

"Fair exchange," I agreed. "What time should I be there?"

"Five too early?" he asked.

"It's a school night," Marianne explained.

"What's Ella got planned for Monday?" I asked Candi.

"That guy who's going to try crossing the Rockies in his hot air balloon. Remember, you're supposed to go up for a ride with him. Ella told us about it last week." I must have repressed this sickening bit of information. I felt myself turn a little green.

"Five o'clock will be fine. If I survive the balloon flight I'll see you then." Even a pack of partying ten-year-olds would look pretty good after an afternoon with nothing between me and the ground but a thousand feet of air and an over-sized picnic basket.

"We might even persuade Ronald McDonald to set an extra place for you at dinner," Ben said.

"Ben, Phoebe's already agreed to come," Marianne said. "There's no need to threaten her."

"What's for dinner tonight?" I asked. "I'm starving."

"No lunch again." Cyrrie shook his head.

"That's not true," I objected. "We had a perfectly good lunch out at the beaver pond."

"We did," Candi backed me up. "Phoebe brought some Cokes and trail mix along in her vest pocket."

"My dear Candida, are you telling me that you ate lunch out of Phoebe's pocket?"

"Really, Cyrrie, it was in a plastic bag," I said.

"Well now, my little marsupials," Cyrrie opened the menu in front of him, "Who's for the teriyaki salmon?"

CHAPTER 13

"I brought along a tape of my work," said Felix. "I thought you might want to take a look at it before we go out to the stream. That way you'll see all my bad habits and know what you're up against." He had been waiting for me in The Ranch's parking lot, leaning against his car in the afternoon sun with his brand new black Stetson cocked at a jaunty angle. "There's a VCR and a television set in the library. We can use them."

I fished my battered work-bag out of the car and we started toward the house. Felix carried a new canvas camera bag, bright red and bristling with pockets and velcro tabs. His khaki hiking jacket had the rustle of newness too, and even more pockets than the bag. "How long have you been doing video photography?" I asked.

"I've only been at it since the summer," he said. "But I always had a secret yen to make movies. I just never did anything about it. I probably wouldn't yet except for Byron. One day when I was down at the stable looking at some of his photographs I happened to mention that I was interested in movies. He offered to lend me his video camera for a couple of weeks and that did it. I was hooked. Then my wife noticed an ad for your friend's class at the community college and here I am."

"I didn't know Byron did video too," I said. "He showed me some of his work when I was out here on Friday. Very impressive. But I thought he was strictly stills."

"He is," Felix said. "I'm pretty sure the video camera was a whim. I don't think he uses it much."

"Where is everybody?" I asked. The house had that empty Sunday afternoon feeling of naps and nothing to do that used to drive me mad with frustration as a child. Two guests sat at a table in the living-room playing backgammon. Another dozed in front of the fire. The others were nowhere to be seen.

"It's their one free afternoon of the week. They're usually exhausted by Sunday so I expect they're all back in their cabins fast asleep," Felix said.

We climbed the stairs to the third floor. The rest of the house seemed deserted too. Felix opened the door to the library. "Damn. Some idiot has borrowed the machine." The television set still sat on the cart in the corner of the room but its companion VCR had vanished. "So much for showing you my brilliant camera work."

"That can't be the only VCR in the house," I said. "I thought I noticed one in the main office."

"That's the one Heather and Phil use. So as long as Heather hasn't hauled it off to preview more of those self-help videos she specializes in we're in luck."

Felix got out his keys but we found the door to the main office ajar. A distraught Margaret Sabbatini stood in the open door of Mr. Reilly's inner office, a file folder clutched in her hand.

"Oh, it's you," she said. A lock of her usually tidy grey hair had escaped its moorings and hung down over one eye. "Your voices startled me."

"What's the matter, Margaret?" he asked. "You look upset."

"It's never going to end, is it?" she said. "First he's murdered, cut down in cold blood. And now his office is ransacked. Look at this mess." She stepped aside and pointed to the interior of Mr. Reilly's office. It looked immaculate to me. One of the filing cabinet drawers was open a crack, a couple of manila envelopes protruded from a desk drawer and a slightly rumpled piece of paper lay in the middle of the floor. That was the sum total of the carnage. The rest of the place was in perfect order.

"Come now, Margaret. This is hardly what I'd call a mess," Felix said.

"Maybe a man as casual as you wouldn't." It was clear that in Mrs. Sabbatini's books casual and slovenly were synonyms. "But Philip liked things organized properly. I know someone has been prowling through his drawers. I can tell."

"Was anything taken?" Felix asked.

"Nothing." She stooped and picked the single sheet of paper off the floor. "This was sheer vandalism."

"Maybe the police disturbed his things," Felix said.

"I straightened the office myself on Friday afternoon after they left."

"Well Margaret, I wouldn't worry if I were you. If someone has been in here, I'm sure there's a simple explanation. Maybe Heather needed something from one of his files and got it herself. Have you asked her?"

"I don't need to ask her." Mrs. Sabbatini glared in the direction of Dr. Morrison's deserted office. "I know who did it. The same person who killed Philip, that's who." Her eyes got that teary look I'd come to know too well. "And I know the police know who that is so why don't they arrest her?" The tears began to spill. "Where's my funeral file? I came here this afternoon to finish the arrangements for Philip's funeral and that's what I'm going to do no matter what kind of mess his office is in. Where's my funeral file?"

I pointed to the folder in her hand. "Maybe it's that one."

She sat down at Mr. Reilly's desk and started to sort

through the file. "Philip's funeral has to be perfect, you know. You must excuse me. I'm very busy. Very busy."

"Is there anything we can do for you?" I asked.

"Oh, no. No thank you." The offer seemed to offend her. "I'm Philip's secretary. I'm the only one who touches things in his office."

Felix collected the VCR from its shelf in the main office. "We're taking this to the library, Margaret. We'll bring it back later in the afternoon." Mrs. Sabbatini didn't look up. I wasn't sure she'd even heard him.

"Do you think we should just leave her?" I opened the library door for Felix. "She seems pretty upset."

"She is," Felix said. "But there's nothing we can do for her so she might as well be fussing the funeral if that's what she wants."

I settled down in one of the easy chairs while he connected the VCR to the television set and turned on both machines. He took a videotape out of his camera bag and tried to insert it in the VCR. It wouldn't go.

"Bloody hell. The machine's broken. Maybe I'm not supposed to show you my work." He shoved the tape at the slot again but still with no success.

"Try the eject button," I suggested. "I think there must already be a tape in it." He pushed eject and out popped one of The Ranch's brightly labelled tapes. *The Sound of Music*. Somehow it didn't strike me as a likely choice for either Dr. Morrison or Mr. Reilly. Maybe Mrs. Sabbatini snuck in the occasional movie on slow afternoons.

"The mechanical whiz. That's me." Felix laughed. He handed The Ranch tape to me and slipped his own into the machine. "Well, at least I remembered to turn the damn thing on. Are you ready to be impressed?" He started his tape.

Felix was about as adept with his camera as he was with the VCR. His work was terrible. Maybe he'd had lots of medical emergencies that forced him to skip classes. Otherwise, it was hard to understand how after two months of Jerry's instruction he could still be that bad. The tape rolled on while Felix burbled an enthusiastic accompaniment, kindly identifying the headless people who stood in front of the skewed horizons. It was pretty grim stuff but I tried my best to make encouraging noises.

"What kind of tripod have you been using?" I asked, knowing full well that he hadn't used a tripod at all. Most of the shots wobbled but in one the camera jerked so badly I was sure he must have tripped over something.

"Actually, it's all hand-held," he confessed proudly. "I haven't got round to buying a tripod yet. O'Neil says they're an absolute necessity but do you really think I need one? Maybe I'll never be as steady a photographer as you are but I don't think I'm all that bad for an amateur." The camera panned one hundred and eighty degrees in a giddy three seconds and then the screen went blank. "Well?" He switched off the television set and turned to me. "Come on. Tell me what you think."

I was spared by Mrs. Sabbatini's appearance at the door.

"I'm brewing a pot of coffee," she announced. "Will you join me in Philip's office or shall we have it in here?"

"Very kind of you, Margaret but Phoebe and I are just on our way out the door. We're going to do some photography down by the stream and we have to get started while the light's still good." Felix swept up our bags with one hand and propelled me out the door with the other. "See you tomorrow," he called and we were off down the hall. Obviously, he had a great deal more experience than I in dealing with the Margaret Sabbatinis of the world.

"What about this?" I held up The Ranch's tape which was still in my hand. "And we left your tape in the machine."

"Not to worry," Felix said. "We'll straighten it out when we come back from the stream. If we go back now we're done for. She'll natter on forever." We walked down the wide front steps. The sunshine had given way to clouds and a sharp breeze blew from the mountains. Felix jammed his hat firmly on his head. "It's getting cold. I wish I'd worn a warmer jacket."

"If you're going to be out here in hunting season you should get a brighter one," I said. "Like this." I zipped up my orange vest, pulled up the collar and fished an equally gaudy toque out of the pocket. "You look too much like a deer in that colour."

"Isn't it illegal to hunt on Sundays?" Felix said.

"Yes," I answered. "It is but . . ."

"Then there's nothing to worry about, is there?"

"Phoebe, you're just the lady I'm looking for." Byron strolled around the corner of the house from the direction of the stable. "I saw you drive in so I went and got my pictures." He handed me a fat brown envelope. "Phoebe's going to show some of my rodeo pictures to a friend of hers who owns an art gallery. Pretty good, eh, Doc?"

"Good luck," Felix said.

"Hey, where'd you guys come across that?" Byron pointed to *The Sound of Music*. "That's one of my all-time favourite movies. You finished with it or are you just taking it out?"

"Neither," I said. "We were watching one of Felix's tapes and this was in the machine. Somebody must have forgotten it."

"No canned entertainment for us today," Felix said. "We're off to make a movie of our own. We're going to shoot a video of the stream for my photography class. I have my own private tutor for the afternoon."

"Looks to me like its gonna snow," Byron said.

"You'd be better off inside watching a movie. You're gonna freeze your butts off down by the stream. But you can't talk sense to photographers."

"It would be one hell of a blizzard that could get me to sit through that schmaltz," Felix said.

"Come on, *The Sound of Music* wasn't all that bad," I said. "I kind of enjoyed it."

"How old were you when you saw it?" Felix asked.

"Seven."

"I rest my case."

"Want me to take it back up to the library for you?" Byron offered. "I'm on my way up there now to get a video for myself."

"That's okay," I said. "We have to go back upstairs later anyway. Besides, if we get back from the stream in time maybe we'll watch some of it. Felix can consider it part of his education as a cinematographer." I stuffed the movie and Byron's package of photos into my work-bag. "Remember how it opens with those great helicopter shots of the Alps?"

"All I remember is that horde of relentlessly cheerful children," Felix grimaced. "They put me off child psychiatry forever. Come on, Phoebe. We'd better get going before it starts to snow."

By the time we reached the stream fifteen minutes later, a few flakes mixed with freezing rain had already started to fall and the breeze had graduated to a wind. It hit us with all its force as we emerged from the shelter of the trees and walked through the couple of hundred yards of open meadow that sloped down to the water. In the spring the stream is swollen with melt waters from the hills but by autumn it is more like a brook—a very fast, very shallow, very cold brook. Ice crystals had already formed along the edges of the eddies.

"I guess we'll have to cross to the other bank," Felix

said. "Then we won't be shooting into the sun." He pointed at some slippery looking rocks protruding from the water. "We can use those as stepping stones."

"Felix, it's snowing. There is no sun to shoot into. We might as well stay on this bank." My toes ached at the thought of risking wet feet in that evil-looking water. "Maybe we should head for that clump of poplars downstream and take our opening shots from there." At least the trees would provide a little shelter from the wind which lashed the ever more abundant wet snowflakes into our faces.

"Actually, Phoebe, I'd prefer to open with a medium shot of that big rock. The one right in the middle of the water." Soon we wouldn't be able to see the rock for snow, let alone photograph it. "I love the way it splits the water. Look at those little whirlpools on either side." The temperature was falling by the minute.

"Let's do it then." I slung my work-bag on to the ground. The snow was falling so hard I could barely see the trees at the top of the meadow. "But we'd better hurry or we're not going to get anything on tape before this turns into a blizzard."

I heard a muffled crack. At the same time, Felix's hat went flying into the middle of the stream. He dropped to his knees. "It's that damn killer owl of yours. He's attacked me again."

"Oh no he didn't, not in the middle of the afternoon," I started to haul him to his feet. "Somebody shot at you."

"That's ridiculous. It's Sunday." He brushed the dirt and snow off his trousers. "Besides, why would anyone want to shoot me?"

"Because you moved. Because they think you're a deer. I don't know why, but believe me that was a shot." I heard another faint crack. The second bullet hit the ground directly in front of us and sent a spray of dirt into the air.

This seemed to convince Felix. "Come on." I grabbed my work-bag and tugged at his arm, "We've got to get to the trees."

"Hi! You idiot." He waved his camera bag over his head. "Do I look like a deer?" he shouted indignantly. "Deer don't carry camera bags, you bloody fool." The next bullet ripped through one side of the red canvas bag and out the other. It hung limply from the strap on his shoulder. He stood staring at it, as if his mind hadn't quite registered the message. "He shot my brand new bag."

"And he's going to shoot you if we don't run." I grabbed his hand. "Come on, Felix. Move." We ran for the trees downstream. There were no more shots. I blessed the white cloak that concealed us from the hunter's view. Thanks to the snow we had been difficult still targets. Now it made us impossible moving ones. Even so, that hundred yard run felt like a hundred miles. We didn't stop until we were safely in the middle of the poplar grove. Adrenalin driven hearts pounding we leaned against a tree and gasped for breath.

"We should be okay here as long as it keeps snowing," I said when I could finally spare the breath for words.

"You're a very cool customer, Phoebe Fairfax," Felix panted. "Thanks. I'd still be standing back there like Joe Egg while that lunatic took pot-shots at me."

"Not so cool," I could hear the quiver in my voice. "I think I'm going to be sick." I started to shake.

"No you're not," Felix said. "Come here." He put his arms around me and held me close to him. "Try to breathe normally. You'll be all right in a minute or two."

I rested my head on his shoulder. Gradually the nausea subsided. "I think I'm better now. Thanks." I disentangled myself from his arms. The wet snow swirled around us and the poplars creaked and groaned in the wind. "We've got to get out of this storm. If we stay out here much longer we'll be soaked to the skin."

"Back to The Ranch?"

"I don't think that's such a hot idea. The shots came from that direction. For all we know that jerk may still be hiding in the trees at the top of the meadow waiting for his funny looking herd of deer to reappear."

"What's the alternative?"

"Follow the stream north for a couple of miles to my place."

"Isn't that a little dangerous?" he asked. "The storm is getting worse. It would be very easy to lose our way."

"We'll have the stream as a guide," I said. "Besides, I'd sooner take my chances with a blizzard than a hunting rifle."

"Having just experienced the wrong end of a hunting rifle, I tend to agree," he said. "Let's go."

By the time we finished the first mile it was snowing so hard that I could only see about fifty feet ahead. I began to wish that I hadn't tipped the odds quite so glibly in favour of the blizzard. As long as we were near the stream we would be all right. It was the last quarter mile from the stream to my house that worried me. If the storm got any worse, which it showed every sign of doing, we could get so lost that we would wander in circles until exhaustion and exposure succeeded where the hunter had failed. We wouldn't be the first. I've read the inscription *Lost in a blizzard* on more than one gravestone in foothills' cemeteries.

"I think it's getting worse," Felix said. His hair was covered with snow. If it got much colder, our wet clothes would freeze.

"We're nearly there. Another fifteen minutes and we're warm and dry." I kept my morbid thoughts to myself.

By the time we reached the barbed wire fence that

marked the beginning of my property, the storm was a full-scale blizzard. Visibility was down to twenty feet and the swirling eddies of snow that blew over us reduced it to zero.

"I don't know what we should do," I said. "If we go on from here we have to leave the stream and finding our way without it to mark our direction could be . . . ," I hesitated, unable to think of a euphemism for impossible. "If we wait here for awhile the storm may fall off a little. Then again, it may get worse." They'd find us in the spring. We'd melt out of a snow bank.

"Why don't we follow the fence?" Felix asked. I stared at him dumbly. "Does it go all the way around your land?" I nodded. "Why can't we follow it until we reach your front gate?" Why indeed. "Then it's two steps down the driveway and we're at your house." Feeling like a total fool, I followed Felix home along the fence.

CHAPTER 14

The dog met us at the mailbox. He'd obviously just emerged from one of his sheltered sleeping places because his fur was still dry. That was more than I could say for Felix and me. Our clothes were sodden and I was chilled to the bone. The dog led the way to the house. He leaned against my legs while I fished the key out of my work-bag. I was grateful for the warmth. I opened the door and switched on a light. It couldn't have been much after four but the storm made it dark as dusk in the house. I turned up the setting on the thermostat. "It's freezing in here."

"You're soaked through. You need a hot bath." Felix peeled off his wet jacket. The melting snow had seeped through to his shirt.

"So do you." I kicked off my soggy shoes and squished over to the closet in my stocking feet.

"Seems a little pointless to take a bath when all I have to wear are the same wet clothes."

"I'll put them in the dryer for you. I've got a robe you can wear in the meantime." I opened the closet and found a dilapidated terrycloth bathrobe Gavin had abandoned when he moved out. I added a pair of woolly grey work socks and passed the whole bundle to Felix. "Here. The hot water's all yours."

"You first," he said. "It's your bathtub."

"Right after I check on the horses." I picked up the phone.

"Shall I build a fire?" he asked. I nodded and pointed

to the kindling box.

Barbara answered and assured me that Elvira and Pete were snug in their stalls. Not that the pair of them couldn't have come through the storm outdoors in fine style but, for my own peace of mind, I prefer them stowed safely in the barn when the weather gets really rough. By the time I hung up, Felix had a very respectable fire burning in the grate. We stood side by side facing the flames, the front of our wet clothes turning steamy from the heat. The dog lay between us luxuriating in the warmth and the company.

"I guess we'd better phone the police and tell them about our Sunday hunter," I said.

"I think you should do it," he said. "You know the district better than I do. Besides, I'm getting very sick of talking to policemen. This week feels like it's been one long conversation with a Mountie."

I looked up the number of our local RCMP detachment and dialed. The officer I spoke to listened to the tale of our brush with death with the usual police sang-froid. We might have been discussing a parking ticket. After five minutes of questions, he concluded that because our lives were no longer in danger and the blizzard had made driving impossible, further investigation of our complaint would have to wait until the storm cleared. That would probably be by tomorrow morning but, knowing the erratic foothills weather, it could even be later tonight. He was glad we weren't hurt. An officer would call on us as soon as possible. Good afternoon, Miss Fairfax. And that was that. So much for almost having your head shot off.

"They didn't seem very worried about us," I said to Felix. "The officer I talked to was more upset about someone breaking the Sunday hunting law. He says they'll want to talk to both of us."

I wanted a long, luxurious wallow in a hot bath, but that didn't seem fair to Felix who was still freezing in his wet clothes. Instead, I stood under the spray of a hot shower for ten minutes. Reluctantly, I got out and towelled dry. I wrapped my wet hair in a towel and put on my warmest robe. It's made of soft grey wool and reaches to the floor. It even has a hood that makes me look like a junior monk.

I found Felix in the bathrobe and socks, sitting in front of the fire drinking a mug of tea. "Your turn," I said. "There are towels in the bathroom cupboard."

"Would you like some tea?" He poured a mug for me. "I hope you don't mind. I helped myself to your kitchen and made us a pot. I used your telephone too. I had to call my wife so she wouldn't worry about me. I let the people at The Ranch know that we're all right, too. I talked to Heather. She said she'd pass the message on to Byron."

Felix stayed in the shower a long time. While he drained the hot water tank, I tossed his clothes in the dryer. I drew the drapes to shut out the storm and put another couple of logs on the fire. The dog decided the hearth had finally become too hot and, with much sighing and a few long-suffering looks, he hauled himself off to resume his nap next to the coolness of the patio doors. The phone rang. It was Byron. Dr. Morrison had not passed Felix's message along. He had seen our cars still sitting in The Ranch's parking lot and was worried.

"I figured I'd try your number first," he said. "If I didn't get you, the next one I called was gonna be the Mounties. Why didn't you guys come back to The Ranch? This is some blizzard."

"We had more than the weather to worry about." I told him about our near-fatal encounter with the hunter. Byron's reaction was much more satisfactory than the policeman's had been.

"Jesus, Phoebe! You coulda been killed. You gotta call the police and report this."

"I did," I said. "They're sending someone out here to talk to us."

"In the storm?" he said. "They're nuts. Nobody could get through this."

"They're going to wait until it eases off a little. Could be tonight, might not be until tomorrow morning. Not that it matters much. I think they just want to get our signatures on a formal complaint or something. They'll never catch the guy now."

"You're sure you guys are all right?"

"I'm fine and so is Felix," I assured him. "And thanks for worrying. It's good to know someone would have come looking for us."

"I couldn't let my favourite lady photographer get herself lost in a blizzard, could I? Especially not before you got a chance to give my pictures to your gallery friend," he laughed.

"Spoken like a true photographer."

"You really are okay? I'm being serious now. I mean it."

"I really am okay."

"Then I'll be seeing you tomorrow afternoon I guess. If the storm's stopped."

"What's tomorrow?" I asked.

"Phil Reilly's funeral," he replied. I had forgotten. "Most of the guys from The Ranch are gonna be there. Mrs. Sabbatini said you'd be coming too. It's at one-thirty."

"I think I have to work then," I said, remembering my scheduled joy-ride with the balloon lunatic. It was odd that Ella hadn't phoned to confirm the assignment. That was unlike her. She usually has me briefed with a shot list in my hand by Friday afternoon. Maybe she was having such a great weekend with Marty she'd forgotten me. It was unlikely but I could always hope. "But I'll try to be there if I can."

"I'd like to keep on talking Phoebe, but I really gotta go now. I got a sick horse on my hands."

"What's wrong?"

"Colic and its pretty bad. We've got to keep walking her."

"An all nighter?"

"Yeah, I think so. But at least I've got some help. One of the wranglers is with me and we're spelling each other off. It's time I was back down there."

"Good luck."

By the time Felix emerged from the shower looking much warmer in the socks and the bathrobe, I was sitting on the rug in front of the fire brushing my hair dry.

"Better?" I asked.

"Much." He sat down beside me on the rug.

"More tea? Or maybe you'd like a drink?"

"I could do justice to some of that Scotch you gave me last time. I don't usually drink in the afternoon but then I don't usually get shot at either." I got up and poured us both a measure of whisky.

"Good health and a long life to you, Phoebe Fairfax." He touched his glass to mine.

"A very, very long life to us both, Felix Sanders." We drank our toast and I sat down in one of the fireside chairs.

"It makes you think, doesn't it?" he said.

"Being shot at?"

"I looked at my camera bag when you were in the shower. A couple of inches lower and he'd have shot off my hand."

"Good thing you didn't get a chance to look at your hat," I said. "A couple of inches there and he'd have shot off your head."

"Like I said before, Phoebe, you're a real comfort." He yawned and stretched out on the rug. We sipped our drinks in silence and stared into the flames. Then he started to snore. Not just polite heavy breathing but great long honking snorts. The dog woke up and glared at him indignantly. I tried not to laugh. Felix didn't wake as I fetched my duvet from the closet and covered him with it. I stood looking down at him. His head rested on his arm. His hair was a little thin on top. The woolly socks peaked out from the bottom of the duvet. If only Candi could see my philandering married man now. So much for her twenty dollars.

I did my best to be quiet while I got one of Cyrrie's care packages out of the freezer. The label said boeuf bourguignonne. I started it thawing in the microwave while I made a salad, put water on to boil for pasta, and set the table. Finally, I opened a bottle of wine, poured myself a glass and settled back in the chair by the fire to wait for Felix to wake up.

"Sorry, I must have dropped off for a minute." He rubbed his eyes and sat up on one elbow.

"Are you hungry? Dinner's almost ready."

"And the wench cooks too. Now all I need is for her dad to own a pub and I'll marry her tomorrow."

"Sorry, no pub. He's a retired banker. And I'm not exactly cooking either," I admitted. "I'm thawing. I'm one of the world's truly great thawers. I'm nuking us some boeuf bourguignonne."

Felix got up and followed me to the kitchen. He walked a little stiffly. "It's a long time since I fell asleep on a floor." He flexed his shoulders and massaged the small of his back.

The microwave emitted its series of insistent little beeps. I poked at the bourguignonne with a wooden spoon. It was very hot. I drained the noodles, dressed the salad and dinner was served in the main salon.

"That bourguignonne was thawed to perfection," Felix

announced as we finished the last forkful. "Thank you, and my congratulations to the cook, whoever the cook was."

"My friend Cyrrie," I said. "He thinks I don't eat properly so he's always sending little packages of food home with me. I think I've got a lasagna, some spinach souffle and two days worth of chicken cacciatore on hand after this. We could be snowed in for a week and still eat. He is a good cook, isn't he?"

"Is that the same Cyrrie you told me about on Monday night. The one who was the friend of your Uncle Andrew whose piano you inherited and whose house this used to be?"

"That's the Cyrrie," I said. "You have an incredible memory."

"Only for things I care to remember. And I care to remember things about you." He poured us each another glass of wine and then went over to the piano and ran his hand silently down the keys. "Won't you make an exception this once and play for me?"

You can hardly refuse to play a tune for someone who's been your companion through the worst of a foothills' blizzard. "What would you like to hear?"

"Anything you'd like to play." He put another log on the fire and sat back in the chair.

I played Gershwin for him. Half a dozen of the old standards, the Gershwin songs that everyone knows. I finished with "Someone to Watch Over Me."

"How did you know that Gershwin is one of my favourites?" he said. "And that that's one of my favourite Gershwins. Do you do encores?"

"Maybe one. On special occasions."

"Do you know 'They Can't Take That Away From Me?'" He came and stood beside the piano while I played. We sang the last chorus together.

"How do you know all these songs?" he asked. "They're from long before your time. Most of them are before my time."

"Uncle Andrew taught them to me," I said. "Besides, everybody knows them. Gershwin tunes are practically part of the air."

"I enjoyed that very much, Phoebe. Thank you. You're very good and you should play for people more often." I made a mental note to give him a ringside seat at one of my Saturday calliope sessions. A few close choruses of "Daisy" might change his mind on that one. He glanced at his watch. "And now I'm afraid I have to use your phone again to check on some of my patients."

One of the difficulties in having just one room in your house is that it makes private phone conversations impossible. For the next fifteen minutes, while Felix sat at my desk and phoned his answering service and the hospital, I busied myself in the kitchen corner doing the dishes. At least that way it felt like I wasn't eavesdropping intentionally. I heard him make arrangements with one of the residents to do his hospital rounds for him that evening. He finished his phoning with another call to his wife. Then he wandered over to join me in the kitchen.

"Can I help?" he asked.

"Your timing is perfect." I put a plate in the dishwasher. "That was the last dish. Finished phoning?"

"Everything's taken care of," he said. "I'm sorry it took so long. I had to find someone to look after my patients tonight. I'm afraid they don't stop being sick just because I'm caught in a blizzard. Have we drunk all the wine?"

I held the bottle up. "We've been very restrained." I poured two more glasses that emptied the bottle. Felix took his wine and wandered over to the part of the room where I do most of my work. He sat down at the chair in front of the editing machine.

"What is this contraption?"

"It's a film editing bench. I spend a lot of my time here these days."

"Is this what you're working on?" He pointed to the strips of film hanging from numbered metal pegs on a rack near the bench. Their ends trailed into a large cloth bin suspended under the rack. "Could I watch a little of it? Would you mind? I've never seen a film being edited."

I threaded a reel of the beaver pond work print on to the optical track and explained the workings of the editing machine. "It has three tracks. Two are for sound editing and this closest one is for the film." A good crisp shot of Clyde-Alfred-Alpha beaver lunching on a poplar twig filled the viewing screen.

"Where was this taken?" he asked.

"At a beaver pond a couple of miles from here." The last succulent bit of twig disappeared behind Clyde's big front teeth.

"You do most of your work nearby, don't you? The films O'Neil showed our class were all shot in the foothills."

"Film's an expensive business. My own backyard is the only place I can afford to work. But even if I were rich, I'd still work here. This is where I grew up. I know the country pretty well. There's lots to be done."

"Why beavers?" he asked. "There must be hundreds of films about beavers already."

"It's not just about beavers. It's about the whole system of life that surrounds the pond. The fish, the plants, the insects. Maybe there are lots of films about beavers," I conceded, "But no one has made a film about these particular beavers and their particular pond."

"And that's important?"

"I think so. You see, at heart I don't think I'm really a

film maker at all," I explained. "What I really am is an archivist. A cataloguer. A recorder of animals' lives. Particular lives. Individual lives. What with logging and mining and tourism, the foothills are under pressure from all sides these days. I guess I'd like there to be a record of what we're going to lose. Of what we've lost already. At least we'll know what we once had."

"You make it sound pretty hopeless," he said. "Is it really that grim? What about all those conservation groups and environmentalists? Don't you think they're having any effect?"

"I'd like to believe that they are," I said. "But when I'm being honest, I find I have very little hope for the natural world. There's too many of us and too little of it. And we have the advantage. We're adaptable. Too adaptable. I think we'll manage to adapt to enormous changes in our natural environment simply because that will be easier for us than stopping them. We need air to breathe and water to drink and food to eat, but the human race does not need beaver ponds in order to survive." Clyde was in the middle of cleaning his whiskers when the last foot of film flickered through the gate and the screen went blank.

"Isn't that a depressing way to think? Especially for someone in your line of work," Felix said.

"I guess maybe it is," I agreed. I rewound the film and switched off the power to the editing bench.

"How can you go on working if you think like that?"

"I try not to think about the implications of my work too much. I just do it. Besides, look at you," I said. "Dealing with crazy people all the time must be depressing but you manage to go on working."

"Give me a little credit," he said. "Some of them do get better."

"And you like your work all the time? It never

depresses you? You're always hopeful?"

"Yes, I do like my work most of the time," he said. "Sometimes it does depress me but I am hopeful. Always. I couldn't work unless I had hope that I'll succeed at least some of the time. What would be the point?"

"The work itself, I guess. It's really all that matters."

"Not for me," he said. "It's not enough. For more years than I care to remember, work was my whole life. I put in eighteen-hour days seven days a week. Nothing mattered but work. I was a classic case, a living example of the kinds of behaviour I warn my patients about all the time. I'm supposed to be something of an expert on stress. That was a joke. One day I collapsed from exhaustion in the hospital elevator. I couldn't move. I could hardly speak. It was humiliating. It took me nearly three months to get well enough to go back to work. Since then I've been very careful to make sure nothing like that ever happens to me again."

"Is that why you took the job at The Ranch?"

"The Ranch is part of my slow down campaign," he said. "It guarantees me two stress free afternoons a week plus a couple of swims in that beautiful old pool."

"Is the video photography part of the same campaign?" I remembered Dr. Morrison's crack about occupational therapy.

"It's why I make the time for it," he said. "But I do it because I enjoy it."

"Even after this afternoon?"

"I'm assuming that the joys of video-making don't usually include getting shot at," he said. "I'll admit that could get a little stressful on a regular basis."

The dog gave one discreet woof and went to stand by the back door. At the same time, the phone rang. "Will you please let him out while I answer this?" I picked up the phone and put my hand over the receiver. "Please don't let him take forever or he'll come in and shake snow all over the house. Just give him enough time for a quick pee then call him in."

"Is that you, Phoebe?" Unfortunately, Ella hadn't forgotten about me. I knew it was too much to hope.

"Have you had a good weekend?" she asked sweetly. The question came as such a surprise I nearly dropped the phone.

"Very nice, thanks. And you?" Ella and I had never had a conversation like this in all the time I'd known her.

"The best. I'm just lying here in bed, looking out the window at the storm." For Ella to divulge such an intimate personal detail was totally out of character. It verged on the strange. "Is it stormy where you are?"

"Very blustery." I wondered if she'd ever get to the point.

"Now, about Mr. Margolis and his hot air balloon." That was better. "He says it's going to be too windy to fly which is very inconvenient of him." We were back to normal. "There's supposed to be a chinook tomorrow and he's afraid his balloon will get wrecked or something." Ella obviously did not have similar fears for her photographer. She'd have sent me up in a tornado if she thought she needed the shots. "He says we can try again on Wednesday." I could have sworn I heard a voice in the background murmur something about why don't we try again right now. I put it down to a momentary electronic muddle on the phone line.

"Wednesday's fine," I said. At least it gave me two days' reprieve. With any luck the wind might hold and we'd have to cancel the whole thing.

"I'll call you to confirm." She gave a high-pitched little giggle, mumbled something I couldn't understand, and hung up. Really, Ella was not herself these days.

"What's his name?" Felix asked.

"Marty, probably," I said. I no sooner put the phone down than it started to ring again.

"Just probably? You don't know for sure? He is your dog."

"You're asking me the dog's name?"

"Remember, you wanted me to call him in," Felix explained patiently. "But I don't know his name and I've never heard you use it. You always call him The Dog."

"It's Albert," I said. "Bertie." I picked up the phone while Felix opened the back door and shouted the dog's name into the wind.

My new caller was Barbara. She and Jack were still planning on leaving in the morning for their two days in Edmonton, weather permitting. She reminded me that Tom would be away too so I'd have to look after the horses myself. And while I was over bringing in the mail and checking the house, would I mind taking a look at the Phoenix? The thermostat on the furnace in the barn had been acting up and Jack would be grateful if I'd make sure the temperature was holding steady. Barbara would leave all the relevant keys in our usual hiding place. She'd call when they got home on Tuesday. I wished them a safe journey.

"Sorry to be so long. I think Bertie had trouble hearing me over the sound of the wind." Felix walked over to the fire and stood warming his hands. A layer of snow covered the dog's fur. He followed Felix into the living-room. The unmistakable pong of wet canine came with him. He stopped beside me and shook himself vigorously, spraying me with melting snow.

"That's what he wanted you to think," I said. "He suffers from the deafness of convenience. His hearing comes and goes as it suits him." I scowled at the dog. He gave me back one of his best martyred looks and then slunk off to sleep in his basket by the door. I joined Felix in front of the fire.

"The blizzard is as bad as ever," he said. "You can't even see the end of the drive. I won't make it home tonight."

"These storms usually blow themselves out by morning. It's supposed to be warm again tomorrow. They're predicting a chinook."

"It's all right if I stay here tonight, isn't it?"

"What do you think? I'm going to take back my socks and toss you out into the storm?"

"Where do we sleep?" He looked around the room.

"I sleep here." I pointed to the sofa. "It opens into a bed. You sleep in the little room next to the bathroom."

"I could get lonely."

"You're a big boy. I'm sure you'll be brave."

"Wouldn't it be cosier if we both slept out here?" He put his arms around me and kissed me gently on the lips. I may be a little slow, but even I knew that Candi had just won herself twenty bucks.

"Felix, this is a really dumb idea." I took his arms and put them by his sides. "You're married."

"And that makes a difference?"

"Never sleep with a married man. It's right up there on my list of rules to lives by."

"Does it come before or after never play poker with a man named Doc?" He smiled and stroked my face.

The age old brew of warmth and wine, hormones and proximity made it very difficult to turn away from him. What I really wanted to do was pull him down to the rug and make long, slow love in front of the fire. Instead, I busied myself by giving the fire a few unnecessary pokes and throwing on an extra log. "It comes right after never eat at a place called Mom's. And the unabridged version says never sleep with a married man, especially one who's called his wife twice since he got here. Come on Felix, who are you trying to kid? You're not the philandering type. I'd just make you feel guilty."

"What you're making me feel is appallingly middle-aged. Come on yourself, Phoebe." He caught me up and began to waltz me around the room. The dog got up and ran beside us barking. "I'm a helluva fellow tonight. I've been shot at. I've been caught in a blizzard. Now I'm stranded in a lonely house with a beautiful young woman. For God's sake, I'm James Bond and I want to make love to you." He stopped dancing and looked at me.

"Sorry 007. Maybe some other time when you're not so married."

"You really mean it, don't you." It wasn't a question and it wasn't said jokingly.

"Yes, I do."

"You really are going to dash my hopes to the ground and risk irreparable damage to my delicate male ego." The bantering tone was back.

"Pretty heartless of me, isn't it?"

"Then I think the least you can do is get me another drink and play that piano of yours some more."

"What'll it be?"

"Scotch on the rocks and more Gershwin." He settled himself in a chair by the fire and stretched his woolly feet out in front of him while I poured the drinks. "You could start with 'They're Writing Songs of Love, But Not For Me.' Seems appropriate under the circumstances, don't you think?"

"What about this one?" I sat down at the piano and launched into "Let's Call the Whole Thing Off."

CHAPTER 15

The roar of the snowplow woke me shortly after six so Felix and I were up and dressed before Constable Lindt arrived to investigate our shooting complaint. I live on a school bus route and the plow is always out here early, much to the disgust of the neighbourhood children. I folded up my bed and opened the drapes. There was no wind and sometime during the night the snow had stopped too. It lay sparkling in the starlight in wind-sculpted drifts.

The snow plow hadn't woken Felix. He was sound asleep when I knocked on his door.

"What's the weather like?" he mumbled.

"The blizzard's over and the plows are out."

"Good. I have a very important meeting at the hospital this morning." He sounded a little more awake. I went to have my shower and by the time I reappeared, he was up, dressed and had the coffee making well in hand. The robe and the woolly socks lay neatly folded on the couch. "Cream and sugar?"

"Black thanks." As he passed the cup I noticed an extra inch or two of hairy wrist extending from his red plaid cuff. I'd managed to shrink his shirt in the dryer. "Sorry about the shirt."

"Not to worry. We'll consider it a small offering to the god of the storm."

I booted the sleepy dog out for his morning patrol and then got dressed while Felix brushed his teeth with one of the extra brushes I keep on hand for guests. I'm not a total loss as a hostess. I even offered him the use of my leg shaving razor but he preferred to wait and shave at the hospital. Much to my relief, he declined my offer of breakfast as well. I could see he was worried about being late for his meeting.

Constable Lindt arrived just as we were about to embark on the long hike down the road back to The Ranch and our deserted cars. The dog scuttled into the house ahead of her and headed back to his basket to resume his interrupted sleep. He believes in at least ten hours a night bolstered by a series of sustaining naps during the day. The constable was her usual brusquely officious self. If she was surprised to see Felix, she didn't let it show. She saved us the walk by offering to drive us back to The Ranch so we could show her the scene of the crime.

It was cold when we left the house and walked through the new snow to the constable's car. There was no sign of Ella's chinook and it was still too dark to look for the sweeping arch of clouds over the mountains, that certain harbinger of the wind's coming. We drove in silence. The police car was so cosy that I nearly fell asleep again. We arrived at The Ranch's parking lot and sat in the car while Constable Lindt led me through a detailed account of the shooting. I was sure this was the first complaint she had handled solo. She took copious careful notes. No detail was too small. Felix practically writhed with impatience.

"Dr. Sanders, is there anything you'd care to add to Miss Fairfax's account of the incident?" The constable turned to Felix.

"That's exactly what happened. There's nothing I can add." He looked pointedly at his watch.

"And where's your hat now, Dr. Sanders?" Constable Lindt ignored the hint.

"Still in the middle of the stream I expect." He ostentatiously zipped up his jacket and jingled his car keys.

"And your camera bag?" The constable remained impervious.

Felix held up the wounded bag which Constable Lindt immediately impounded as evidence. She did allow him to keep the contents. He sat with his video camera on his lap and filled his numerous jacket pockets with the remaining bits of paraphernalia.

"Are we finished now?" Felix abandoned subtlety.

"One of you has to stay and go over the ground with me." Clearly, she regarded our Sunday hunter as her first Big Case.

"Miss Fairfax will be of far more help to you out there than I would, Constable." Felix climbed out of the car. "She knows the countryside very well." The we had suddenly become me. "You don't mind, do you, Phoebe?" I did. "My meeting really is very important." And your work isn't so it can wait, he might as well have added. "I'll call you later." Felix brushed the snow from his car and drove off to his meeting and his morning rounds leaving me to complete the constable's maddeningly thorough investigation.

We waited until the first grey light of dawn began to show before we trudged through the snow drifts back out to the stream. The constable found Felix's hat caught on the branches of a bush a few yards downstream from where we'd stood when I heard the first shot. Its brim was partly frozen into the stream so she bashed it free with a rock. She shook the ice shards off the felt and pointed to a neat round hole near the crown. I felt a little sick when I saw how close the bullet had come to Felix's head. Even the constable looked a bit green. Nevertheless, it took over an hour to convince her that the storm had obliterated every other trace of our hunter. Finally we walked back to our cars and I followed her to the local RCMP office where I spent another couple of hours drinking bad coffee and waiting to sign various official forms and statements. Our morning together ended with Constable Lindt's lecture on the importance of safe attire for hunting season. Then, at last, she walked me to my car.

It felt much warmer outside and the wind had freshened. The tell-tale arch swept over the mountains. The warm dry chinook wind had begun to melt the snow and fill the air with the damp earth smells of its counterfeit spring. A gust nearly blew the car door out of my hand. The constable held on to it while I climbed into the driver's seat.

"Please be careful, Miss Fairfax," she warned. "Be very careful. And if you feel afraid for any reason, call us. Don't wait. Call us right away." For a moment Constable Lindt forgot to be pompous. She was genuinely concerned for my safety.

"I'm sure there's really nothing to worry about now, Constable." She sounded so worried that I found myself trying to reassure her. "Whoever shot at us is long gone by now and I don't want to overreact to this."

"It might be better than underreacting. Here." She handed me a card with a telephone number written on it. "You can use this number." I stuffed the card in the pocket of my jeans. "The line is always open." The constable closed my car door and walked back into the station. Her usually well-disciplined black hair billowed loose in the wind.

Back at home I made myself a peanut butter sandwich and heated a cup of the leftover breakfast coffee in the microwave oven. I listened to my telephone messages while I ate my lunch. There were four, all of them from Ben. The first was a reminder about Lisa's birthday party that afternoon. The next one invited me to dinner with him and Marianne after the party. The one after that told me that I shouldn't bother to bring a present. The last warned me to wear jeans because there might be games. I hoped Lisa was as excited about her party as her father.

I changed into my funeral clothes and was on my way out the door when the phone rang. It was Ella. By the time she finished giving me the particulars on Wednesday's balloon assignment I had only ten minutes to make the fifteen-minute drive from my house to the church.

That afternoon, five minutes made a difference. The sensation surrounding Mr. Reilly's murder had packed Christ Church's pews to capacity and if Mrs. Sabbatini hadn't included me on her official list I wouldn't have got a seat. The invited guests occupied the front pews. Except for me. The service was just about to begin when the usher led me to one of the last seats at the back of the small church.

I wasn't the only person from our station in the congregation. Cheryl, the news reporter who'd handled the Reilly murder, sat two pews ahead of me. One of the staff photographers waited for her in the churchyard. Instead of retreating to the shelter of his van to drink coffee and read the newspaper like a normal person, he was out in the gusty chinook wind behaving like a photographer, taking cover shots of the church exterior from every conceivable angle.

Christ Church is worth a foot or two of tape. It's tucked away on a quiet little secondary road where the view of the ranch country's rolling hills sweeps to a meeting of mountains and sky on the western horizon. The church was built in 1896 by our district's first residents, so by Alberta standards, it's old, especially for a log structure. However, what makes the building truly unusual is the placement of the logs themselves. In Christ Church, the logs run vertically rather than horizontally which means that they function as weight-bearing pillars.

Standing tightly side by side, the wooden columns support a system of open rafters that make the peaked ceiling seem higher than it really is.

Originally, the logs were left unpeeled. However, when the parishioners noticed with some alarm that armies of wood boring insects had been busy under the bark and the church was in danger of being eaten away, they quickly stripped the logs and treated them with insecticide. The treatment worked. The insects vanished, leaving nothing behind but thousands upon thousands of small rounded grooves preserved in the surface of the wood, a graceful maze tracing the paths of their dark journeys under the bark. As a child, I had occupied many a sermon by trying to count all the worm paths in a single log. I'd never succeeded.

"O God, whose days are without end, and whose mercies cannot be numbered: Make us, we beseech thee, deeply sensible of the shortness and uncertainty of human life."

Cranmers' towering prose filled the little church with the finality of death. Mr. Reilly's coffin sat in the centre aisle near the front. Light from the stained glass windows played over its polished oak surface. On the lid stood a small, velvet-lined box containing some American war medals, one of them a Purple Heart. Private Philip Reilly had been wounded on a Normandy beach. At least that's what it said in the two paragraph biography I read in the little pamphlet provided by the funeral director.

"We are here today to celebrate the life of Philip David Reilly." Christ Church's regular minister was at home sick with the flu. A pinch hitter, the Reverend Robert (Bob) Davis, had been sent out from Calgary to dispatch Mr. Reilly. He made no mention of murder. He conducted the service as if Mr. Reilly had been some old duffer of ninety-nine who'd popped off quietly in his sleep one night. We had arrived at the part in the Order For The Burial Of The Dead which provides an optional space for the Minister to deliver a little extemporaneous chat about the deceased.

"I didn't have the privilege of knowing Phil personally but I did get a chance to talk to a few of his close friends just before we began this afternoon's service and I can tell he must have been quite a guy." Sometimes I think this provision for occasional ministerial originality is one of *The Book of Common Prayer's* few lapses in judgement. The Rev. Bob barged on. "I only had a couple of minutes with them but I think I got a real feeling for the warm and caring person that Phil was all about." "Right now I'd like to take a little time to share a few of their feelings for Phil." I stopped listening. The word share has the same effect on me that the word fuck has on my mother. I made a silent apology to Mr. Reilly's memory and closed my ears to any more funereal warm fuzzies.

The back of the church was a good spot to check out the rest of the congregation. That's probably why Inspector Debarets and Constable Lindt were there with me. The constable was in mufti for the occasion, a smartly tailored navy suit that made her look like a junior version of Ella. I wondered if the police were here to investigate the old cliché—the one about murderers showing up at their victim's funerals. The four front pews seemed to have been staked out by The Ranch. Mrs. Sabbatini was there, of course, in the first pew, along with Dr. Morrison. A grey haired man sat between them. Perhaps he was the mysterious Mr. Sabbatini. Reg and Deanne and Byron and a selection of The Ranch Apollos occupied the next three pews. I recognized some of the other employees from The Ranch scattered through the congregation, including Felix. In his dark blue, pin-striped suit, he looked remarkably groomed and composed for a man who had spent his morning dashing between my place, Calgary meetings, and a foothills funeral. I decided the equally well-dressed pleasant looking woman beside him must be his wife. They looked about the same age. Other people's marriages are no business of mine, but for some reason seeing her made me feel uncomfortable. I concentrated on a handy log and started counting worm paths.

"Miss Fairfax." Constable Lindt tapped me lightly on the arm and brought me back to earth. The Rev. Bob had stopped sharing and the church was very quiet. We seemed to have hit a lull in the service. "Miss Fairfax," the constable whispered. "The Minister wants us to turn to our neighbour and share our favourite memory of Mr. Reilly."

"You're joking." But I knew she wasn't. Most of the congregation now sat staring straight ahead in mute discomfort.

"I only ever saw him dead." So much for Constable Lindt's favourite memory. "What about you?" Her whispered question boomed like a cannon over the sea of silence in front of us. Even the Rev. Bob realized that this one had failed dismally. He hustled us back to the regular order of service.

Ten minutes later we stood in the churchyard and watched the dove grey hearse drive off with Mr. Reilly's coffin. Only Reg and the minister went along to complete the service at the crematorium. I edged my way through the crowd towards my car taking care to avoid Felix and his wife. I had decided that my uncomfortable feeling was guilt and that made me angry. What did I have to feel guilty about? It wasn't my fault Felix had come on to me. For all I knew he made a habit of being unfaithful to his wife. So why was I the one feeling guilty? It was his marriage, not mine.

"How was *The Sound of Music*?" Byron caught up to me in the parking lot.

"We never got a chance to watch it," I said. "I meant to bring it with me this afternoon. I wanted to give it to you to take back to The Ranch for me but I forgot it at home. Damn."

"Aren't you coming back to The Ranch now? There's coffee and sandwiches in the staff dining-room."

"I can't. I have to do some taping in Calgary tonight and I want to stop at the gallery and drop off your photographs first. I'd better get going." He opened the car door for me

"I'm real pleased about that gallery, Phoebe. Will your friend take some of my pictures? Do you think I have a chance?"

"I think you have more than a chance," I said.

"Can I phone you tonight sometime and find out what she thinks?" he asked.

"She may not have had time to look at them by tonight. She might not even be in. Besides, I don't know what time I'll be home. I'll probably be late."

"I guess I'm acting like a jerk," he laughed. "I never done nothing like this before. I don't know the rules."

"You don't sound like a jerk to me. I feel exactly the same when I send any of my films away," I said truthfully. "Tell you what. I'll phone the gallery in the morning and then I'll call you and let you know what she says. Where can I reach you about eleven?"

"I'm usually out on a trail ride then so don't worry about it, I'll call you."

"Hey, I almost forgot. How's your sick horse?"

"She kept us up all night but she's okay now. Better than me on no sleep, anyways." I moved to get into the car but he put a hand on my arm and held me back. Once again the clear blue eyes smiled into mine and once again my hormones responded right on cue. I don't think Byron even tried to be sexy. The lad just couldn't help himself.

He was a natural turn on. "And Phoebe, no matter what happens, thanks. You're the first person who ever was serious about my pictures. Thanks a lot."

The dog met me at the gate. He was a mess. His fur was soaked and filthy and his feet were heavy with mud. He'd been out enjoying the chinook. I changed into my jeans and went to feed and stable the horses. It was early for them but they'd simply have to put up with an early night for once. All three of the animals were excited by the wind. The dog pranced beside me sniffing the air. Elvira was positively giddy with friendliness, nudging me with her head and searching my pockets for carrots. Even the normally docile Pete decided to have a frolic through the corral. By the time he finished we were all covered with mud. I don't know why, but a good chinook really gets them going and this was a good one. Except for the deeper drifts, it had already melted most of the snow. The smell of melting snow makes me a little high myself so I could hardly blame the creatures for feeling frisky. It seemed to take forever to get the horses cleaned up, fed and watered, and in their stalls.

It was nearly four by the time I walked down the path through the poplar woods over to Barbara and Jack's house to collect their mail. I was really going to have to hustle to make Lisa's birthday party on time. I climbed over the stile on the fence between our properties and stopped to collect the keys that Barbara had left in the wooden box hidden under the stile's hinged top step. I took the house key and, with only the slightest pang of conscience, left the key to the calliope's barn sitting in the box. I'd check the Phoenix's furnace in the morning. Everyone knows that Jack is an over-anxious mother. I collected the mail, put it on their kitchen table and locked the door behind me.

By the time I fed the dog and changed into a clean sweater and fresh jeans I knew I was going to be late. I found some fancy paper and wrapped the birthday present I'd bought for Lisa, a sweatshirt with a zebra face on the front and a corresponding zebra rear and tail on the back. I tied the package with a bow made from a few feet of film from my shots-that-didn't-quite-make-it bin. There were lots to choose from. I stuffed it in my work-bag along with my video camera and a fresh tape. Byron's photographs still sat at the bottom of the bag along with *The Sound of Music*. I made a mental note to remember to return The Ranch's tape the next day.

The roads to Calgary were bare and dry and there was almost no snow on the ground. It was hard to believe we'd been in the midst of a blizzard less than twenty-four hours ago. The gallery was closed for the day when I arrived so I wrote a note on the package and tossed Byron's photos through the mail slot. I was only twenty minutes late when I finally pulled up in front of the Sugamotos' neat suburban bungalow. Ben saw me coming up the walk and opened the door. For someone who had been looking forward to a party he looked pretty gloomy.

"Something wrong?" I asked.

"Nobody came to the party, that's what's wrong. Their parents phoned and begged off. We have a grand total of two guests. The word got around."

"I'm sorry, Ben."

"Three dental appointments, two colds, one flu and an ear ache. Nobody wants their kids partying at a murderer's house." He shrugged. "I should have known this would happen."

"Where's Marianne?"

"Out getting the pizza. Lisa's downstairs."

"So let's go take some pictures of the kids who did come." I loaded a tape in the camera and followed him down the flight of stairs to the rec-room. Lisa and her two guests sat on the floor in front of a television set at the far end of the room. They were in the midst of some shoot-'em-up video game. Balloons and party streamers flowed from the ceiling in what had turned out to be inappropriate profusion.

"Hey Phoebe, am I ever glad you came." Lisa ran over and gave me a hug. "These are my best friends Sarah and Toby." Sarah looked up from the screen long enough to say hi but Toby stared straight ahead and continued zapping Martians at a spectacular rate. "Do you want a turn?" Lisa asked.

Toby gallantly relinquished the controls. It took less than a minute for the Martians to zap me. Then Sarah took over the joystick and once again the interplanetary tables turned in our favour. Defunct space monsters littered the video landscape. If anything, Sarah's hand-eye coordination was even more impressive than Toby's. Her gimlet gaze of absolute concentration didn't waver even when I moved the camera in for a close-up. I was pretty sure Ben wasn't very interested in recording this party for posterity, but he was doing his best for the kids' sake to pretend there still was a party. I took a few shots of the decorations, but mostly I kept the camera in fairly tight on the children. Wide shots would only emphasize the room's emptiness.

Marianne arrived home with the pizza and Lisa's two younger sisters Anna and Jane. I went upstairs to help her.

"Poor old Lisa." Marianne put the pizzas in the oven to keep hot. "Phoebe, would you mind if we ate with the kids? That way it might look a little more like a party."

We were eight at the table, five Sugamotos and three guests. Two year old Jane sat opposite me in her high chair, her face covered in tomato sauce and an empty pizza crust draped demurely over her left ear. Eating with children is like pain. Between episodes, one tends to forget how grim it can be. I tried not to watch while the other juniors washed down enormous wedges of pineapple pizza with buckets of chocolate milk. It's hard to take pictures with your eyes closed, but I did my best.

A huge birthday cake followed the pizza. Evidently, it had been made before the guests cancelled. We did our best to sound like a crowd while we sang "Happy Birthday" and Lisa blew out her candles and cut us each a piece of her cake. The pieces were pretty substantial but the cake still looked like it hadn't been touched. Present opening was a little jollier and the zebra shirt made a big hit. Finally, the three party animals adjourned to the rec-room to watch a horror video while Ben and Marianne tucked the two little girls in bed and I cleaned up the dining-room and loaded the dishwasher.

"Thanks, Phoebe. You shouldn't have bothered but I'm glad you did. I don't think I could have faced that mess tonight." Marianne looked ready to drop from weariness.

"How's Ben doing?" I asked.

"He's exhausted and half off his head with worry. I don't think he can take much more of this. The police want to talk to him again tomorrow. What more can they ask him? When are they going to leave him alone?" Marianne leaned against the counter. She looked like she couldn't take much more either.

"They're both asleep," Ben joined us in the kitchen and flopped down in the chair beside me at the table. "I damn near fell asleep myself when I was reading them their story. Let's have some coffee."

"None for me thanks," I said. "I should go home."

"But it's early," Marianne protested. "You must have time for one cup."

"Please, stay Phoeb. Just for half an hour. We could use a little cheering up."

My one cup of coffee turned into three and the half

hour stretched into two full hours, but I didn't manage any cheering up. All I did was sit and listen. Ben and Marianne had discussed the murder between themselves to the point of exhaustion. They'd stopped listening to each other. I was a new audience. Around nine o'clock Toby and Sarah's respective parents came to fetch them home from the party. Ben and Marianne hardly paused for breath. There was a distance between them that I'd never seen before as if each had retreated to a private misery. This was not a conversation, it was a lament for two solo voices and a pair of ears.

"If they're going to arrest me, I wish they'd do it and get it over with."

"I keep telling Ben they'd have arrested him by now if they had enough evidence and there isn't ever going to be enough evidence because he's innocent."

"It's the waiting around that's really driving me crazy, Phoeb. I can take everything but the waiting."

"Every time I see a policeman I think they've come to arrest him. I could take almost anything, but I don't think I could take that."

Their voices chased each other like squirrels in a cage. Perhaps it did them some good to talk. I'd probably be there still if Lisa hadn't come into the kitchen around nine-thirty looking for more cake and milk. That shut them up immediately but Lisa knew what they had been talking about. Anna and Jane were too young to understand what was happening but Lisa understood and she was afraid. I hoped Ben and Marianne hadn't stopped listening to her too.

By the time I drove home, the chinook wind had dropped to a light breeze and the night air was warm and moist. I put a Rolling Stones tape on the car stereo and jacked up the volume to an appropriate level. For the Stones, appropriate comes just at the point where the car windows begin to bulge slightly outward in the louder bits. I arrived at my gate a little before midnight. I was surprised that the dog wasn't there to meet me until I remembered I'd left him locked in the house to dry off. I said good night to Mick, put the car in the garage, and walked to the house through what felt like a soft spring night. The world still smelled of mud and melted snow. The owl hooted from a nearby tree. Maybe he was out celebrating the chinook too. I wished I'd worn a hat for him.

There was a foul smell in the house. It hit me as soon as I opened the door. I switched on the lights. Something was wrong. Something was so wrong that my brain refused to acknowledge what my eyes saw. I stood for an instant that was an eternity in the pile of rubble that had once been my possessions. Then the protective dam of the first shock burst and the reality of the room flooded in. Someone had trashed my house.

Every drawer in the place stood open, the contents strewn over the floor. The desk drawers had been thrown across the room. One had cracked the glass in the patio door. Hundreds of feet of tangled film from the editing bins lay on the floor muddled with papers and folders from the filing cabinet. All the books and videotapes had been swept off the shelves. Each of the tapes had been taken out of its case and tossed into a heap of clothes near the empty closet. Even the piano had suffered. A deep gouge scarred its curved side and the lid had been thrown back with a force that ripped the hinges out of the wood.

I nearly tripped over the source of the smell. The dog lay in a puddle of blood and urine—a whimpering, half-conscious heap of tan fur, partly buried by rubble.

CHAPTER 16

I found the phone on the floor beside my desk. It still worked. I called the vet and then the police. The vet arrived first. She took one look at the bloody gash on the dog's head and bundled him into the back of her van. He lay there shivering in a blanket, conscious but inert, and somehow managing to look very small. The vet thought he had been hit over the head with something heavy and sharp-edged like a length of two-by-four. Whoever trashed my place had trashed the dog first. She took him back to her clinic for x-rays and stitches.

Fifteen minutes later an RCMP patrol car pulled into my drive. It was Constable Lindt. Again. This was our third meeting of the day. Much more of this and the constable and I would be old friends.

"Don't you ever go home, Constable?" I walked out to the car to meet her.

"How can I, Miss Fairfax," she said. "You're a full time job. Besides, half the detachment has the flu. We're all on overtime right now. What's the trouble?"

The police investigate messes, they do not clean them up. An hour later, Constable Lindt had completed her investigation. She'd searched carefully through the house and the barn and then asked her questions and taken her careful notes. There was nothing more for her to do but she seemed reluctant to leave. I could see that it bothered her that nothing had been taken. Even the television set and the VCR were still in place.

"Do you keep large sums of money in the house?" she asked. I laughed. "What about jewelry?"

"The only valuable stuff I own is my photography equipment and it's all here. Whoever did this picked the wrong house to burgle."

"What about illegal drugs, Miss Fairfax?"

"I don't use drugs. No one ransacked my house to find my private coke stash." The constable didn't look convinced. "I'd hardly have called the police if I thought you might find something you could toss me in jail for, would I?"

"So you're positive there's nothing missing?"

"I can't be positive in this mess but I'm reasonably certain that nothing's been stolen."

"Do you have the card with the phone number that I gave you this morning?" she asked. I nodded. "Keep it by the phone." She stood in the doorway, ready to leave. "Maybe you'd like to go stay the night with a friend. Get out of this mess for awhile."

"Constable, this mess is my home. I'm not going to let whoever did this to it drive me out. I've got to get it cleaned up."

"Don't try to clean it yourself, Miss Fairfax," she said. "Go to bed and call a cleaning service in the morning. Give yourself a break."

There was one mess I couldn't leave for a cleaning service. After the constable left, I sponged the rug where I'd found the dog and then sprayed the stain with carpet cleaner. The cloying floral scent made me gag. Before, the room had stunk of urine. Now it smelled like the dog had peed in a perfume factory. The vet had said that if nothing serious showed up on his x-rays I could bring him home tomorrow. She figured he'd probably be all right in a couple of days, but head injuries could be tricky. I missed the old idiot. Especially now.

I scooped the snarled mounds of film off the floor and into a sheet. I'd be a long time sorting the mass of knots and loops back into some semblance of order. I tied the sheet at the corners and put the whole bundle on top of the editing bench. Somewhere in the heap under my feet were Candi's shot lists. I'd have to sort all the papers too. But not now. Now I couldn't face any more of the confusion.

I was exhausted but still wired tight and twitchy. I knew I wouldn't sleep so there was no point going to bed. My intruder had managed to miss the shelf where I keep my liquor. I grabbed the first bottle that came to hand. I couldn't be bothered to search for an unbroken glass. I sat on the couch sipping neat gin out of the bottle and pondering the mess. According to certain of the more introspective Eastern religions, there are some things that are simply unprofitable to contemplate and meditation upon them is pointless. I decided my trashed house was one of those things. What I needed was a little mindless escape and a lot more gin. I turned on the television but all I got was a screen full of snow. I looked behind the set and checked the connections. The burglar must have tripped over the wires while he was messing around with the tapes on the shelf above because the antenna's lead had been ripped out of the wall. My escape route to the vast wasteland was severed at the socket.

I looked at the tapes scattered on the floor. There wasn't any escape there either. They were mostly stuff I'd shot while I was making my own films. The remainder belonged to Gavin. He'd bought them for a course he'd taken on film and politics. *Battleship Potemkin* may be great art, but it's not much help to someone in need of mindless fluff. Then I remembered that I still had The Ranch's copy of *The Sound of Music* lurking in the bottom of my work-bag. Now there was fluff. I fished it out, slapped it into the VCR and collected my gin bottle. I wrapped the duvet around my shoulders and lay down on the couch to watch alpine peaks and singing nuns until either they or the gin put me to sleep.

I sat up again. Fast. There were plenty of peaks on this tape all right but they had nothing to do with mountains. The high points in this production were two hard nippled breasts, two raised knees and a pair of buttocks. The owner of the breasts and knees lay back on a bed. She was no nun, singing or otherwise. The owner of the buttocks had his face buried in her crotch. The back of his head blocked the main action but her ecstatic moans on the sound track told exactly what he was doing. Then he raised his head and stared straight into the camera. I choked on my gin. It was Byron. But that was nothing compared to what came next. The woman sat up, pushed Byron on to his back and climbed on top of him. This time, it was the late Janet Benedict's turn to smile into the lens.

I switched off the VCR. I'd just learned a whole lot of stuff I didn't want to know. I'd watched the tape for about ninety seconds. In that time the camera remained motionless. It never zoomed or panned or changed shots in any way. What I'd seen was a badly framed fixed shot, the kind of shot that a hidden camera with no operator takes. Ben hadn't caught Mr. Reilly watching a pornographic video in his office the afternoon before his murder. Mr. Reilly had been screening one of Byron's own home movies, the one starring the late Janet Benedict. He'd been watching the tape Byron used to blackmail her. The tape Byron trashed my place to find. The tape Byron had murdered him for. Now I understood. But percipience comes with a price tag and, when I heard the knock at my window, I knew I was about to pay the cost in full. Byron stood staring in at me. He carried a rifle.

Fear hits the pit of your stomach first. It slams you

one to the gut with the old falling elevator sensation. Then your heart tries to burst out of your chest and your lungs heave to gulp every foot of air in the room in one breath. That's the adrenalin inspired flight response. The whole thing lasts less than a second or two. Except for the taste. The taste of fear lingers in the back of your throat. Its acrid aftermath is like the smell of overheated electrical wires. I know. When Byron tapped on my window with the butt of his rifle, I became an instant expert on the fear-flight response. Trouble was, I had no place to flee. He motioned for me to open the patio door. Heart thundering in my ears, I obeyed.

"I want my tape, Phoebe. Where've you hid it?" He stood with the rifle balanced on his hip. The clear blue eyes regarded me from under the brim of his Stetson. He looked tall and blond and fresh as the night air that entered the room with him. Byron did not look like a murderer.

"You trashed my place." My voice surprised me. It was steady.

"I'm real sorry about that. But if you hadn't of hid the tape then I wouldn't of had to look for it." He sounded calm and reasonable, like·an adult doing his best to explain something difficult to a particularly obtuse child.

"You hurt my dog. You almost killed him."

"He wouldn't let me come in the house. He damn near took my arm off." Byron raised his arm to show me the jagged rip in the sleeve of his jacket. "So I had to tap him a little one with the butt of my gun. I'm sorry if I hurt him but I need that tape."

"What tape?"

"You're not a dumb lady, Phoebe, so don't pretend." An edge of exasperation crept into his voice. "You know what tape I'm talking about. I know you watched it. You know what you got or you wouldn't of hid it. Now tell me where it is." He pulled the bolt on his rifle and I heard a bullet click into the firing chamber. "Please, I don't want to hurt you." The elevator in my stomach fell a few more floors.

"I hid it in the barn," I lied. The tape was all I had. The instant Byron got his hands on it I'd be dead. As dead as Janet Benedict and Mr. Reilly. Maybe the lie would buy me a little time. Handing over the tape would buy me a bullet in the head.

"Then let's go to the barn," Byron said. He believed me. I'd just won myself a trip to the barn. I practically sang with relief. It might not seem like much, but when you're calculating your life expectancy in terms of the next five minutes a trip to the barn can double your long-term future. Maybe I could keep us moving around the place for the rest of the night before he gave up in frustration and blew my brains out.

"I've got to put some shoes on." It was simple. The longer I kept him away from the tape, the longer I'd live. I laced my runners with painstaking care. The right lace broke so I had to start over.

"Come on. Hurry up with the laces. Haven't you got any boots you can pull on?"

The left lace developed a very complicated knot. "How did you shoot that tape, Byron?"

"I stuck the camera on a tripod in my closet and made sure I kept the lights on when I was screwing her. It was easy. She never knew nothing about it."

"Then why did you kill her? What did Janet Benedict ever do to you?" I concentrated on the knot.

"I had to kill her. I felt real bad about it, but she was going to tell. She was going to tell Reilly and the police everything."

"You were blackmailing her, weren't you? What were you going to do? Send the tape to her husband if she didn't pay up." I attacked the lace with my teeth. It was a very stubborn knot.

"I mailed her a letter and a copy of the tape. The very next night she come out to The Ranch looking for me. She come straight to my place. She said she didn't give a shit if I sent that tape to her husband. She said I could play it on the national news for all she cared. Then she called me a lot of names and said she was gonna tell Reilly everything. How could she do that, Phoebe? You tell me. You're a woman. How could she do that after we'd made love and all?" I think he was genuinely puzzled. "She made it so's I had to kill her."

"How did you do it?" The lace slid free of its snarls but Byron was so engrossed in his story that he didn't notice.

"I made her swallow a whole bottle of the pain killers I keep on hand for my leg. I made her drink a lot of whisky with them so it wasn't so bad. Then I just sort of sat around with my gun on her until she wasn't moving much any more. I waited a long time. I wanted to make sure everybody at The Ranch would be asleep. Then I carried her up to the pool and dumped her in.

"It must've been the middle of the night but I didn't turn any lights on. She kept bobbing up so I had to get one of those long poles Marty uses for lifeguarding and poke her head under the water with it. After ten, fifteen minutes I figured she had to be dead. Then I set the pill bottle and the rest of the whisky down by the edge of the pool and took off.

"She was going to tell Reilly I was a blackmailer. I'm not a blackmailer. I just wanted some money, that's all." In his own mind, Byron probably wasn't a murderer either. He'd just killed a couple of people, that's all. "Janet was rich, too. All the women at The Ranch are rich. She didn't have to be so cheap. I only asked for five thousand. Why would a rich lady be so fucking cheap?" He looked bewildered. "People are weird, aren't they Phoebe?"

I had to agree. People could be unreasonable. I was unreasonable. I didn't want to die. Please brain, think of something so I don't have to die. That's probably what Janet Benedict had said to herself too.

"If Janet Benedict didn't tell him then how did Mr. Reilly find out you were blackmailing her?" Keep him talking. I had to keep him talking.

"Somehow he got hold of the tape," Byron said. "I don't think he knew I asked her for money, but he was a smart guy. He'd have figured it out. You did."

"So you killed him too."

"What else could I do?"

"Why did you use Ben Sugamoto's knife?"

"Because it was there. I hid in the trees at the back of the house until everyone left the kitchen. Then I went inside to get a knife. I thought if I used one of the kitchen knives they'd figure anyone could've done it. Then I saw Ben's knife sitting on the counter so I picked it up."

"You took a pretty big risk with all those people around, didn't you Byron? Weren't you afraid someone might see you go into the kitchen?"

"Sometimes you gotta take big risks or you don't get anywhere in life." He seemed to regard my comment as a compliment. "It's like you gotta play big to win big."

"What have you won?"

"It's not working out like I had it figured. Janet should've paid and then Reilly would never have got a hold of the tape. He must've hid it pretty good. After the police left, I looked all through his stuff but I never found nothing. Then you and the doc show up with it yesterday afternoon. What a fuck-up."

"So then you tried to kill us too. You're the one who shot at us, aren't you?"

"I never tried to kill you guys, Phoebe. I just wanted

to scare you. I only wanted my tape. You see everything's gonna work out fine as soon as I get back that tape."

"If you didn't want to kill Felix and me you sure made it look like you were trying."

"If I'd wanted to kill you, you and the doc would be dead right now. Honest," he assured me earnestly. "Shooting at you guys was a real dumb idea. I know that now. But I figured if I scared you enough you'd run for cover and I was right because that's what you did. That's why I waited until I saw you put that big bag of yours down on the ground before I shot. But instead of just taking off, you stopped to pick the fucking thing up like it was a part of your arm or something. Why didn't you leave that bag where it was lying? Then everything would've been okay. Now it's all fucked up. Why'd you have to do that, Phoebe? Why'd you have to go fuck everything up?" I assumed this appeal to reason was purely rhetorical.

"Are you going to let Ben go to jail for you?"

"I don't think they'll send Ben to jail. I'd feel real bad if they did." Byron shook his head sympathetically.

"You feel bad about a lot of stuff, don't you Byron? How bad are you going to feel about murdering me?" As soon as it left my lips, I knew this was not my brightest remark of the evening.

"You can tie that shoe right now or go in your sock feet." I tied my shoe. "Get moving." Byron opened the patio door and stepped on to the deck. "Walk ahead where I can see you. You got a flashlight?"

"There's a light in the barn." I started down the dark path. Byron followed with his rifle pointed at my back and his finger on the trigger.

"Don't do nothing stupid, Phoebe. I don't want to have to hurt you." I wished he'd stop telling me that.

It was dark in the trees but a small sliver of moon lit

the clearing near the corral. Byron's self-absorbed voice droned out of the darkness as we walked.

"You know, Phoebe, talking to you has done me a lot of good. I feel way better now. I couldn't tell anyone this stuff before. They wouldn't of understood. Not like you. Talking to you has made me see things a lot clearer. You know, everything would've been okay if. . ."

I felt a rush of air on my face and heard the whoosh of wings as the owl swooped over my head hunting for a hat. Byron cursed and stumbled as the great talons connected with his Stetson. The big bird hooted. I ran. I ran expecting a bullet in the back with every stride I took though the moonlit clearing. I fled past the corral, back into the dark safety of the trees and on to the stile and its cache of keys. If I could make it to Jack and Barbara's house I could phone the police. I might be able to hide there long enough for the police to find me before Byron and his rifle did.

"Hey, Phoebe! Wait up. I don't want to have to start shooting." I heard him stumbling along the path behind me. He couldn't be much of a runner with that leg. I reached the stile, lifted the top step, and scrabbled for the key. It wasn't there. It was still in the pocket of my other jeans. The only key in the box was the one to the calliope's barn.

"Please, Phoebe, don't do this," Byron pleaded. "Don't make everything go wrong again." Maybe he was a better runner than I thought. His voice sounded too close.

I grabbed the key, hopped the stile, and ran for the Phoenix's log barn. I stood at the door fumbling with the key. I couldn't control the shaking of my hands long enough to shove the damn thing in the lock. I held my breath to steady myself and concentrated on the small brass circle in the huge plank door.

"I see you Phoebe. I've got you all sighted up." Byron's words came in uneven gasps. I could hear him panting for breath. I didn't want to think how close he might be. Besides, I knew he was bluffing. The night was too dark. He couldn't possibly see me. At least not clearly enough to get a good shot. "Please don't make me pull the trigger." He was bluffing. I knew he was bluffing.

A bullet slammed into the lintel and buried itself in the wood. The crack of the shot echoed off the hills. Byron wasn't bluffing. The key slid in and I turned the smooth oiled lock. I heaved the door shut behind me and shot the deadbolt home. Then my knees relaxed and I slid to the floor. I sat with my back against the door while I caught my breath and tried not to wet my pants with relief. I was safe with the Phoenix. The barn's log walls were a foot thick and the door was made of four-inch planks. The big double doors at the back where the Phoenix came in and out were made of the same planking reinforced with diagonal strips and held shut by a steel braced crossbar. Jack had fitted the one tiny window with burglar bars. Byron and his rifle couldn't hurt me here. God bless and keep all great horned owls. I was safe.

Byron rattled the door handle. I felt my heart lurch. He knocked on the planks with the butt of the gun. "You gotta come out of there Phoebe." I didn't answer. "There's a window. Come out or I'll shoot you through the window."

"You have to see me to shoot me. It's dark in here."

"Maybe I'll just start blasting and hope I get lucky."

"You've already shot once. You probably woke half my neighbours with that one. You start banging away and they're going to call the cops. You'd better make sure your next shot counts." That wasn't a bluff and Byron knew it.

"Tell me where my tape is and I'll leave you alone. I

promise. I won't hurt you. I didn't mean it about shooting you. I couldn't do that." Byron wheedled at the door a little longer but I didn't bother to answer. I don't know how I could ever have found him attractive. Now, even the sound of his voice repelled me.

Aside from a faint glow of moonlight at the window, it was very dark in the barn. Still, I could sense the bulk of the Phoenix on its wagon looming above me. I heard Byron scrabbling around near the window for a minute or two but it didn't worry me much. Then everything was quiet again and I settled back against the door. All I had to do was wait here where it was warm and safe until Jack and Barbara came home.

I don't know how long I sat there in the dark before I heard the sound of a car engine approaching the barn. I got up and felt my way carefully around the calliope wagon and over to the window. I climbed up on the bin where Jack stores the wood that fuels the Phoenix's boiler and looked out. Byron had managed to get Jack's battered old pick-up truck started. I watched while he backed it to within ten feet of the window. He got out and attached a tow-chain to the truck's trailer hitch. Then he walked toward the barn, rifle in one hand and chain in the other. I knew what was coming next. The bastard was going to tie the chain to the burglar bars and use the truck to pull them off the window.

I fished a birch log out of the wood bin. It was about as big around as a baseball bat and half as long. I crouched against the wall to one side of the window while Byron knocked out the glass with the butt of his rifle. He was so close I could hear him breathing. He tapped out the last shard and reached through the opening to loop the chain around the bars. I swung the log with all my strength and smashed it into his hand.

He screamed, a strange drawn out scream, high-pitched and wild. I'd never heard a sound like it before. At least not a human sound. It was the howl of an animal in agony. And I didn't care. If Byron had stuck his other hand through the window I'd have smashed it too. Maybe I'd even have done his head if I'd had the chance. I don't know.

I think he must have fainted because the scream stopped as abruptly as it had begun. Then he started moaning and muttering to himself. "That fucking bitch, she broke my hand. That fucking bitch, she broke my hand." He repeated it over and over. I heard him open the truck door so I risked another look out the window. His left arm hung useless at his side. He leaned against the open door and shoved the rifle into the truck. Then he climbed in and drove off without bothering to shut the door. The tow-chain, still dangling from the trailer hitch, snaked along behind. The headlights disappeared around the side of the barn but I could still hear the engine.

The truck pulled up in front of the big double doors. I heard it edge forward until the bumper hit the wood with a gentle thud. Then the engine roared and the tires spun as Byron tried to push the doors open. The thick planks creaked a little, but neither the doors nor their old iron hinges budged an inch. The crossbar in its big steel cradles held firm too. It would take more power than Jack's old pick-up could muster to muscle through that barrier.

The noise of the engine faded but Byron hadn't given up. He shifted into reverse and backed the truck away from the barn. He revved the engine in neutral for a few seconds, then slammed into first gear and drove straight for the doors. I heard the glassy crash of head lights and the crunch of metal. Again, the barn doors didn't shift. In all, Byron tried four times to break in with his motorized battering ram. Judging from the sound effects, the fourth attempt must have been pretty spectacular. I could hear that he'd backed up farther than before in order to get an extra long run. He gunned the engine and the old truck shot forward. It hit the doors with a crash that must have buckled every bit of metal on its body. Even the barn doors creaked inward a fraction at this one. A few more blows like that and Byron might have made some headway. But there were no more blows. Jack's truck had battered its last. The force of the impact silenced its old engine for good.

I dropped the log back into the wood bin and leaned against the Phoenix's wagon. I'd won. There was no way Byron could get me now. He'd need a bazooka to blast his way into the barn. There wasn't a thing he could do to me in here short of setting the place on fire.

Fire. Fire and a tinder dry log barn. He was going to set the barn on fire. I knew it. Byron wasn't just a murderer. Byron was a smart murderer. If I could think of fire, so could he. The shit was probably busy collecting kindling and dipping rags in the truck's gas tank right this minute. This time he had me. If I left the barn he'd shoot me, if I stayed inside he'd roast me. Either way, Byron came up a winner and there was nothing I could do. If screams could bring the neighbours, Byron's performance would have had them lined up outside right now. I could shout all I liked while he practiced his pyrotechnics. No one would hear me. Especially not from inside the barn.

I started feeling my way back to the door. I'd have to risk leaving the barn and that was that. I might not have much chance of survival outside, but in here I was as good as dead. Besides, I'd sooner die from a fast bullet to the brain than be trapped in a fire with nothing for company but an old circus machine. The Phoenix might rise from the barn's ashes but I sure as hell wouldn't. I edged around the corner of the calliope's wagon and tripped over the shaft. I stubbed my toe so hard it felt like I'd broken every bone in my foot. I leaned against the Phoenix and wept.

Obviously, if I am any example, Dr. Johnson was wrong. The prospect of imminent demise does not concentrate the mind quite so wonderfully as he claimed. Pain, however, does. The pain of a well-stubbed toe banishes everything else from its sufferer's consciousness. It wipes the slate clean. The lightening bolt that rippled up and down my foot occupied my thoughts completely. But at last, when the first flash of pain had faded, a tiny thought managed to flit across the back of my mind. An equally minute frisson of hope flickered after it. Two heartbeats later, the floodgates of elation opened. I was leaning on my salvation. Maybe I couldn't shout loud enough to be heard but the Phoenix could. I had everything I needed to stoke up the calliope and wake the entire neighbourhood. I'd give them the calliope concert to end all calliope concerts.

I hobbled to the light switch by the door. Unfortunately, I couldn't stoke up the calliope in the dark. I was going to have enough trouble managing it in the light. I turned on the two banks of overhead fluorescents. The sudden glare hurt my eyes. It also made me a well-lit target. I had to cover the window or Byron would shoot me while I worked. I pulled the canvas cover off the Phoenix's keyboard and lashed it to the window bars with my shoe laces. My impromptu blind was pretty flimsy, but at least Byron would have to pull it down before he could get a clear aim. Besides, he only had one good arm. He couldn't pull and shoot at the same time. I'd have lots of warning. At least enough to dive for cover behind the calliope. Or so I told myself.

The next part was harder. How to get the calliope working. It looked so easy when Jack filled the boiler and poked at the fire box. He'd open a few valves here and close a couple more there, and soon the first hiss of steam would rush through the yards of brass tubes, bringing the whistles to life with a wheeze and a sputter. I didn't know where to start. How do you make music out of a mound of brass spaghetti? On the other hand, how long would it be before I heard the crackle of burning barn? Byron's task was as simple as gasoline and a match which meant I didn't have a lot of time to study the finer points of steam engineering. So what if I screwed up? At the very worst, the Phoenix would blow my head off. Since Byron and his rifle were going to do that for me anyway, I hadn't much to lose.

There isn't much point in heating a dry kettle, so I began by filling the boiler. I actually remembered the location of the calliope's water intake so it was just a matter of running the long hose over from the barn's storage tank and turning on the tap. I didn't want the boiler too full on the theory that the more water I used the more time it would take to heat. Ten minutes of steam pressure would do. If ten minutes of the calliope's racket in the middle of the night wasn't enough to call help then I was finished. The tinny sound of splashing water echoed in the empty boiler. I couldn't find the water gauge so I made do with a long stick from the kindling box that I dipped down into the boiler from time to time. When it came out wet to a depth of a couple of inches, I arbitrarily decided that would do, turned off the pump, and closed the intake.

Before the boiler started producing steam, I'd have to decide which valves needed turning and what pipes went where, but I'd take care of all that while the water heated. Right now I was a long way from the steam stage. First I needed a fire. I collected an armload of birch and some kindling from the wood box, tossed it on to the floor of the wagon and climbed up after it. The boiler sits below and in front of the calliope's keyboard, nestled under the open arms of the *V* shaped bank of whistles. The fire box is tucked underneath it. You have to shove the logs in from the end opposite the keyboard. As I discovered, it's an incredibly awkward task. The space in front of the box's door is low and cramped and the part of the calliope surrounding it bristles with brass bits just waiting to cosh the unwary. I crouched down carefully, opened the door, and laid the fire.

Then came the search for a match. In the old days when everyone smoked there was always a box of matches lying around. Now try to find one. I looked everywhere in that stupid barn. Nothing. I was almost ready to start rubbing two sticks together when I heard the gas furnace's fan kick on. Who needs matches when they've got a whole furnace full of nice blue gas flames? I ripped a strip of bark from one of the birch logs and rolled it into a tube. I opened the small metal door on the side of the furnace and held the bark over the burning gas jets. Its papery edges caught and flared. I carried my little torch slowly over to the calliope's fire box and pushed it gently under the kindling. The dry twigs flamed within seconds. I helped them along with a little gentle blowing until the logs caught and the fire burned vigorously enough to suck its own oxygen. Soon heat began to blast from the fire box door. It was time to worry about valves and gauges.

As it turned out, this was the easiest part of the operation. The calliope conducts its steam from the boiler to the whistles through a system of branched lines. It looked simple enough. A few inches from the boiler, the main line split in two. One large pipe ran left, the other right. Much smaller tubes connected the individual whistles to these feeder pipes. Before every branch in the line, there were valves to shut off the flow of steam. Right now, all the valves were open. I decided I only needed to shut the one nearest the boiler. I thought that with the main valve closed, the steam would have less space to fill. That meant the pressure might build up more quickly. I'd leave all the other valves open. Then, when the pressure looked right, I'd open the main valve, the steam would rush to the whistles and I would start playing my way to rescue. It was a good theory. Some of it may even have been true.

Watched calliopes never boil. I waited for what seemed an eternity but the gauge I concluded must be the one that measured the boiler's steam pressure hadn't budged a millimetre. Probably only a couple of minutes had passed. I checked the fire for the fifth time. It was burning well. I rummaged around in the storage box under the operator's seat and found a set of ear protectors. The calliope would be unimaginably loud in this closed little space. I placed them carefully on the keyboard and then fished out one of the yellow rain slickers and put it on. I was ready to play. The Phoenix wasn't. Another thirty seconds ticked by. I checked the fire again. This time I added four good sized birch logs to the blaze. That would get the water boiling. I knelt in front of the fire box and watched their bark catch with a satisfying flash.

"Phoebe, you bitch," Byron called from the door. "Either you open this fucking door or I'm gonna chop it down." I heard something heavy thunk against the door. He must have found an axe in Jack's woodshed.

I jumped to my feet and that's the last thing I remember until I woke up I don't know how much later. My head had connected with one of the bits of protruding brass above the fire box. It knocked me out cold.

Consciousness did not come rushing back. It crept along in dribs and drabs, reality and dreams muddled together in a curious buzzing noise. I opened my eyes and lay on the floor of the calliope wagon trying to remember where I was. When I finally figured that out, I moved on to why. The answer was not encouraging. I knew I had to get moving. I sat up and wished I hadn't. I put my hand to my head. That was a big mistake too. It came away covered in blood. The whole left side of my head was sticky with blood. It had even soaked under the yellow slicker and down into my sweatshirt. Much more of this and Byron wouldn't need to bother killing me. I'd do the job for him.

His axe still thudded against the door. Chopping through those planks with one hand would be a slow job but a man who'd already murdered two people wasn't going to give up on his third without a fight. Too bad I hadn't smashed both his hands.

I looked at the fire. Its embers glowed red hot. I hauled myself up and clutched the side of the wagon while the barn spun round and round and the floor tilted at all kinds of crazy angles. I waited until the spinning decelerated a little before I looked at the dial on the steam pressure gauge. It still registered zero. I pounded a frustrated fist on its glass face and the needle shot up into the red. The Phoenix was ready for business. More than ready. It was going to explode if I didn't get playing and release some of the pressure. The needle was so far into the red that they'd be mopping up bits of me from here to Banff.

The tap on the main valve behind the boiler was too hot to touch so I bunched up the sleeve of my sweatshirt and wrapped it round the handle. Then I turned. The tap gave way with an almighty whoosh and spun open. Steam roared past the valve and down the brass pipes. It slammed through the system with such force that the whole calliope shuddered and the wagon rocked. Right then, Banff looked pretty close. But the pipes held. Jack could be proud of his brassy babe. She was one tough old trouper.

I climbed into the operator's chair and sat for a moment. I wished the barn would stop spinning, even a little. At least the keyboard and I seemed to be twirling in the same direction —that was something. I eased the ear protectors gingerly on to my head and felt the warm ooze of fresh blood. The wound on my head didn't hurt much but the ear protectors must have opened it again. At least they blocked the sound of Byron's axe chopping steadily at the door.

I stared at the keyboard. This was the final exam. Would the Phoenix make music for me? I pushed the key for middle C. The connecting rod clicked, the whistle opened and the note shrilled out loud and clear. I'd passed. I was a steam engineer. I put my hands over the keys and then hesitated. If this didn't work then Byron and his axe would win. The Phoenix was my last chance but I'd be damned if I'd die to the tune of Daisy and her bicycle built for two. If I were going out, it would be in a blaze of glory. *The Hallelujah Chorus* and nothing less. And so, together, the Phoenix and I blasted out the most glorious rendition of Handel's masterpiece ever played on a circus calliope. We were magnificent. We were transcendent. We were sublime. We were loud.

In the barn's confined space the Phoenix's roar was a palpable force. I heard Handel with every part of my body. In the midst of the heat and the clouds of condensing steam, I became a part of the noise. I breathed and my lungs sucked in noise. My heart beat and noise pumped through my veins. I sang and the voice of the Phoenix poured from my throat. Our hallelujahs were a physical force, towering waves of sound that crashed and beat at the walls of barn. I played until the whistles sputtered and their screams turned to gurgles. I played until they dribbled out their last gasps of watery steam and the pressure in the boiler dropped to zero. That was it. The concert was finished and, unless the cavalry rode over the hill at that very moment, so was I.

I took off the ear protectors and put them down on the keyboard. The pad on the left one was soaked with blood but I was too dizzy and exhausted to fret about a quart of blood here or there even if it was my own. I leaned back in the operator's seat. My ears roared and the barn banked sharp left on its way into another spin. I closed my eyes. Just for a moment.

CHAPTER 17

"Phoebe. Phoebe Fairfax. Wake up!" My tenth-grade algebra teacher stood looking down at me. Funny, Miss Rose had an axe in her hand. "Wake up. You have to wake up." I wondered when Miss Rose had started wearing a uniform to class. How odd. A peaked cap. Even a gun. Maybe she'd run away from school and joined the Foreign Legion. "Don't close your eyes again." Come to think of it, Miss Rose looked a lot like Constable Lindt. "Are you awake, Miss Fairfax?" The constable persisted.

I gave the question some serious thought. "I think so. If you're real then I'm awake. Are you real?"

"I'm beginning to wonder." Constable Lindt put down the axe and called to someone over by the door. "We need an ambulance here."

"Has someone been hurt?"

"Had a look at yourself lately, Miss Fairfax?"

"We have to get out of here." I tried to stand but a burst of pain filled every cubic inch of my skull. The constable put a restraining hand on my shoulder.

"I don't think you should move until the ambulance comes."

"We have to move or he'll kill us both. He has a gun. He tried to kill me."

"Nobody's going to hurt you, Miss Fairfax. You're safe. Right now half your neighbours are standing outside this barn. The other half are probably at home phoning the police. Who tried to kill you?"

"Byron."

"Who?"

"Byron Wilke. From The Ranch. He murdered Mr. Reilly and Janet Benedict. I have the blackmail tape."

"You're not making sense, Miss Fairfax. Let's take it from the top."

I took it from top to bottom as fast as I could and, to her credit, Constable Lindt didn't make me waste a lot of time on details. She waited until I was finished my story before she asked me how I got my bloody head. I was in the middle of my explanation when two more Mounties appeared in the barn. Then the ambulance came. They took me out on a stretcher. The pain in my head registered every movement. My own private seismograph. The constable walked beside me. Jack's yard was full of vehicles and flashing lights. At least three of my neighbours said hello to me between the barn and the ambulance.

"I can't go yet. I have to get that videotape from my house," I said.

"An officer is going to do that right now. Don't worry, Miss Fairfax. It's all over. You won. You and that crazy pile of whistles in there. *The Hallelujah Chorus.*" Constable Lindt shook her head in disbelief. "We'll pick Byron up before he gets very far. All you need to worry about is getting your head patched up. Everything's okay. I'll see you at the hospital." The ambulance doors closed.

At the hospital in Calgary they shaved four inches of hair from above my ear and stitched the gash in my scalp. The hair around my new bald spot was matted with blood. They also ran me through a whole series of tests they said were standard treatment for people with head injuries. I must have passed, because a little after six they finally let me phone Cyrrie. I knew he'd be frantic with worry if he found out about my nocturnal adventures from one of the neighbours.

"It's always delightful to hear from you, my dear, but why are you calling in the middle of the night? Is something wrong?"

I told him my story. "So I'm fine now. They've stitched my head and they figure it's a pretty minor concussion so I can go home tomorrow. They're keeping me for observation but there's nothing to worry about."

"Nothing to worry about!" Cyrrie shouted down the phone. "You've been chased by a homicidal maniac. You damn near blew yourself up with that heap of brass hooters. Now you're in the hospital with a concussion and you say there's nothing to worry about?"

It took me another ten minutes to convince him I was all right and that he shouldn't come roaring over to the hospital that very minute.

"I'm too old for this, Phoebe."

"Really, Cyrrie, I'm fine. They say I need some sleep, that's all. I'll see you this afternoon. I think the visiting hours start at two. Now go back to bed."

After they finished with me in the emergency department they found me a bed on a regular ward. I don't think I've ever been so exhausted. I don't remember changing into a hospital gown or getting into bed. I do remember that they woke me at least once every hour. I'd no sooner get to sleep than a nurse would shine a light in my eyes, take my hand in hers and ask me to squeeze her fingers. Then, before she let me go back to sleep, she'd ask me to name the first prime minister of Canada or the capital of Manitoba or the highest mountain in the world. Apparently hourly games of Trivial Pursuit are also standard treatment for patients with head injuries. Once, I woke on my own and thought I saw Cyrrie sitting in the chair near the window. I decided I must still be asleep and that he was part of a dream.

The chair was empty when I heard the door to my room open for what seemed like the hundredth time. "Sir John A. MacDonald, Winnipeg, and Everest," I mumbled into the pillow.

"Good morning to you too, Miss Fairfax." Constable Lindt opened the curtains and sunlight flooded the room.

"What time is it?" The light made my eyes water.

"Nearly noon." Noon. I'd been in bed over five hours. I was still exhausted.

"Have you caught Byron yet?" I asked.

"They arrested him on the highway near Lethbridge. He was heading for the border."

"What about the tape?"

"We found it in your VCR just like you said. Inspector Debarets has it." The constable's nostrils flared as she struggled to suppress a yawn. "The inspector's here. He sent me in to wake you. He'd like to talk to you now. The doctor said it was okay." She turned to leave.

"Please, wait a minute, Constable Lindt." She came back and stood beside my bed. "Thanks," I said. "Thanks for the rescue mission."

"It's my job, Miss Fairfax."

"For my money they can make you commissioner tomorrow."

"Right now I'd settle for eight hours sleep." This time she didn't manage to hold back the yawn.

"What made you come back?" I asked.

"I don't know. I guess I felt uncomfortable about leaving you alone." After she left me in my trashed house, Constable Lindt had gone home. Thanks to the detachment's staff shortage, she'd been on duty since seven o'clock that morning so she was more than ready for bed. Nevertheless, she couldn't sleep.

"I couldn't turn my mind off. Everything kept

churning around in my brain. You'd been at The Ranch when Philip Reilly was murdered. A few days later you and Dr. Sanders had been shot at. Then your house was vandalized. All that in one week? It was too much. It didn't make sense to me to treat them as isolated incidents."

The constable had given up trying to sleep. Instead, she got up and drove back to my place. She saw that the lights were still on in the house so she parked in my driveway and knocked at the back door. When no one answered she went to the front and found the patio door standing open. By this time, Constable Lindt was very worried indeed. Even so, she hesitated to call for reinforcements. What if I'd simply left my trashed house and gone to stay the night with a friend like she'd suggested? She'd look like a jerk, a junior officer who'd overreacted.

"I nearly gave up and went home again, but then I heard the calliope." At the sound of the first hallelujah, Constable Lindt was out of my driveway and on her way to Jack's place. She found Byron's abandoned axe in front of the barn door. He'd nearly made it through the planks so she simply carried on where he'd left off. By the time the calliope ran out of steam, she had managed to finish chopping a hole big enough to stick her hand through and turn the dead bolt.

"You gave me one hell of a fright, Miss Fairfax." The constable found me slumped over in the operator's seat, my head covered with blood. "I thought you were dead."

"If you hadn't come back I would have been. Another few minutes and Byron would have made it into the barn."

"I don't think so," she said. "I think he ran at the first note from the calliope. He must have known that your neighbours would be along any minute. I just got there a little earlier than they did, that's all." There was a knock at the door. "That's the inspector. I have to go now." She touched my hand. "Take care of yourself, Phoebe."

Inspector Debarets looked as fresh and elegant as the bouquet of purple and white iris he carried in his hand. "How are you, Miss Fairfax?"

"Alive thanks to Constable Lindt," I said. The inspector put the flowers in the water jug by my bed. "I didn't know the RCMP sent people flowers."

"They don't," he said. "But I do. The flowers are here unofficially. Unfortunately, I am not. The doctor says you have a slight concussion. I'll try not to take too much time." He pulled a chair over beside the bed and sat down.

"Don't worry. I'm okay," I said. "The stitches make it look much worse than it is. Constable Lindt told me you've arrested Byron."

The inspector nodded. "And I've looked at the videotape. Did the constable tell you that we found five others like it in his apartment? They were on a shelf in his bookcase right beside the VCR all labelled to look like tapes from The Ranch's library. There are five women who are going to be very grateful to you, Miss Fairfax."

"He was blackmailing all of them?"

"We won't know for certain until we talk to the women but I think that's a fairly safe assumption. We're tracing them now. It's likely they were all guests at The Ranch so it won't take long. In the meantime, the cowboy has been charged with both of The Ranch murders and with attempting to murder you."

"How did Mr. Reilly get that tape in the first place?" I asked.

"According to Margaret Sabbatini it came in the mail on the morning of his murder. Apparently Janet Benedict's husband came across it on a bookshelf at his home. He thought that his wife had simply borrowed it during her stay at The Ranch and forgotten to return it. He had his secretary mail it back to The Ranch with a note of explanation. Mrs. Sabbatini said she'd put it on her desk with the intention of returning it to the library when Mr. Reilly came along and saw it. *The Sound of Music* had been his wife's favourite film. He found it overly sentimental and used to tease her about it. It seems to have been a bit of a joke between them. Mr. Reilly decided to watch the tape for old time's sake. He took it and the VCR to his office and that's the last Mrs. Sabbatini thought of it. She worked late that evening but, before she left, she tidied his office as she usually did and returned the VCR to its place in the outer office."

"That's why the tape was still in the machine when Felix and I went to The Ranch on Sunday," I said.

"I think you're getting ahead of me, Miss Fairfax. I would like you to start at the beginning and tell me exactly what happened." The inspector pulled his tape recorder out of his brief case, placed it on the bedside table and pushed the record button. "How did you come to have the tape in your possession?"

I told him the whole story. Occasionally he asked a question to clarify a detail but, for the most part, he listened silently. By the time I finished, my head throbbed abominably. No pain killers. That's another part of the standard treatment for concussion. "Then the calliope ran out of steam and I'm afraid I don't remember anything more until Constable Lindt found me."

"I think you've remembered enough for today, Miss Fairfax." Inspector Debarets turned off the tape recorder and returned it to his briefcase. "You'll have to answer more questions and make this all official, but I can leave you to rest for now. You need more sleep, I think."

I thought so too, but nobody else did. I had more visitors that afternoon in the hospital than I would in a month at home. They all brought flowers. Even the nurse who delivered my lunch tray.

"This might be a little cold." She plunked the tray on a table and wheeled it over to the bed. "We couldn't interrupt you while the police were here but we tried to keep it hot." She whisked off the plate cover and exposed two small slabs of congealed liver flanked by some watery green beans and a cold potato. "If you can't manage the main course, at least try the dessert." A dish of orange Jello glistened malevolently from under its squirt of whipped whatever. "The rose is from the man who spent the morning in your room. He left a note." A single yellow rose in a bud vase was the most appetizing item on the tray. The nurse took my pulse and checked my stitches and then left me to ignore my lunch and read my note.

"They say you'll live, so I've gone to fetch Bertie and see about having your house cleaned up. I'll make arrangements for Elvira and Pete too. Be back to see you later today. Sleep well. Cyrrie." So I hadn't dreamed him after all.

I pushed the tray away, pulled up the covers and closed my eyes. The door opened again. This time it was Felix and a dozen red roses.

"I hear you had a pretty close call. You're the talk of the hospital." I had forgotten that this was the hospital where he worked. He put the roses on the table by my abandoned lunch.

"I'll be all right in a day or two. At least that's what the doctor in the emergency ward said."

"He's right. You will. I looked at your chart before I came in. But you're going to have one hell of a headache for awhile. How does it feel now?" He sat on the edge of the bed and took my hand in his.

"I could use an aspirin," I said. "Thank you for the flowers. They're very beautiful."

"You've burned your hand." He pointed to a small

blister on one of my knuckles.

"You were right about Janet Benedict," I said. "Byron murdered her. He told me how he did it. He held a gun to her head while he doped her up with booze and pills. Then he dumped her in the pool and held her head under." I started to cry. "He was going to shoot me." By now I was trying to talk between sobs. "At least that would have been quicker." I gave up and lay back on the pillows and wept. Felix sat and stroked my hand. He waited until I was more or less coherent before he spoke.

"The hospital has a very good counselling service," he said. "You should talk to them. The cut on your head will heal in a week or two, but the psychological wounds inflicted by an experience like yours can last a long time. I think it would help you to talk to someone."

"I'll be okay. I'm just tired. That's why I lost control." He passed me the Kleenex box. I blew my nose and a stab of pain shot through my head. "Besides, couldn't we swap? My free photography lessons for your free shrink time. If I found myself feeling delicate, I'd give you a call."

"I don't think that's possible for us any more," he said. "You see, Phoebe, I've gone and done a foolish thing. I think I'm falling in love with you." He must have noticed the look of alarm that I'm certain crossed my face. "Don't worry. I know you don't feel the same way about me. No, please." He held up his hand. "You don't have to say anything. I don't want to hear that you think I'm a very nice man and that you like me very much and hope we can be friends. I don't think we can be friends."

"Felix, I'm sorry."

"And I'm sorry too. I'm fifty-three years old. I'm going to be a grandfather in February. I love my wife." He shook his head. "I wish I could be more like some of my colleagues. They seem to thrive on discreet affairs with beautiful young women. I guess I thought I could too, but the first time I try it I bugger it up by falling in love."

"I don't know what to say."

"Then don't say anything. Let me go on believing that the only reason you didn't leap into bed with me is because I'm such a lousy photographer." He smiled. "Don't look so surprised. I know I'm terrible. You should have seen the look on your face when you were watching my tape. Take my advice, Phoebe—don't ever play poker."

"Felix, you're the nicest lousy photographer I know. I'll miss you. I wish we could be friends."

"Maybe someday."

"Good grief, Phoebe! What did that creep do to you?" Candi swept into the room flourishing a billowy bouquet of pink sweetheart roses and baby's breath. "Hello Felix." She greeted him in passing as she leaned over the bed and scrutinized my stitches. "How long does it take hair to grow?" Felix waved to me over her shoulder and tiptoed out the door. Candi settled herself in the chair by my bed. At least she didn't expect me to make conversation. She did all the talking which was good because simply keeping my eyes open was becoming a major task. Just when it seemed Candi might be running down, the door opened and reinforcements in the form of Reg arrived. A wicker basket full of lilies swung from his arm. And so it went for the rest of the afternoon.

Reg and Candi were followed by Jack and Barbara and a pot of autumn crocus. They had stopped at Cyrrie's on their way home from Edmonton and heard the news. Jack fidgeted for the entire fifteen minutes they spent in my room, worried to a frenzy about the Phoenix. It was obvious whose health really concerned him. He could hardly wait to get home. He tried to make a tactfully oblique enquiry about the calliope's condition but all this got him was a look from Barbara that could have dropped a charging rhino in its tracks.

Jack was spared further agony by Dr. Morrison's appearance at the door. I really don't know why she came. After Jack and Barbara left, she stood awkwardly at the foot of the bed clutching a single, gawky bird-of-paradise flower. She looked at my head, informed me the doctor had done an excellent job of stitching it up and then left, still holding her flower.

I may have dozed off for a minute or two before Ben and Marianne arrived. They were virtually incoherent with delight. They seemed to have the impression that I had single-handedly snatched Ben from the shadow of the prison gates. At one point a nurse came in and told Ben to keep the noise level down to a roar. He gave her one of the orchids from the bouquet he and Marianne had brought. The nurse shooed them out so she could do more pulse taking and head checking. They left with promises of parties and champagne to come.

Then Ella marched in carrying a pot of sensible bronze chrysanthemums. The mums were her only claim to sense that day. She was giddy with news.

"Phoebe, guess what? Marty and I are getting married." She beamed.

"Ella, that's terrific. I'm very happy for you."

"My God, your head looks awful." She peered closely at my stitches. "Never mind. It's in the afternoon. You can wear a hat."

"What are you talking about?"

"To my wedding. You can wear a hat. The wedding is in two weeks and I want you and Candi to be my bridesmaids. Will you, Phoebe? Please?"

I was glad I was lying down. I'd had enough shocks for one day. As it was, I was so weakened by lack of sleep that I said yes.

"When do you get your stitches out?" she asked. I told her. "Then I'm sorry but you really will have to wear a hat. We can't have you looking like the Bridesmaid of Frankenstein."

"Actually Ella, that's Frankenstein's matron of honour. Fomerly married persons can't be bridesmaids." I do enjoy correcting Ella. It's such an infrequent pleasure. By the time she left I had given up the idea of ever sleeping again. At least I'd given up all hope of sleeping in the hospital. I simply had to get out of the place before the next wave of visitors washed through the door. I needed some rest. I climbed out of bed, found my clothes and got dressed. I bent over to put on my shoes and a burst of pain ricocheted around my skull. I sat on the bed and waited for the worst to pass. I'd have to remember not to bend over for a day or two.

I shuffled out to the corridor and slopped along to the elevators in my laceless runners. I walked past the nursing station. No one noticed me. That is, none of the hospital staff noticed me. I did get some pretty funny looks from my fellow passengers on the way down in the elevator. Even the taxi driver wasn't too certain. I couldn't blame him. I knew I looked disgusting. As if my new punk hairdo weren't enough, my sweatshirt was stiff with dried blood and my jeans were covered with soot and grease. Somewhere along the way I'd lost my socks.

"Where to lady?"

I gave the driver Cyrrie's address and lowered myself gently into the back seat of his cab. My head had started to pound again with real enthusiasm.

I found Cyrrie sitting at his kitchen island with half a dozen back issues of *The Blood Horse* and two computer printouts spread in front of him.

"Phoebe, what on earth are you doing out of bed? You

look terrible. Why did those idiots let you leave the hospital."

The dog lay on a mohair throw by Cyrrie's feet. A huge, cone-shaped plastic collar fanned around his head to prevent him from scratching the stitches above his ear. He tottered over to greet me. He looked like his head hurt as much as mine. We were a matched set.

"They didn't let me out," I admitted. "I left. Would you pay my taxi, Cyrrie? I don't have any money with me." I pulled a stool over to the island and sat. The dog lay down on the floor beside me and rested his plastic contraption on my foot.

"Even the cab driver's worried about you." Cyrrie came back to the kitchen. "He thought you'd been in a fight. You wait here and I'll get my car."

"What for?"

"To take you back to the hospital, that's what for. Really, Phoebe, sometimes you behave as if you're still ten years old."

"Cyrrie, I'm all right. The doctor said I could leave tomorrow morning anyway so what's a few hours? I can't sleep there."

"You were very sound asleep when I came to visit you this afternoon."

"I'll be better off at home."

"Home is totally out of the question. Your house is still a mess. I booked a cleaning service but the first appointment I could get is for tomorrow afternoon."

"Then can I please stay with you? I really am okay. All I need is some sleep."

"You should at least phone the hospital and let them know where you are. It probably upsets them when they misplace patients."

As it turned out, this misplaced patient really didn't bother the hospital all that much. I got a few bleats about leaving without signing the proper papers and they made it pretty clear that if I dropped dead before morning I needn't come complaining to them but that was it.

"Are you hungry?" Cyrrie asked. "What about a bowl of soup?"

"I don't think I could stay awake long enough to eat it. What are you up to?" I pointed to the papers in front of him.

"My dear, I've found Elvira a husband." Cyrrie held up a full-page colour spread in *The Blood Horse* for my inspection. "Won't this be a match? God, I feel like the Dolly Levi of the horse world. What a matchmaker! Take a look at this." It was an ad for the services of a very famous stallion, one of whose offspring had won the Kentucky Derby.

"Won't he be expensive?" I asked. "He's a pretty classy fellow."

"To hell with the expense," Cyrrie said. "This is Elvira. You only live once. We're going to win the Queen's Plate with this foal, Phoebe. Those guineas are as good as ours. We'll stick with the Noel Coward names, I think. We'll call her Madame Arcati. How's that sound for a Blithe Spirit filly?"

"There's a fifty-fifty chance that she'll be a he. What if it's a colt?" I said.

"Then we'll call him Madame Arcati anyway. He can win the Drag Queen's Plate."

I laughed and set the pain in my head off again.

"You should be in bed," Cyrrie said. "Go remove those disgusting clothes. I'll get you a pair of pajamas."

One hot bath and a pair of Cyrrie's clean pajamas later, I climbed between the sheets in the little guest room and turned the electric blanket up to six. The dog lay on the rug beside the bed. For some reason, he refused to let me out of his sight. He'd even napped on the bath mat while I was in the tub. Cyrrie knocked on the door.

"I've brought you a mug of soup and some biscuits." He put a tray down on the bedside table. "If you want anything else, give me a call. Come on, Bertie," he held the door open for the dog. "You know Sergeant-Major Fairfax here has very strict rules. No sleeping with people. March."

"It's okay," I said. "Let him stay here if he wants to. Just for tonight." Cyrrie raised his eyebrows and closed the door.

I drank a little of the soup and fed the dog one of the crackers. I had forgotten to pull the drapes but I didn't feel like making the effort to get out of bed. Instead, I lay and looked out the window at the view over the city. The sun had already set but there was still a glow behind the mountains. In the southwest sky, the bright white lights of an airplane coming in to land shone above the peaks. Although the light looked very close, the plane must have been quite far away because it seemed to hover in the same place for a long time. But maybe I was mistaken. Maybe it wasn't even an airplane. After all, the gloaming is the light of illusion. I got up and closed the drapes.

"We've got to get back to work on those beavers, Bertie." I reached inside the silly plastic cone and stroked his silken muzzle. "At least you can depend on a beaver to behave like a beaver. Can't you?" Bertie thumped his tail on the rug in agreement. I climbed back into bed and pulled up the covers. "Castor canadensis, Bertie. The good old Canadian beaver. Now there's a face you can really trust. I think."